TOURNAMENT OF CHANCE

DRAGON REBEL

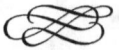

SUZANNE G. ROGERS

IDUNN COURT PUBLISHING

CONTENTS

Idunn Court Publishing
7 Ramshorn Court
Savannah, GA 31411

ISBN: 978-1-947463-25-7

Tournament of Chance first published by Musa Publishing, September 2012
Published by Idunn Court Publishing, March 2015

Published in the United States of America
Cover Design: Suzanne G. Rogers
Editor: Jaime-Kristal Lott

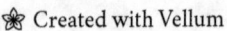 Created with Vellum

THE HORSE AND THE CARROT

*T*he guards at the castle gates were rude and brusque, but Heather hadn't let it check her enthusiasm for what lay ahead. The men had searched her father's pelt-laden cart and made him turn his pockets out. Fortunately they hadn't searched her, or they might have discovered the hunting knife she kept inside her boot. Even though she was only eight years old, her father had taught her never to be without a weapon of some kind. "Nobody cares more about your well-being than you do," Saltimar would often say. "Always make sure you're in a position to survive, no matter the company you keep." Her eyes forward, Heather held her breath until the cart was finally waved through. Her father glanced over and gave her a little nod and wink. After she let her breath out, a giggle escaped her lips. The castle guards would doubtless have been surprised to learn her father had a hunting knife secreted inside his boot as well.

Now that the danger was past, Heather couldn't stop smiling. Saltimar of the Jagged Peaks and his daughter were on their way to the castle of King Chance! She bounced and wriggled on the wooden seat, unable to contain her excitement at visiting the castle grounds. The horse-drawn cart crossed over a meandering creek, upon which floated elegant white swans. Heather gaped, enthralled by the sophisticated creatures. After they reached the far side of the bridge, however, she spied something even better. "Stop the cart, Papa!" she cried, clutching her father's arm.

Saltimar reined in his horse and allowed his daughter a moment to retrieve a vibrantly hued tail feather shining in a field a few yards away. With her long auburn braid streaming behind her like a streak of joy, Heather scooped up the plume and dashed back to the cart. Saltimar chuckled at her enchanted expression.

"Look at the wonderful colors, Papa. Is it from a magical bird?"

"There's no such thing as magic, Heather. It's a peacock feather. Peacocks roam the grounds. See over there." Saltimar pointed to one of the males, in full iridescent display, visible in between the trees. Heather gasped in delight.

"Oh, how fantastic!"

"Some people think peacocks are lucky."

"Oh, they *are*, I just know it. A creature that beautiful could only bring good fortune."

Upon reaching the seaside castle a few minutes later, Heather heard the rhythmic crashing of ocean waves. She took a deep breath of salty air. Seagulls made lazy circles against the azure sky overhead.

"It looks and smells...and *feels* so different than Jagged Peaks," she said. "I want to live here."

"I love the mountains, but I admit this does make a refreshing change."

A servant directed him to drive the cart to a loading dock in the back of the fortress. As her father transacted his business with the castle steward there, Heather drank in the glorious alabaster towers and terra-cotta-colored turrets thrusting skyward, each flying the red and gold flag of Destiny. She simply had to have a peek inside the castle, however brief. Before anyone could stop her, she scrambled onto the dock and flew toward the open doorway. Almost as soon as she set foot over the threshold, the porter appeared. Clad in a spotless uniform accented with red and gold braid, his gaze raked her slender frame with a contemptuous glare. "*Commoners* aren't allowed."

Heather lifted her chin. "Why not? My father pays taxes—more and more every year."

"What a stupid ignorant question, child. That's just the way it is."

When the man reached for a broom to shoo her away, Heather turned to leave. "It's a stupid ignorant rule, and it's not fair! Royal chamber pots smell just as bad as the ones commoners use."

A harried scullery maid walked past, weighed down by a bucket of soapy water. "Hear! Hear!" she muttered.

Frustrated, Heather bounded into the daylight once more. Maybe she couldn't see inside the blasted castle, but the magnificent gardens beckoned. Still clutching her peacock feather, she sprinted for freedom.

"Don't go too far," Saltimar called after her.

Heather entered the garden through a vine-covered archway, heavy with fragrant, pale flowers. She immediately encountered a topiary shrub in the shape of an elephant—just like the wooden carving Uncle Latimar had brought her from his travels. For the life of her, she couldn't imagine how somebody could get a bush to grow that way without magic. She circled the elephant, awestruck.

A young boy sauntered over, perhaps a year younger than Heather. "That's nothing. You should see the one that looks like a lion."

"Show me."

The boy took off running, and Heather followed. Moments later, he skidded to a stop next to a fantastic topiary lion, complete with a shaggy fern mane. The boy grinned with satisfaction at Heather's stunned reaction. "The gardeners here are quite clever. They can cut the bushes into almost any shape you can imagine." He noticed the peacock feather in Heather's hand. "You like those? I know where you can get more."

They raced through a maze of garden hedges together, their boots crunching on the white gravel-covered pathways. The boy led her to a large, open space with a manicured lawn. Dropped tail plumes decorated the mossy grass, glowing with color under the sunlight.

"The royals go lawn bowling here every so often, but the peacocks enjoy the moss," he said.

Together they assembled a bouquet of the magnificent feathers.

"Are you sure nobody will mind?" she asked.

He shrugged. "They just end up burning the feathers with the lawn cuttings anyway. Take as many as you want."

Suddenly Heather tossed the feathers to the ground and pulled her hunting knife from her boot. The boy's eyes grew wide as he held up his hands. "Whoa," he said, stumbling backward.

"Don't move."

Grasping the knife by its tip, she hurled it in the boy's direction. The blade impaled a large, poisonous snake not more than a yard off. The lad gulped at the sight of the long gray reptile. "I-I've never seen one of those around here before."

"It's a diamond crested aldersnake," Heather said, puzzled. "I see them all the time, but only in the mountains." She retrieved her knife, stowed it in her boot, and handed the limp reptile to the boy. "You might want to give this to the cook. The meat is delicious."

"My name is Jovander, by the way." He draped the snake over his shoulders. "Thanks for saving my life."

They exchanged a firm handshake.

"Heather. And you're welcome." She gathered up her feathers. "You're lucky to live in Destiny Castle. Although I love Jagged Peaks, I'd do anything to grow up in a place like this."

She extended her hand, palm outward, and closed her eyes.

"What are you doing?" Jovander asked.

"My father says magic doesn't exist, but I can *feel* it here." Heather shivered and opened her eyes. "Can't you?"

The boy chewed his lower lip. "Maybe. Wanna hear a secret?"

"I love secrets."

"A long, long time ago, Destiny was called Ormaria. Back then, Ormaria was ruled by an ancient people, the Ormvalders, who were able to speak to dragons."

"That's silly. No one can talk to dragons," Heather scoffed.

Ignoring her skepticism, Jovander went on with his story. "Under Ormvalder rule, the citizens had great prosperity and happiness. But when the last Ormarian king fell ill, the country was invaded. The dragons were hunted down and killed, and the Ormvalders were forced into hiding."

"If that's true, where are they now?"

"There's a legend that says the Ormvalders will return to power someday, when the time's right. I hope so, because I'm one of their descendants."

"Really?" Wide-eyed, Heather leaned closer. "What happens if the king learns your secret?"

"I'd be hunted down and killed for sure." He showed her a pendant hidden underneath his shirt, a small stone carving in the shape of a dragon. "This is the symbol of the Ormvalders, but my mother told me not to tell anyone, *especially* not King Chance."

Just then, Saltimar's voice rang out. "Heather!"

"That's me. Bye."

As she darted away, she bumped into a tall, thin man behind a nearby hedge with a covered basket over his arm.

"Oh, I'm terribly sorry. I didn't see you there," she gasped.

"You're not supposed to have weapons on the castle grounds. I should call the guards."

When the man seized her arm, Heather grew pale. Suddenly Jovander jumped from behind the hedge and shoved the dead snake toward the man's face with a hissing noise.

"Watch out, Wexler!"

The man stumbled backward and dropped his basket. The lid opened, but the basket was empty. With a filthy glance at Jovander, Wexler snatched the basket from the ground and hastened toward the castle. Heather and Jovander shared a nervous laugh.

"That's one of the king's men. He's always spying on me. I think I'll leave this snake in his bed tonight," he said.

"Heather!" came Saltimar's voice again, more insistently.

She gave Jovander an impulsive kiss on the cheek. "Bye again."

A few minutes later, Heather reached the cart. After she'd scrambled inside, she stowed her feathers away and picked up the reins. When she gave the leather a sharp snap, the horse lurched forward. Saltimar peered at her, surprised. "In a hurry to leave so soon?"

"Oh…well I saw the gardens. That was the best part."

"You found more treasures. I hope the birds were willing?"

Heather laughed. "Of course. A nice boy helped me gather them up."

After she handed the reins to her father, she cast a nervous glance over her shoulder. Jovander stood in the road swinging the snake over his head like a trophy. Heather giggled and waved at him until a curve in the road broke her line of sight.

With the castle out of view, her fear of Wexler eased. A sigh of relief escaped her lips.

"Papa, Destiny Castle is a magical place."

"There's no such thing as—"

"Oh, yes, I know. There's no such thing as magic," she interrupted. "It's not fair that only royalty should be allowed to live there. I want to be a member of court. Maybe it sounds silly, but I have the strangest feeling I belong here."

"Perhaps you *shall* live here someday."

Heather frowned. "Not likely. The mean porter told me commoners aren't permitted inside the castle."

"That isn't exactly so," Saltimar said. "Noblemen and soldiers, distinguished in battle, may win a place at court."

"But I'm not a man, nor highborn."

"No, but good King Chance also offers the same opportunity to *any* maiden, be they high or lowborn."

"Really?" Heather sat up straight and squared her shoulders. "Will I have to prove myself in battle?"

"Not exactly," Saltimar chuckled. "The king hosts an archery competition once a year, called the Tournament of Chance. The winner is awarded the title of Lady and is invited to live at the castle. You must work hard, little one, but when you are eighteen, you could win that tournament."

"I'll win; you'll see. I'm going to be a champion and make you proud."

Saltimar gave his daughter a hug. "I'm already proud of you."

On their return to Jagged Peaks, Saltimar drove into Destiny Village. He passed a grain mill, powered by horse harnessed to a large wheel. The unattended animal walked around and around in a never-ending circle, causing a belt to move inside the mill.

"What makes the horse go?" Heather asked.

"You see the carrot dangling off that pole?" Saltimar said, pointing. "The horse wants the carrot, so he walks."

"But no matter how hard he tries, he won't get it."

Saltimar chuckled. "Don't tell the horse, or he might file a grievance."

"Do the owners of the mill ever give the carrot to the poor thing?"

"If they did, the horse would have no incentive to work."

Heather frowned. "It's cruel. Just *once* the horse should win."

A few moments later, Saltimar stopped the cart at the general store. He pulled a scrap of bark from his pocket, with writing on it.

"Your mother gave me a shopping list. I dare not return home without these things or I'll be sleeping in the stable with the dogs."

She giggled. Her father tied the horse's reins to a hitching post and disappeared into the store to shop. While she waited, Heather observed the grain mill horse toil away in fruitless, solitary labor. Leaving her peacock feathers stowed safely under the seat, she slid down from the cart and headed toward the mill. No one was around, so she ducked under the spokes of the rotating wheel and used her hunting knife to cut down the carrot. Confused, the horse slowed and then stopped altogether. Heather snapped the carrot into pieces and fed them to the old workhorse, patting his neck as he chewed. Sudden, loud shouting from inside the grain mill made Heather flinch. She took cover behind the shoemaker's shop and peeked around the corner to watch.

The owner of the mill emerged, cursing. He slapped the cut end of the rope and kicked the dirt in frustration. Heather gasped when the man loosened a whip coiled on his belt, and cracked it at the horse's flanks. The horse strained at his harness, and with a terrified neigh, he began to move at a faster pace than before.

"Keep it moving, ye old nag."

Wracked with guilt, Heather crept back toward the general store. She'd meant to help the horse, but instead she'd made things worse. When she arrived, she found her father loading parcels in the back of the cart.

"There you are. I sold every one of my pelts today, so I bought you a present."

He presented her with a handsome leather quiver full of arrows and a matching child-sized bow. Heather's eyes shone with joy.

"Oh, Papa, thank you. How perfect!"

"I'll make you a better one myself, come winter. Until then, you can use this one to practice. There's a target in the back of the cart that goes with it."

As her fingertips explored the polished wood, Heather's determination became even more firmly fixed than before. "Papa, how many commoners have won the Tournament of Chance?"

"None yet," he replied. "But I've heard there are some strong competitors this year."

"I expect the first commoner to win the tournament will be famous."

"I'm sure you're right about that."

As they headed back to the main road, Saltimar and Heather passed the grain mill again. Another carrot had been procured and was now hanging off the stick. The horse had settled into a nice, comfortable pace, and the owner had disappeared inside the mill.

"Between you and me, I'd like to see the horse get the carrot, too. Just once," Saltimar confided.

Abashed, Heather managed to nod.

DRAGON REBELS

*B*efore sighting her target, Heather touched the lucky peacock feather in her lapel. *"I am the arrow, and I will find my mark,"* she whispered. Her loosed arrow soared through the air to earn another perfect score. Although it remained for the head judge, Sir Fitzelle, to verify the results, Heather had won the Eastern Regional championship.

Slinging her wooden recurve bow across her back, Heather marveled as always at its majestic lines. Saltimar had made the bow himself out of horn, wood, and sinew. Its compact design lent power to the accompanying footed arrows. Her father had become an artisan in the craft of bow and arrow making over the last ten years, so much so that hunters from miles around sought his expertise. The ornate stamped leather quiver hanging from Heather's belt was one he'd given her on her eighteenth birthday, nearly a year ago. She wore it with pride.

She reported to the judges' stand to receive her bona fides, the scroll that would admit her to the final match of the Tournament of Chance. Mounting the makeshift dais, she held the scroll aloft in triumph. The spectators roared their appreciation, but Heather scanned the multitude of faces for those of her parents. She returned her mother's wave, but she sought her father's approval. Even at this distance, his eyes were twinkling. The single nod of his head filled her with pleasure.

As she beamed at the huge crowd celebrating her Eastern Regional Championship win, her cousin, Obie, appeared at the dais.

"I had the utmost confidence in your victory. In fact, I just won myself a pocketful of silver taking wagers."

"I'm glad I could help line your purse, Obie. What would you have done if I'd lost?"

"Run."

Several young men from her village arrived just then, including the raw-boned blacksmith's apprentice, Ustin.

"Congratulations, Heather. We're here to escort you home."

"So soon? Can't you give me a moment to bask in the glory and all that?"

People were stamping their feet and whistling with infectious enthusiasm.

"It's getting a bit rowdy, wouldn't you say? Besides, I hear there's to be a party in your honor. We can't keep your admirers waiting."

With one final wave, Heather allowed herself to be coaxed into leaving. She took a few steps toward her parents, but Ustin held her back.

"We brought your horse for you, Heather. I've spoken to Saltimar and Rose. They'll drive the wagon home, and you'll be riding with us."

She glanced over, but her parents had already disappeared into the crowd. Heather laughed and gave a little shrug.

"I have little choice, do I?"

She accompanied her friends to the railing where they'd tied the mounts. The journey was a merry one for her and Obie. As they rode their horses down the road, her cousin kept her entertained with amusing anecdotes about the parts of the day's competition she hadn't seen. But Ustin and the others swiveled their necks as if scanning the horizon for pheasants.

"Give it a rest, lads," Heather said finally. "You're making me nervous. Do you expect to be set upon by bandits?"

To her surprise, Obie didn't laugh. "Can't be too careful, Heather. Dragon Rebels have been spotted around here."

"Ugh...Dragon Rebels. They're all about the 'restoration of Ormaria,' aren't they? I've never heard anything so ridiculous."

"You don't believe the legends?" Obie asked.

"Romantic nonsense. What a waste of time."

"If you manage to win the Tournament of Chance next week, I expect we won't hear from the rebels for a while," Obie said.

"Why would that be?"

"You'll have proven the king is as good as his word."

"If my victory will secure peace in Destiny, I'll redouble my efforts."

THAT NIGHT, Heather's father hosted a party at the local tavern. Spirits were high, and most of the town showed up to partake of free-flowing ale and roasted wild boar. Even the staid Vicar Jenns and his two daughters put in an appearance.

Saltimar raised his tankard for a toast. "To my extraordinary daughter, the next winner of the Tournament of Chance!"

"We're counting on you, Heather," Vicar Jenns added. "You've become an inspiration for common folk everywhere."

Heather grinned. "I'll do my best."

"Let us also drink to King Chance. It's because of his tournament that our Heather has the opportunity to become a Lady," Saltimar said.

At that, Ustin stood. "You're daft, every one of you. Don't

you realize the tournament is for show? The king will never let a commoner win."

The tavern roof nearly lifted off its rafters with the echo of boos, but Saltimar raised his hands for quiet. "The lass with the truest aim will be the winner, Ustin. Arrows don't lie."

Ustin folded his arms across his chest. "No commoner has ever won the tournament. How do you explain that?"

"Cream rises, Ustin. This year, it's Heather's turn," the vicar said.

"Heather will never be made a member of the nobility under this monarch. Mark my words," Ustin said.

"Better be careful, lad. With talk like that, you might be mistaken for a rebel," Saltimar chortled.

Everyone laughed except for Ustin, and the celebration continued unabated. Casting a dark glance around the room, Ustin left the tavern without another word. Obie leaned over to Heather. "I'd better go see what's got into him." After he drained his tankard, he followed Ustin outside.

Heather glanced at Kitty, Ustin's younger sister. "What's wrong with your brother? You don't suppose he's actually joined the rebels, do you?"

Kitty shrugged. "Ustin's had his eye on you for ages. He's probably upset because when you win the tournament, you'll be living at court, and he'll be stuck with one of the vicar's daughters. He doubtless finds it an unappetizing prospect."

She had a good point. The eldest of the vicar's two girls was plagued with boils and lacked her two front teeth. The younger was not quite so homely, but she was known to be pious in the extreme.

"I wish Ustin luck. I have no desire to settle down...not for a long while," Heather said.

"Once you get to court, there will likely be many handsome men to change your mind."

"It would take more than a handsome face to tempt me, Kitty; I can safely promise you that."

Kitty gave her a teasing glance. "We'll see. You'll live in the castle, marry a nobleman, and live a charmed life. Even though I'm happy for you, I'll miss you terribly."

She paused a moment.

"So will Ustin," she added.

Kitty and Heather burst into laughter.

OVER THE NEXT WEEK, Heather spent most of her waking hours with her bow and arrows. She practiced in a pasture outside of town. The field was surrounded by trees, which made it quite private—and isolated. The morning before the competition, Heather was working on accuracy. When her arrows were spent, she set off for the target to retrieve them.

Three strangers emerged from the forest. They fanned out, as if encircling their prey. Heather was schooled enough in hunting to recognize predators on sight. A ripple of fear traveled down her spine. Dropping her bow, she pulled her knife from her boot and searched for a means of escape.

"Oi, now, no need for that. Yer Heather, aren't ye? Such pretty red hair ye got," the first man said. His lips pulled back over his teeth, blackened by poor hygiene and tobacco.

"Yer father done broke his leg. We come to fetch ye home," the second said.

The third man said nothing, but he unfastened the bullwhip hanging from his belt and gave it an experimental crack.

"My friend don't like yer little stickpin. Put it down, there's a good girl," the first man said.

Heather kept her eyes trained on the bullwhip. When the man pulled back his arm, poised to strike, she hurled her knife at his chest. Even before he'd hit the ground, she was sprinting past him toward the forest. Her only hope of evading capture would be to lose the other two men in the woods. Although she was fleet-footed, her assailants closed the distance in the open field rapidly. Several yards away from the tree line, the twang of arrows being loosed reached her ears. The men behind her cried out, but Heather didn't slow down—until she slammed into Ustin. He grabbed her by the arms.

"You're safe, Heather. They're dead."

"Ustin! I'm so lucky you were here," she panted, gasping for breath. "Were those men Dragon Rebels?"

"No. I'm absolutely certain they weren't."

Obie came crashing through the forest with his bow in hand. His friends Cor and Lane followed. Lane handed Heather her hunting knife, now wiped clean. "Good throw, that. Saved me the trouble of wasting an arrow."

"Were you lads here the whole time?"

Ustin nodded. "You were never in any real danger, but we waited to make sure there weren't others lurking about."

"Others? Like who?"

"The king's goons, of course." Obie rubbed his hands together with enthusiasm. "I suddenly feel the need for a bonfire."

"Nothing like a fire to get rid of pesky deadwood, eh?" Cor snickered.

While Cor, Lane, and Obie dragged the three bodies into the center of the pasture and set them ablaze, Ustin and Heather retrieved her bow, arrows, and practice target.

"What's happening, Ustin? Why are you following me, and what makes you think those horrible men were sent by the king?"

"Nine years ago, a commoner won a place in the final competition. She fell ill at the tournament and died. Many people believe she was poisoned."

"Idle gossip and speculation. What does her misfortune have to do with me?"

"Six years ago, there was another exceptional contestant—a commoner from the north. She won several preliminary archery competitions, and it was widely believed she would win the tournament. One day, she was attacked. The men stole nothing, but the girl had her fingers broken so badly she could never again hold a bow properly."

"If the king was truly determined to fix the outcome of the tournament, Ustin, I would've been attacked long before now."

Ustin smiled, but he wasn't amused. "You stayed safe because you've secretly been protected by Dragon Rebels all year. There are more of us than anyone realizes, and we've thwarted at least six attacks so far. You'll be escorted to the tournament tomorrow by rebels, and we'll be watching the outcome closely."

Stunned, Heather found it difficult to accept what Ustin had told her. Her closest friends were Dragon Rebels, and she'd had no idea. She'd had gone hunting with Obie several times over the last few months, and he never said a word.

A LOUD INSISTENT pounding at the front door startled Heather awake the next morning. A few moments later, she heard Ustin having a row with her father in the kitchen. Heather's mother, still clad in a dressing gown, stepped into the bedchamber. She held a lantern aloft.

"Get up, Heather."

"What's happening, Mother?"

"Ustin and Kitty are here."

"Kitty, too?"

"Aye. Put on your hunting gear, quickly."

Aghast, Heather stared at Rose, wide-eyed. "But I'm going to the tournament today. I'm to wear my best clothes."

"Don't argue with me. Ustin says you're in danger."

"What?"

"There are men canvassing the town for you right now, so there is no time to waste. You must travel in disguise."

Heather grasped a hank of her thick auburn waist-length hair. "How are we going to hide this?"

Rose produced a pair of shears. "We can't."

Not too long after that, Heather and Rose hastened into the kitchen. Ustin nodded his approval at Heather's appearance. Kitty and Saltimar were less discreet in their reactions. Heather's father flat out moaned, and Kitty put her hand to her mouth in shock. Although Heather wore the same breeches and leather boots she always wore when hunting, her wavy mane had been closely cropped. With her slender figure and her newly shorn hair, she could have passed for a boy. Rose tossed the hair clippings into the fire. Tears stung Heather's eyes, but she blinked them away.

"That's that. No one searching for Heather will be looking for a lad," Rose said.

"Well done, Rose," Ustin said.

Saltimar averted his gaze from his daughter's mutilated appearance. "I'll get my hunting gear and saddle the horses."

Ustin shook his head. "No, Saltimar, you can't come with us. They'll be watching for you in particular."

"You'd have me leave my own daughter unprotected?"

"Heather will arrive at the tournament safely. Obie and I would give our lives to make sure of it," Ustin said.

"Surely that won't be necessary," Heather said.

Saltimar stared at Ustin for a few moments, and then wrapped his daughter in his arms. "Winning this competition isn't worth the price, child. Forfeit and we will go on as before."

"Aye, your father is right, Heather," Kitty said. "Just walk away. None of your friends will think the less of you for it."

"I will *not* forfeit. I believe Ustin is sincere, but I'm certain the king himself cannot be responsible for this mischief. Once I reach the castle grounds, I'll be under his protection. All will be well."

Everyone jumped when a knock sounded at the door. A deep, growling voice called out. "Open up, Saltimar. We must have a word with you."

"The king's men," murmured Ustin.

As Saltimar hurriedly pressed money into his daughter's hands, Rose thrust a sleep cap at Kitty. "Put this on and get into Heather's bed."

Kitty gave Heather a quick hug. Tucking her brown tresses into the cap, she scrambled toward Heather's bedroom. Ustin pulled Heather toward the back door, but she suddenly froze.

"I almost forgot my bona fides! I can't leave without that scroll."

Heather's saddlebag was sitting by the front door. As she slung it over her shoulder, the door burst open, and five men poured into the house. One seized her by the arm.

"Where's yer sister, boy?"

She gulped. "Lazy girl isn't awake yet," she replied, in a slightly lower register than she was used to.

Saltimar advanced. "Get your hands off my son," he boomed, without missing a beat. "And what do you mean by knocking my door in?"

The men pushed forward to confront Saltimar while Heather backed out of the house and headed for the stables. Ustin was already there, saddling her horse.

"That was close," she gasped.

"Obie will join us on the outskirts of town," he said.

"We can't leave Kitty and my parents there alone!"

"Don't be concerned," Ustin replied. "Lane, Cor, and several other rebels are hiding outside. When they see we're safely away, the king's men will mysteriously disappear, and an early morning bonfire will be lit."

Heather retrieved her archery gear from the tack room. She slung her bow across her body, as if she were going on an ordinary hunting trip—but this time she was the one being hunted. She and Ustin rode out of the stable and down the road at a slow walk, to belay any suspicions. A quarter mile or so from the house, Ustin urged their horses into a trot.

Dawn was glimmering at their backs when they met up with Obie. He stared at Heather, open-mouthed. "Ye look like a boy!"

"Yes, thanks, Obie. That's the whole point," she replied.

Ustin glared at Obie. "I think her hair looks better this way."

"Oh—yeah, you're right," Obie lied, with a vigorous nod. "Much better."

Heather sighed.

DREAMS AND NIGHTMARES

*T*hey rode west toward the coast, stopping once at a roadside inn to eat. None of them had had the luxury of breakfast, so they ate with enthusiasm. A serving maid, who called herself Pansy, came by to refill their cups. "You lads heading to the tournament?"

"Aye. It'll be the first time a commoner has won," Obie said.

"I'll believe it when I see it," Pansy said. She gave Heather's cheek a caress. "Be sure to stop here on your way home. I fancy lads with ginger hair."

With a wink at Heather, Pansy returned to the kitchen.

Ustin stuck an elbow in Heather's ribs. "You've made a conquest."

Heather flushed the color of the scarlet table covering. Ustin burst out laughing, but Obie wasn't amused. "I've got ginger hair, too. Why can't I ever get the girl?"

When the trio resumed their westward trek, the road was increasingly filled with people making the sojourn to the tournament. They passed uniformed guardsmen from time to time, who were searching for something or someone. But to Heather's relief, their eyes skimmed over her without a pause.

She tried to remain calm, but each beat of her horse's hooves brought her ever closer to an uncertain future.

~

THE FINAL COMPETITION of the Tournament of Chance had been set up some distance from Destiny Castle, in a field nestled next to an apple orchard. The beautiful castle was still visible through the trees, and many a visitor strained their neck trying to get a better look.

"I'd give a lot to see that castle up close some day," Obie said.

"Better hope it's not from the prospect of the dungeons," joked Ustin.

On one side of the tournament field, cushioned benches had been erected underneath opulent canopies. Those seats were reserved for the royals, members of the king's court, and other nobility. The far side of the field was roped off for commoners. Many commoners had camped out overnight to get a good spot, and tents dotted the field. Several colorfully clad entertainers roamed through the crowds, playing instruments, juggling, or walking on stilts. When Heather, Obie, and Ustin arrived, the far side of the field was already nearly full.

Obie took charge of the horses as Heather and Ustin pressed their way toward the competition staging area. Heather recognized the head judge from the regional competition and pointed him out to Ustin. "There's Sir Fitzelle. I guess I'll go present myself."

Ustin gave her a one-armed hug. "Good luck. Just remember, Dragon Rebels are here. If the king tries *anything*, he'll be very sorry."

With her bona fides stuck in her belt, Heather approached Sir Fitzelle. "I'm here for the competition. Where shall I wait?"

Sir Fitzelle spared her the briefest of glances as he flicked his fingers. "Go over there with the rest of the commoners. This area is for competitors only."

"You don't understand, Sir Fitzelle. I'm Heather of the Jagged Peaks. I'm a tournament finalist."

The man beckoned to a couple of guardsmen. "Take this boy and put him elsewhere."

Just then, a well-dressed young man lounging nearby stood up and inserted himself between Heather and the guardsmen.

"Open your eyes, Fitzy. That's no boy," he drawled.

The judge peered at Heather as she presented her bona fides. "My heavens, child, what did you do to your hair?"

Her spine stiffened. "I think it looks better this way."

"Indeed, I don't know how your hair looked before, but I daresay it couldn't have been more fetching," the young man interjected.

Sir Fitzelle rolled his eyes skyward and sent the guardsmen back to their posts. After examining Heather's bona fides, he walked over to confer with the other judges. The young man bowed. "Call me Joe. I'm at your service."

"Thank you, Joe. Are you a member of court?"

"Not a member, exactly. You might, perhaps, call me a pest. No, that won't do. Maybe a mascot or fixture or…an annoyance. Yes, that's it; I am the official Court Annoyance."

She giggled.

"I hope you win this tournament, Heather of the Jagged Peaks," he said.

"I shall do my best. I just wish I had my lucky peacock feather with me."

The boy gave Heather a peculiar glance. "What did you say?"

"I know it's daft, but I came to the castle once before and collected an armful of peacock feathers. I've kept the tip of one in my pocket for luck ever since."

A ripple of excitement greeted the arrival of the young woman who was to be Heather's adversary. Her long, gently flowing locks shone more brightly than newly threshed wheat, and the gown that adorned her willowy figure was a marvel of light blue silk and silver embroidery. As she handed Sir Fitzelle her bona fides, the beautiful girl personified elegance and nobility. Dismay washed over Heather. With her short hair, breeches, and leather boots, she suddenly felt dreadfully self-conscious and out of place. After her morning's journey, she also suspected she smelled a lot like horse.

Glancing over to gauge Joe's reaction, Heather was disappointed to see her new friend had disappeared. Moments later, however, the king, queen, and members of court arrived with the pomp and circumstance she would have expected from royalty. After a bracing musical flourish from a quartet of trumpeters, the king and queen took their places under the canopy.

As they passed, Felicia sank into a sweeping, graceful curtsey so low she could almost have brushed the grass with her pert, dainty nose. Having never curtsied in her life, Heather didn't know how. Embarrassed, she finally made an awkward dip. It mattered little since the royal pair took no notice of anyone.

"Today is a momentous occasion," said King Chance, after he'd settled himself on a cushion. His booming voice resonated across the field. "Let the finalists for the Tournament of Chance come forward."

"Your Majesty, I present Lady Felicia of the Valley and Heather of the Jagged Peaks," announced Sir Fitzelle.

Felicia glided toward the king as if to greet an old friend, but Heather hung back. Now that the moment had arrived to actually meet the king and queen, her feet were frozen to the ground. Suddenly wishing for invisibility, she forced herself to move toward the king's canopy. All eyes swiveled in her direction as she stood next to Felicia. Murmurings and titters rippled through the royals at Heather's appearance. Although Felicia ignored her altogether, the queen openly laughed, as did many of the courtiers. A rosy blush crept toward Heather's hairline.

The king beamed at Felicia. "How splendid to see you again, dear girl."

"And you, Your Majesty," Felicia responded. Her smile showed the lovely dimples in her cheeks.

Queen Chelsea frowned—far less pleased to see Felicia than was her husband. King Chance next focused his attention on Heather. His welcoming expression did not slip one bit, but Heather was taken aback. His eyes resembled those of a cold, poisonous snake.

"And who might you be again?"

She gulped. "Heather of the Jagged Peaks, Your Majesty."

"Well done, Heather of the Jagged Peaks. It has been many years since we had a commoner compete in the final competition of the Tournament of Chance, but all are equals on the field. Let the most skilled maiden prevail."

A toss of a gold coin determined that Felicia would go first. As she stepped onto the field, a wave of enthusiasm rose from the canopied seats. Heather noticed that Felicia's elegant recurve bow bore a striking resemblance to one of her father's creations. Since Saltimar never sold his weapons to anyone other than huntsmen, someone must have purchased it from him on her behalf. Her ground quiver, at least, was Felicia's own; made from a rubbed wood, the flag of Destiny was painted on the side.

Felicia's arrow found the center of the target at fifty paces without any trouble. The nobles applauded, and many of the ladies waved scarves in approval. Heather admired her form. In her opinion, the girl had definitely earned her spot as a finalist. *But then, so have I.* When Heather took her place, a huge roar went up from the throng on the far side of the field. The greeting was much louder and more sustained than that which had welcomed the king, and she flushed with pleasure.

Joe appeared at her elbow, out of breath from running. He handed her the tip of a peacock feather. "For luck."

After accepting the feather from him, she tucked it into her pocket. To the delight of the crowd, she kissed the boy on the cheek.

"Thanks," she whispered.

Heather knelt and gathered a small fistful of soil. As she let it run through her fingers, the way the dirt fell indicated a slight westerly breeze. She adjusted her aim.

"I am the arrow, and I will find my mark," she murmured.

She released her arrow. When it sank into the target, dead center, the commoners erupted in excitement.

"This round is yours," Joe chortled.

Heather permitted herself a slight nod of satisfaction. She'd beaten Felicia, even if by the width of a hair. Headed by Sir Fitzelle, the trio of judges examined both targets and pronounced the results. "Tie."

Murmurs of approval came from the vicinity of the canopies, in stark contrast to mutters from the commoners. Several cried, "Boo!" Heather shrugged off the call. Felicia's aim had been true; perhaps the results *had* been too close to rule in her favor. The stuck arrows were removed, and the targets were walked out another twenty-five paces. A whisper of a smile flirted with Heather's lips. *The bigger the challenge, the better I like it.*

Once again Felicia scored a bull's eye, but from her vantage point Heather thought her aim was slightly off center. Stepping up to take her turn, Heather checked the wind and found it had grown still. *I am the arrow, and I will find my mark.* With a satisfying thwack, her arrow hit the exact center of the target. The commoners cheered and punched the air in victory. Their screams roiled the air like a bull stampede, but everyone held their collective breaths as the judges examined the targets.

"Tie."

As the commoners went wild, the royals shifted in their seats and exchanged uncomfortable glances amongst themselves. The targets were walked back an additional twenty-five paces, and several more guardsmen positioned themselves next to the ropes. Heather appraised the new challenge, undaunted. At home, she could hit the knothole of a tree at one hundred paces, even in a stiff wind. The only issue now was whether Felicia could do the same.

The king gave Heather a beneficent smile while his eyes glittered with dislike. She recoiled from the chill. Two footmen trotted out from the royal canopy, goblets in hand. They brought one to Felicia and the other to Heather.

"Wine to refresh yourself, compliments of the king."

Although her throat was parched, Ustin's warning about poison echoed in her ears. She pretended to sip from the cup, but kept her lips tightly compressed. Feigning satisfaction afterwards, she wiped her mouth on her sleeve and returned the cup to the footman. He peered down his long nose into the goblet.

"The king bids you drain the cup. It will be a great insult otherwise."

"I would not wish to insult His Majesty."

Heather grasped the goblet from the bottom, causing it to tip over. The contents spilled to the ground, splashing the footman's shoes.

"Oh, no. I'm so sorry. How amazingly clumsy of me."

The man scowled but left with the cup. Heather hoped he wouldn't return. Felicia gave her a gracious smile.

"Your friends are quite keen to watch you shoot," she said, referring to the hordes of commoners. "You may have the next turn, if you like."

Felicia's flaxen locks shone in the sun. Even from several yards away, her huge, cornflower blue eyes radiated sweetness. Heather had always imagined girls like her existed only in tales of princesses and unicorns.

"All right," Heather said.

Kneeling for what she hoped would be the last time, she

scraped together a handful of dirt. Its drift indicated the westerly wind had kicked up again. Heather stood and adjusted her aim accordingly. *I am the arrow, and I will find my mark.*

Her arrow pierced the canvas of her target in the same hole as before. Even over the whoops and whistles of her supporters, Heather heard Joe yelling, "Yes!" behind her. She tried to give him a smile, but he was busy turning a handspring.

Then Felicia loosed her arrow. It hit the bull's eye, but off-center. The royals gasped in horror, and the commoners screamed in excitement. Heather's shock turned to bliss. She'd won the tournament at long last! Everyone fell silent when Felicia's head bent forward. She cupped her delicate fingertips over one of her lovely eyes. The royal surgeon examined Felicia and then had a word with the king. Heather was bewildered, as was Joe.

"What's going on?" he muttered.

Sir Fitzelle approached, a peculiar expression on his face. "I'm afraid you have been disqualified for cheating, Heather. You threw dirt in your opponent's eyes. Her aim was off because of it."

Heather couldn't believe her ears. "I did no such thing!"

Joe was even more vocal. "That's complete dragon dung. Heather didn't cheat; I swear it! I was standing here the whole time."

Sir Fitzelle shot him a warning glance. "That's enough. It has been decided." He paused. "It's out of my hands."

Vibrating with shock, Heather stared at the ground. As Lady Felicia was declared this year's winner of the Tournament of Chance, the commoners began to boo. The sound began low but built until it resembled the groan of a hurricane. To show their dissatisfaction with the decision, people threw apple cores and rocks onto the field. Pushing and fighting broke out. When a few of the men stumbled through the rope barricades, the king's guardsmen closed ranks. Within short order, a phalanx of mounted guards joined the melee and created a buffer between the commoners and the royals. Even so, the booing grew louder.

In the meantime, the king, queen, and other members of court rose from their seats and filed toward the castle as quickly as their dignity would allow. The queen made no effort to mask her disgust. "Listen to those thugs! We try to be nice to the commoners, but they don't appreciate it."

"You don't understand, Chelsea. Commoners lack the capacity for higher thought. It's best to treat them like beasts in the field," the king replied.

If she'd been slapped, Heather could not have been more wounded. Tears pricked her eyelids. The king and queen were talking about her family, her friends—and her. When the king pointed an accusatory finger in her direction, however, she preferred the insults to what came next.

"Arrest her for inciting a riot," he told his guardsmen.

"What!" Heather gasped.

King's guards strode over to confiscate her bow and quiver. Ustin and Obie tried to push through the crowd to come to Heather's aid, but they were intercepted by guardsmen. Despite Joe's protests, the guards took her into custody. As she was hauled away, Heather shook her head in disbelief. If this were a nightmare or some kind of joke, she'd long since ceased to be amused.

THE ORMVALDERS

*H*eather shivered on the floor of an unlit, desolate dungeon. She hugged her knees for comfort and warmth but received little of either. The distant sound of the ocean filtered through the tiny slit that passed for a window, but the smell of saltwater was mixed with other, more unpleasant odors. The darkness of her cell didn't prevent Heather from discerning her situation with clarity.

She'd been an utter fool to believe she could break free from her humble roots. Ustin was right—the Tournament of Chance was a sham and a lie, now laid bare for everyone to see. King Chance had never intended to let her win—not her or anyone like her. Despite her complete and utter faith otherwise, the king wasn't egalitarian at all. The tournament had been a clever ruse designed to keep the commoners in their place.

The creaking of the dungeon door made her flinch. To her surprise, Joe appeared.

"How did you get in here?" she whispered.

"I stole the key. You've got to go now."

"I'll be executed if I'm caught trying to escape!"

"I hate to break it to you, but you're going to be executed

either way. The commoners are right angry about the tournament. You've become a symbol now, and a danger to the monarchy."

Heather followed him out of her cell and into the unoccupied corridor. As they crept through the dungeons, she expected Joe to lead her up the stairs. She winced when he lifted a heavy metal grate and slipped into a sewer trench instead. With few other options, she did likewise. They sloshed through the smelly waste, toward a sliver of light she guessed led to the outside.

"Do you swim?" Joe asked.

"Huh?"

"The castle is built on a cliff, and this trench spills down into the ocean below. We'll have to jump from the opening to escape."

"What!" Heather only had a moment for his words to register because a cacophony of shouting and torchlight at the far end of the trench indicated they'd been discovered.

"Oops," Joe said. "Be sure to dive away from the cliff so you don't get crushed on the rocks below."

He bounded the last few feet and launched himself fearlessly out into space. Heather blanched as he dove into the ocean, a hideously long way down. When an arrow whizzed past her ear, she could hesitate no longer. Bending her knees, she jumped with all the strength she could muster. As a hail of arrows rained all around her, it seemingly took forever to reach the safety of the water.

Heather plunged into the cold waves, feet first. Although she could swim, she'd never been in the ocean before. Salt water rushed up her nose and stung her eyes. She floated to the surface, sputtering. Joe treaded water a few yards away. He pointed to a large, triangular indentation in the cliff directly underneath the castle. "Swim to that cave."

As she swam into the mouth of the cave, Heather took care to avoid an enormous, barnacle-encrusted ship's anchor lodged to one side. Although the surf was relatively calm, she was relieved to reach solid ground. Exhausted, she climbed onto the flat rocks at the cave opening, shed her boots and collapsed in the late afternoon sun. Joe kicked off his boots, then removed his shirt and twisted it to squeeze out the excess moisture. If Heather had been alone, she would have done the same.

"Are we safe here? Won't the king's guards follow us?" she asked.

"Nah," he replied. "They don't want to run into my little friend."

"Who do you mean?"

"You'll see." Joe turned his head toward the cave, cupped his hands over his mouth and yelled, "Hey, Lizard Lips!"

Something stirred in the depths of the cave. Despite her fatigue, Heather jumped to her feet in alarm. As she peered into the darkness, she saw an enormous creature undulating in her direction. Lunging for her boot, she pulled her hunting knife from its hidden sheath and took a fighting stance. Joe's laughter was disconcerting.

"Relax. Shimmer won't hurt you as long as you're with me."

The creature emerging from the darkness was a dragon with a wingspan large enough to span her family's stone cottage back home. Its smooth black scales covered a barrel-shaped chest, and its head resembled a cross between a snake and a stallion. Heather's jaw dropped open, but the dragon ignored her and bent his long neck down toward Joe.

"Hello, Your Highness. Is this female my dinner?" the dragon said.

Heather bristled with fear, but she wasn't going into that gullet without a fight. Barefooted and soaking wet, she brandished the knife in her hand.

"Just who're you calling *dinner?*"

The dragon merely cocked his head, but Joe stared at Heather, wide-eyed.

"You're dragon-apt? You understood what Shimmer just said?"

"Yeah, and why did he call you *Your Highness?*"

"Oh, it's our little joke."

Shimmer supplied the answer. "Jovander Chance Hennings is the son of the king."

Heather gasped.

"Unacknowledged," Joe admitted. "The king wasn't married to my mother when I was born, you see. I'm kind of like an open secret around the castle."

Heather remembered the jealous expression on Queen Chelsea's face when she'd greeted Felicia. "Does the queen know?"

Joe grinned. "Indeed, Queen *Cheesy* is well aware of my existence. She tried to kill me a couple of times. When I was seven, the king and queen had my mother and me thrown off the cliff into the ocean."

At that, his cocky smile slipped.

"My mother drowned, but Shimmer here managed to fish me out of the water and bring me back to the castle. Once my dear father realized an enormous dragon was my protector, he didn't dare try anything after that."

"How awful for you. And by helping me, you've made your situation worse."

"Not at all. The king has revealed himself at last. It is time for the Ormvalders to retake the throne."

"You're a Dragon Rebel!"

"And an Ormvalder. My mother was one of the last direct descendants."

As Heather peered at the dragon pendant hanging from Joe's neck, an old memory bubbled to the surface. "Wait a minute...I remember you now. We met in the castle garden when I was eight."

"I was wondering when you'd figure that out. For me, it was

the peacock feather that did it. You saved me from a snake back then, and it's only fair that I return the favor."

"Did you ever put the dead aldersnake in that man's bed?"

"Wexler? No, I didn't get the opportunity. When he overheard me tell you about the Ormvalders, he went straight to my father. My mother was drowned that night."

Speechless, Heather's mouth hung open. "Joe, I'm so sorry. If I hadn't been there, she might still be alive."

"It's not your fault. The king suspected my mother's secret already, when she spoke to a wild dragon. He sent Wexler to poison me with the snake." Joe turned to Shimmer. "Wake the sleeping dragons, my friend."

"As you wish, Jovander."

The black dragon zoomed into the depths of the cavern. Heather gaped in amazement.

"I thought dragons had mostly died out. I've only ever seen one other dragon, and it wasn't that big."

"Shimmer told me the dragons have been in deep slumber for generations, waiting for the Ormvalders to return. Heather of the Jagged Peaks, you're the spark that ignites a revolution." He reached out to touch her fiery hair. "Fate most certainly has a sense of humor."

A pair of dragons, one midnight blue and the other iridescent green, erupted from the depths of the cave. As Heather and Joe ducked for cover, the two handsome, well-muscled dragons zoomed past and took wing out over the ocean.

"How exquisite. Blue is my favorite color," Heather said.

"My favorite color is anything that's not red and gold," Joe quipped.

Shimmer returned moments later.

"You awakened only two dragons?" Joe asked, puzzled.

"For the moment. I will explain when they return," Shimmer replied.

Joe patted the dragon's snout. "Will you take Heather home for me?"

"No. I don't want to leave." Heather stood tall and squared her shoulders. "I've proven myself an expert archer. If there's going to be a revolution, I want to join the fight."

"I was hoping you'd say that," Joe said, grinning broadly. He offered her his hand. "To Ormaria."

Heather grasped his hand in hers. "To Ormaria."

Shimmer spoke. Although his deep voice was recognizable, the dragon suddenly was not.

"To Ormaria."

An elderly man stood where the dragon had been a moment before. Heather gasped. Joe was so startled that he tripped over the uneven rocks and landed on his posterior.

"Oh, sorry about that, Jovander." The man helped Joe to stand. "I always did like to make a dramatic entrance. It's a personal failing, I admit."

Elegantly tailored clothes accentuated the older man's still-imposing physique. His full beard and mane of long white hair contrasted with the sweeping black fabric of his tunic, and he wore a dark crystal pendant around his neck.

"Shimmer?" Joe asked.

"Prince Shimmeris Augustus Ormvalder, to be precise. I am the younger brother of the last Ormarian king, at your service." He gave them a courtly bow.

Heather gaped. "You're human?"

"Completely. To extend my life, I had to choose between transforming myself into an elegant dragon or an ungainly turtle. The choice seemed obvious."

The two other dragons returned just then and landed next to Shimmer. The creatures morphed into young men, both wearing crystal pendants of their own. The shorter one sported a shaggy beard and a mischievous attitude. He exchanged an embrace with Shimmer but stepped back afterwards to peer into his face.

"I say, old boy, you've aged an awful lot."

Shimmer laughed. "And you, Manfred, not at all."

Manfred stretched and then jumped up onto a nearby ledge to sit. He dangled his feet, his face wreathed in merriment as if he were enjoying himself. The taller man had a short sandy beard, with a shock of blonde hair that fell over his brow. In appearance and reserved demeanor, he presented himself as wholly opposite to his friend. His cool blue eyes examined Heather and Joe with something approaching disdain.

"Shimmer, you were supposed to wake us for the revolution. Surely these two boys are not our best and brightest hope for the restoration of Ormaria?"

Both Joe and Heather bristled.

"One of the boys is a *girl*," Heather replied.

The man glanced at her, askance. "If this is what women look like after all this time, Shimmer, perhaps you should return me to my dragon crystal stasis."

"You conceited popinjay," Joe exploded. "Heather's more woman than *you* could handle."

With lightning-fast reflexes, the man drew his sword and leveled it at Joe's throat. "Greater men than you have died for less, lad."

Inexplicably, Shimmer chuckled. "Oh, put your sword away. We are all friends here. Jovander Chance and Heather of the Jagged Peaks, allow me to present Prince Dane and Prince Manfred."

Manfred raised his hand. "Hallo. Just call me Manny."

Heather liked Manny right away, but she itched to slap Prince Dane across his smirking, superior face. His straight nose sniffed the air, delicately.

"What's that stench? It's like an outhouse."

Heather and Joe exchanged an embarrassed glance.

SUZANNE G. ROGERS

"We were obliged to escape the castle through a sewer trench," Joe admitted. "I'd hoped our ocean swim had removed the smell."

"I have precious little magic left, but I can at least remedy that," Shimmer said.

As Shimmer waved his hand, Heather and Joe were suddenly clean, dry, and odor-free. Joe admired his fresh clothes, impressed.

"That's amazing, Shimmer. You're a wizard."

"*Your Highness*," corrected Dane. "He's Ormarian royalty, you insolent pup."

"Shimmer will do. Dane, Jovander is also of royal blood."

"If that is so, the kingdom has deteriorated more than I would have believed possible," Dane said.

When Heather gasped at the prince's rudeness, a distinct flush crept over his cheekbones. Nevertheless, he walked off a few paces and folded his arms over his chest, defiantly.

"How long *has* it been?" Manny asked.

"Two hundred thirty-six years," Shimmer said.

"That long?" Dane closed his eyes, as if he had a headache. "It feels like only days have passed."

Manny jumped down from his perch. "Why haven't you awakened any of the others, old boy?" he asked Shimmer.

"The people of Destiny may be ready for revolution, but the Ormvalders are not. We must restore our magic if we are to prevail."

The violent growling of Manny's stomach was audible even over the pounding surf. He glanced around, sheepishly. "Oh... sorry, but I haven't eaten in two hundred thirty-six years."

"I can guide you to a rebel stronghold north of here where we can get food and shelter, but I had rather hoped to fly. If we walk, it will take hours," Joe said.

"Let us fly then," Shimmer said.

38

Heather caught hold of Joe's sleeve. "What about my parents? Is there any way to get word to them that I'm safe?"

"Don't worry. Someone at the stronghold will be willing to carry news to Jagged Peaks."

As Dane and Manny leaped off the rocks, they transformed into dragons. Shimmer retook his dragon shape and allowed Joe and Heather to climb onto his back. Although she was hesitant at first, Heather gamely sat behind Joe and wrapped her arms around his waist. When Shimmer jumped into the air, he seemed to float for a moment before rapidly accelerating over the water. The three dragons hugged the coastline as they streaked north.

"You're shivering, Heather. Are you cold?" Joe asked.

"A little, I suppose. This is all so exciting. I had no idea the Ormvalders could work magic."

"Nor did I."

Shimmer laughed. "If our quest is successful, you won't have seen anything yet."

HEATHER'S FOLLY

hen the Ormvalder dragons finally landed in a mountainside clearing next to a stream, the last glimmer of daylight was blinking out.

"Bad luck," Joe said, peering at the nighttime sky. "But the stronghold is not too far from here, if we can avoid breaking our necks in the dark."

To his surprise, three strong circles of light suddenly shone from the crystals hanging around the necks of the Ormvalders. Joe and Heather stared in amazement.

"Our crystals are useful for many things, although the strength of our magic is greatly diminished at present," Shimmer said.

Heather cocked her head as she heard rushing water. "Is that a waterfall up ahead?"

"Yes. The Dragon Rebel stronghold is hidden behind it," Joe said. "We're probably being watched right now. Until I can identify us as friends, we should keep our hands where they can be seen."

"I will not!" exclaimed Dane. "I'm an Ormvalder, not some prisoner of war."

"Have it your way," Joe said. He took his dragon pendant from around his neck and held it up like a white flag. "We'll see how you feel when you have a spear through your eye."

Dane reluctantly put his hands up.

"And it would probably be better to dispense with any titles, *Dane*. Dragon Rebels aren't real fond of royalty at the moment," Joe said.

Joe led the way, but as they drew near the stronghold, an arrow landed in the dirt at his feet. He held his dragon pendant higher and called out. "I'm Jovander Chance. I have Heather of the Jagged Peaks and three warriors with me who want to join the cause."

"Throw down your weapons," came a voice from the darkness. "I warn you, you'll be thoroughly searched."

Apart from their dragon crystals, Manny and Shimmer were unarmed. Dane slowly removed his sword belt and laid it on the ground. Heather merely folded her arms across her chest.

"As I recall, Heather, you used to keep a hunting knife in your boot," Joe murmured.

"I don't feel comfortable giving up my only means of self-defense."

Dane gave her an appraising glance. "I cannot help but agree with Heather. If we give up all our weapons, we'll be too vulnerable."

"What are you talking about? You gave up your sword right away," Heather said.

"That was only my most visible weapon."

Her chin lifted. "I'll wait here."

"Don't be daft, Heather! You look half dead on your feet," Joe said. "Besides which, there are friends to be made and food to be had."

Manny grabbed his stomach. "Don't talk about food."

Dane made a sound of frustration deep inside his throat. He removed a knife secreted in his own boot and threw it down. "I can offer you magical protection, Heather, which is considerably more powerful than any knife."

"You haven't seen what I can do with a knife."

"If your skills with a blade are half as sharp as your tongue, I would be amazed." Despite her misgivings, Heather reluctantly tossed her hunting knife into the dirt next to Dane's. In the next moment, Joe, Heather, and the Ormvalders were set upon by rough hands and dragged toward the stronghold.

TORCHLIGHT ILLUMINATED THE EXTENSIVE CAVE, which was crowded with rebels. When Heather appeared, two voices called out her name. Ustin and Obie pushed their way forward, but Dane stepped in between, with a fierce glare.

"The lady is under my protection."

"It's all right, Dane," Heather said. "I know them."

Still bristling, the prince stepped aside. She threw herself into Ustin and Obie's arms.

"I'm so glad to see you!" she exclaimed.

"We thought for sure you were in irons—or worse. How'd you manage to escape?" Obie asked.

"Not now, Obie. Let Heather rest and have a bite to eat before you grill her for details," Ustin said.

Ustin guided her to the long trestle table in the center of the cave. One of the rebels brought the newcomers bowls of stew and coarse bread. Thankful for even the simplest of fare, she ate quickly. Ustin told the rebels how they'd slipped past the king's men that morning. He left nothing out, including the fact that Heather had cut her hair to assume a disguise. While Ustin spoke, a great many eyes fell upon Heather. Her color rose when she noticed Dane's among them. Ustin narrated the story up to the competition. Joe took over then. Although Heather interjected comments every so often, he relished the limelight. He detailed their escape from the castle with enthusiasm, and everyone gasped when he described their harrowing leap off the cliff amidst a barrage of arrows. Embarrassed, Heather hastened to change the subject.

"What happened after the king arrested me, Ustin?"

"Rebels set up a vigil outside the castle, backed by the massive crowds that had witnessed your victory," he replied. "To quell the uprising, the king sent an emissary to announce you'd been released and—"

"And as a goodwill gesture, King Chance bestowed upon you the title of Lady," Obie interrupted. "My fellow rebels, we are amongst nobility."

Cheering and laughter followed his remarks, but Heather frowned and shook her head in disgust. "For me to accept the title now would be a hollow victory. The king would sooner have me killed than welcome a commoner into his castle. And I would rather die than kiss his ring."

"Well said, Heather. There are probably many whose allegiance could be bought in exchange for a title," Ustin said.

"For me, the revolution is more about deposing King Chance than anything else." Heather avoided Dane's gaze. "I'm afraid I've become disillusioned with royalty."

Joe stood and cleared his throat. "Gentlemen, I would like to present to you the greatest weapon we have against the king... the Ormvalders themselves."

Many of the rebels laughed.

"You hit your head in that cliff dive, Joe?"

Shimmer rose. "The lad speaks the truth. Dane, Manfred, and I are direct descendants of the Ormvalders."

Direct descendants? They are *the Ormvalders.* Heather shot Joe a quizzical glance. Bemused, he could only shrug.

"We've been living abroad, but when we heard rumors about an insurrection, we came to see for ourselves. There is much you do not yet understand about the surviving Ormvalders. We are enchanters and wizards who can magnify our power through our dragon crystals."

His words were greeted with blank stares.

"What's a dragon crystal?" Ustin asked finally.

Shimmer tapped the long rectangular crystal hanging from a cord around his neck. A dim light emanated from the stone's core. "*This* is a dragon crystal, lad. It allows us to focus our magic. We can even transform ourselves into animals—most often dragons."

Outright laughter and cries of "nonsense" ensued. Heather shot to her feet and gave the rebels a scorching glare.

"Open your minds and listen to Shimmer. I've seen the magic for myself."

"As have I," Joe said.

"After the contempt I endured from royals this day, I didn't expect this kind of reception from friends." Trembling with anger, Heather sank back onto the hard wooden bench.

The men grew quiet.

"We're wasting our time on this lot, Shimmer," drawled Dane. "Let them attack King Chance and his army with their little arrows and sledgehammers. After the slaughter, they'll beg for our help."

One of the bigger brutes raised his fists and advanced on the prince. "We've had enough of your superior attitude."

"You tell 'em, Zed."

Dane merely raised his hand, and Zed stopped in his tracks. Although he railed, cursed, and pushed against an unseen force, he couldn't break through. Everybody stared, awestruck.

"Imagine having that kind of power on your side, only ten times larger," Manny said. "We could remove the current monarchy, and none of us has to die."

"And in return?"

"We require only the orderly restoration of the Ormvalders

SUZANNE G. ROGERS

as the rightful rulers of Ormaria. As I understand it, that's what you're fighting for," Dane said.

"If the Ormvalders are so powerful, how were they routed in the first place?" Obie asked.

"When King Ansgar Ormvalder was dying, the illness took its toll on his mind," Shimmer said. "He bound up most of the Ormvalder magic in the original Dragonstone and hid it, even as hordes of Great Faturian invaders breached the borders of Ormaria."

"Without their magical powers at full strength, the Ormvalders would have been exterminated. Wizards had no choice but to go into hiding with their families," Manny added.

"We must locate the Dragonstone and destroy it. Only then will the magic of the Ormvalders be released and flow back into our individual dragon crystals," Shimmer said.

"But if the Dragonstone is hidden, how are we to find it?" Heather asked.

"I searched for the Dragonstone for many, many years. I finally traced it to Boravagg," Shimmer said.

A stunned silence ensued, and many rebels exchanged glances. Stories about the evil trolls roaming the volcanic island of Boravagg were common knowledge.

"The Dragonstone is guarded," Shimmer continued. "We must destroy it from afar to release its power."

"Then you need my skills," Heather said. "I can shatter the Dragonstone with an arrow."

"You're utterly mad!" Ustin exclaimed.

The cave seemed to explode with a cacophony of raised voices. Ustin and Obie were determined to convince Heather to return to Jagged Peaks, while she was equally determined to throw in with the Ormvalders.

"Dane, Manny, and I will travel with Heather to Boravagg and protect her with our magic," Shimmer said.

"No harm will come to her while she's with me," Dane said.

"It's out of the question," Ustin said.

"With all due respect, Ustin, I'm not asking your permission," Heather murmured.

The color rose in Ustin's cheeks, and the Dragon Rebels hooted softly.

"You'd be going on a fool's errand. Saltimar would forbid it," Obie cried.

"It's not my father's decision, Obie," Heather said. "It's mine."

"If you're going, then I'm going too," Joe said.

"You're needed here, Joe," Ustin said. "If we decide to move against King Chance, you know the castle better than anyone else."

Again the rebels erupted into fierce debate. Heather stifled a yawn. Although she tried drinking water to stay awake, she was fighting a losing battle. Finally, she folded her arms on the table, rested her head on her arms, and drifted off. A few moments later, she stirred when a man picked her up effortlessly and carried her through the cave. Surrounded by strong, muscular arms, Heather felt so safe she didn't bother to open her eyes. As the man set her down gently on a pallet of straw, a smile of gratitude lifted the corners of her lips.

"Thank you, Ustin."

But the voice that answered did not belong to her old friend.

"Sleep well, Heather," said Dane. "You've earned a warrior's rest this day."

Startled, her eyes popped open. She watched the prince's retreating back until her lids fell closed once more.

HEATHER WOKE the next morning to eerie silence. She rolled from the straw and hastened into the central cavern, where she discovered all the rebels except for Ustin and Obie had already departed. The color left her face. *Have Joe and the Ormvalders left*

without me? She breathed a sigh of relief when she spied Dane's sword belt draped over a chair next to his shirt. As she sat down at the table, Obie gave Heather a crust of leftover bread and a cup of warmed-over coffee.

"Thanks, Obie. Where is everyone?"

"Your friends are outside taking a swim with Joe. Everyone else has their orders," Obie replied.

"We stayed up late last night making plans. The rebels have decided to stand down for the moment," Ustin said.

"We don't have much choice, actually," Obie admitted. "The crowd cheered when King Chance granted you your title, so he has managed to turn public opinion once again. But rebels are traveling throughout the country as we speak, spreading the true story. It would help if you told it yourself, Heather."

"And so I shall, upon my return."

Ustin covered her hand with his. "Can we not dissuade you from this folly? Boravagg is no place for a woman. And how well do you know these foreigners?"

"I can't explain it, Ustin, but I feel secure with them. If you truly wish to see the Ormvalders return to power, you'll give me your blessing."

"And what if you fail to destroy the Dragonstone?" Obie asked.

"Then the rebels will be in the same position as before. King Chance thinks his subjects are no better than cattle. I mean to stand against him any way I can."

Obie and Ustin exchanged a glance.

"Then I wonder how you can be comfortable with these Ormvalder descendants," Ustin said. "It's clear they consider themselves far above their company."

Heather laughed. "That's only Prince Dane."

"He's a prince, is he? I suppose he *is* far above his company." Obie gave his cousin a mocking bow.

"I cannot make apologies for his attitude. I don't know him well enough for that."

"Well, the other two are all right," Ustin said. "And I've always liked Joe."

"Yeah, Joe's great. He drew us a map of the castle in case he doesn't…well, in case we need it," Obie said.

"We'll destroy the Dragonstone and return unharmed."

Ustin sighed. "No one can say we didn't try to talk you out of this insanity." He produced a distinctive bow and quiver of arrows from a wooden crate. "I believe these belong to you."

She gasped in delight. "How did you manage to wrest them away from the guards?"

"Obie liberated them in his own unique fashion."

Obie feigned a little shadow boxing. "There are a few royal guardsmen who don't look very pretty this morning. Not as pretty as me, anyway."

"No one is as pretty as you, Cousin," Heather teased.

Obie pouted. "Tell that to the girls."

AFTER PROMISING to bring word of her wellbeing to Saltimar, Rose, and Kitty, Ustin and Obie set off down the mountain. Shortly thereafter, Shimmer returned to the cave.

"Good, you're awake, Heather. You slept nearly twelve hours, poor child."

"Shimmer, I'm a bit confused. Why didn't you want the rebels to know who you really are? Why pretend to be foreigners?"

"It isn't wise to tell people too much incredible information at once. I told them what they needed to know to keep them from rushing into an armed conflict they couldn't win. They'll learn the whole truth in due course."

Heather cocked her head. "And this quest to Boravagg? Have you told me only what I need to know?"

Before Shimmer could answer, Dane, Manny, and Joe appeared. The sleek muscles of Dane's bare arms and torso glistened from his recent swim. Blushing, Heather averted her eyes.

"I wish to be completely honest, Heather. This venture is horribly dangerous, potentially fatal, and with an uncertain outcome," Shimmer said. "Knowing that, do you want to change your mind?"

"No."

"That proves one thing," Dane said, reaching for his shirt. "She's as worthy as any Ormvalder."

"Or she's as insane as we are," Manny said.

"Or both," Joe added.

Heather hoped the poor lighting in the cave hid her flaming face. "So where are we heading first?"

"A port city north of here," Shimmer replied. "If we leave now, we'll make it well before dark."

"And from there?" Joe asked.

Shimmer untied a bag of gold hanging from his belt and tossed it onto the table. As it landed, the coins inside made a heavy, clinking noise.

"We procure a ship and set sail for Boravagg."

"Can't we fly there as dragons?" asked Manny.

"I've done it, but I wasn't carrying a human being on my back. I can't guarantee good weather the entire way, and it's entirely too risky for Heather and Jovander."

Dane shook his head. "Sailing all the way to Boravagg will take too long."

Shimmer's beard twitched with amusement. "Not with a little magical assistance."

THE BONNY HEATHER

$\mathcal{A}$s the Ormvalders were preparing to leave the cave, Dane abruptly offered to carry Heather. "We should spare Shimmer the extra burden," he added.

Heather became exasperated. "Do you have to speak to me like that?"

"Like what?"

"Like I'm a bag of cats to be drowned. I may be a commoner, but I'm still a human being with feelings. At times I see little difference between you and King Chance."

A muscle worked in Dane's jaw. "You take her then," he said to Manny. "I've had my share of insults for one morning."

He stormed out.

"What's *wrong* with him, Manny? Doesn't he understand I'm trying to help?"

"Dane's a good man, Heather, but he's had no opportunity to grieve the loss of his father. Although many years have passed since he and I went into crystal stasis, it feels to us like yesterday. Emotionally, he just lost his father *and* a kingdom, so he's a bit on edge."

She was taken aback. "Dane is the crown prince? I thought he was Shimmer's son."

"No, he's my cousin. The old boy is *my* father."

A sense of shame washed over her. The Ormvalders had retreated into crystal stasis as an act of desperation. Dane and Manny had been catapulted forward in time and were now reliant on others to help restore their kingdom. For a proud man like Prince Dane, it was likely an unbearable predicament. *If it were me, I'd be out of sorts too. Perhaps I should have held my tongue.*

Deep in thought, Heather prepared her few belongings for the trip ahead. She attached her quiver to her belt and slung her bow across her back to free her hands. As she accompanied Manny from the cave, she vowed to be more kind, understanding—and temperate.

The Ormvalders transformed into dragons in a clearing next to the river. As they flew to Port Providence, Shimmer and Joe took point. Manny and Heather stayed a few wing lengths to his right. Dane, on the other hand, kept his distance. The flight was hours long, and by the time they reached their destination, Heather was shivering. The dragons landed outside of town and morphed into their human shapes so as to make a more discreet entrance.

Dane peered at Heather's hands with concern. "Your fingers are white." The prince grabbed her hands and warmed them with his own. He said a quick spell, and the blood returned to her fingertips. "Better?"

Heather nodded and somewhat awkwardly pulled away. "Thank you."

"You should have told me you were cold, Heather. *I* would have held your hands," Joe muttered.

Dane openly smirked. Despite her vow, Heather felt like giving him a swift kick.

"Next time I will, Joe," she said.

Shimmer frowned at Heather's hair. "Just in case there are soldiers around, let's change your appearance a bit. King Chance will be looking for a girl with short red hair."

In the next moment, her hair was waist-length again. The color was that of the meadow brown butterfly fluttering nearby. Shimmer nodded in satisfaction.

"That should throw them off. Your original color will begin to return after we set sail."

As they walked into town, Heather pulled her hair over one shoulder and rapidly braided it. When she finished, however, she had no way to bind the end. Joe held out the leather strip he used to keep his shirt pocket closed. At the same time, Dane produced a bit of blue ribbon he'd conjured. Heather took them both. "Er—thanks." She used Joe's leather strip to bind her braid and tied Dane's ribbon on top.

After he'd rented them rooms at a seaside inn, Shimmer headed with Manny to the docks. To kill time, Joe went down to the beach to search for seashells. Heather still had Saltimar's money, so she stowed her bow and quiver in her room and searched the town for a general store. Pausing outside a dress shop, Heather drank in the beautiful window display. One of the jackets in particular caught her eye. Fashioned in sumptuous floral brocade in muted colors, it had a blue-ribbon closure that matched the new ribbon in her hair. Heather bit her lip in frustration at being unable to afford such a beautiful garment. With a sigh, she moved on. Perhaps she'd find an inexpensive shawl to keep the chill away.

At the general store, Heather's purchases included a comb, lavender-scented soap, a toothbrush, a tin of tooth powder, and a few things for Joe as well. She sorted through a table heaped with pretty shawls made of silk, but they were far too expensive. With the last of her money, she bought a practical woolen scarf in brown.

When she emerged, Heather was surprised to find Dane

waiting for her, his fair hair glinting in the afternoon sun. His face was turned away as he followed the progress of a carriage down the street. Apparently he'd been shopping, too, since he carried a box under his arm. The sight of him leaning against a post made her catch her breath in a way Ustin never had. *Stop it. You want nothing to do with royalty, remember?*

Dane straightened when Heather appeared and took a half-step back. Unfortunately, he stepped completely off the boardwalk and nearly lost his balance. Heather hastened to grab his arm before he landed in a puddle.

"Are you all right?"

Flushed with embarrassment, he regained his footing. His blush had turned even the tips of his ears red, and Heather found herself feeling almost sorry for him.

"Er—thanks. That was clumsy." He reached for her parcel. "May I?"

She allowed him to take the parcel. Dane fell into step with her as she headed for the inn.

"You ought not be walking around by yourself."

"You're probably right," she replied, with perfunctory politeness. "I appreciate your concern."

Dane laughed. "That wasn't terribly sincere. You're an independent girl."

"I suppose so. My father raised me that way."

"So did mine, but he didn't raise me to be rude." He caught her eye. "I've been behaving quite badly, and I'm very sorry."

"Manny told me a little about your circumstances, Your Highness—"

"Just call me Dane."

"I cannot imagine what you've endured."

"Whatever my troubles, they're no excuse for bad manners."

"There's no reason we can't put that behind us…if you like."

"I would like that very much."

When they reached the inn, Joe was pacing outside her door. "There you are, Heather! I knocked, but you didn't answer."

"I went out shopping. Actually, I brought you some things for the voyage, too."

Dane returned her parcel. She unfolded the wrappings and produced a toothbrush, a tin of tooth powder, a cake of soap, and a straight-edged razor for Joe.

"I guess that's a hint." Joe scratched the stubble on his chin. "Thanks."

A crooked smile lifted the corner of Dane's mouth. "I didn't realize you were actually shaving yet, lad."

"I'm not the only one who needs a shave," Joe retorted.

Dane stroked his beard, grinning with good humor. "I suppose fashion has changed."

"I'm sorry, but I didn't get a razor for you, Dane," Heather apologized.

"Oh, but you did." With a wave of his fingers, the prince magically duplicated everything in Joe's hands. He took one of each item before Joe could drop them.

"I should freshen up before dinner then," Dane said. "If you'll excuse me." He made Heather and Joe a slight bow. "Oh, and this is yours, Heather."

Puzzled, she took the box he proffered and opened it. Inside was the brocade jacket she'd admired in the store window.

"Oh, Dane! Why, I—"

"Consider it an apology."

Dane disappeared down the hall and into his room.

"That's as cheerful as I've ever seen him. What could account for it I wonder?" Joe mused.

"I think you have that effect on people."

～

CLAD IN HER NEW JACKET, Heather was already seated with Shimmer, Manny, and a clean-shaven Joe by the time Dane entered the dining room. A physical shock went through Heather at the sight of the prince. With his beard gone, he was incredibly handsome. Although she tried not to stare, none of the serving girls in the room made any effort to disguise their admiration. She reached for a glass of water to cover her reaction and was dismayed to see her hand tremble. As Dane slid into his seat, Manny shook his head in mock disgust. "Must you make such a spectacle of yourself, Cousin? You've put all the ladies in the room in a dither with that unfortunate face of yours."

Shimmer stifled a laugh, but Joe wasn't amused.

"I'm sorry to cause you distress, Manny, but I gather that beards are somewhat out of fashion these days," Dane said.

"What gave you that idea?" Manny stroked his own whiskers.

"Heather bought a razor for young Jovander here. I thought I would make an effort to fit in." His gaze slid to Heather.

Manny glanced at her as well. "What say you, lass? Do you prefer Dane bearded or clean-shaven?"

Fortunately, she was spared from answering by the arrival of their meal. While they enjoyed roast beef and potatoes, Manny shared other good news.

"We found a lovely ship. We'll have to sail her ourselves, and she cost us a fair bit of gold, but she's worth it."

"You *bought* a ship?" Joe asked. "Couldn't you find a captain willing to take us?"

"Not unless we wanted to lie about our destination," Shimmer replied. "I daresay no one would take us to Boravagg willingly."

"I'm quite fond of sailing. I had my own boat called the *Phoenix*. It wasn't nearly as big as this one, but I don't expect the basics have changed that much in two hundred and thirty-six years," Manny said.

"Shimmer, why in the world did you go to Boravagg in the first place?" Heather asked.

"It was because of an argument I'd had with my brother when we were children. Dragonstones don't occur naturally within the borders of Ormaria, you see. Whenever a new wizard was born, a piece of the original was cut away for his or her use."

"Why do you wear the dragon crystals around your neck?" Heather asked.

"For a wizard to work magic, the dragon crystal must touch his skin," Shimmer replied.

"I've often thought about strapping mine to my forehead, but it just didn't seem dignified," Manny said.

Dane laughed. "Lack of dignity never stopped you before."

"Indeed, it has not. I invite you to shed your dignity and have some fun, Cousin—if you can remember how."

Joe wrinkled his nose in confusion. "Doesn't chopping up the Dragonstone into smaller crystals diminish its power?"

"No, and that's the beauty of it," Shimmer said. "Each dragon crystal remains magically connected to the original Dragon-stone, as if it were never severed."

"The original stone must have been quite large," Heather said.

"I imagine so. The last time I saw it, the Dragonstone was the size of an anvil. I argued that it had been created long ago with a spell, but Ansgar didn't agree. He scoured the library for records on where it had been found. As it turned out, the Dragonstone was discovered in the cave underneath the castle."

"The dragon cave?" Joe asked, startled.

"The very same. Anyway, I accompanied Ansgar to the cave in order to prove that the crystal had grown there. But to my surprise, I was wrong. There was evidence of an ancient shipwreck. Most of the wood had been worn away by time and the tide, but we discovered an anchor and the remains of a mast. We also found the bones of a creature who was not human."

Dane and Manny were as rapt as Joe and Heather.

"I've never heard this story before," Dane said.

"Nor I," Manny added.

"Were the bones possibly those of a troll?" Dane ventured.

"Indeed they were."

"Are you serious, old boy? I've always believed the Dragon-stone was created by the first Ormarian monarch, King Liam," Manny said.

"Indeed, Ansgar and I never told anyone what we had found, because all Ormarians are taught the crystal had been created by Liam Ormvalder," Shimmer said. "They would not have enjoyed knowing we, in some way, owe our magical abilities to a troll."

"Now I understand why my father was always doing research on trolls," Dane said, shaking his head.

"What did he learn?" Manny asked.

"Trolls don't like outsiders, for one, and that's why not much is known about them. They're half again as big as humans, and their eyesight isn't very good. But they make up for that with a keen sense of smell. They don't use magic, and they aren't terribly civilized," Dane said. "That's all I know."

"They're also afraid of water. Boravagg is an island, albeit a rather large one. That fact may explain why trolls haven't spread to other continents," Shimmer said.

"And yet, there was at least one attempt to cross the ocean in the distant past," Heather observed. "I wonder why?"

"Ansgar was always curious about that same question, but when he fell ill, he became obsessed with it," Shimmer said.

"He had help with that obsession," Dane muttered, the bitterness in his voice palpable.

"What do you mean?" Heather asked.

58

"My brother's malady was magical in origin," Shimmer said. "There was a plot to overthrow the monarchy."

"We had a traitor in our midst," Dane said.

"You think this traitor encouraged the king to bind up Ormaria's power and then take the crystal to Boravagg?" Joe asked.

"Shortly after my brother and the Dragonstone went missing, Ormaria was invaded—just as our magic was at its lowest level. It could not have been a coincidence," Shimmer said.

Dane frowned. "The invaders began slaughtering anyone suspected of being a wizard."

"We gathered together every wizard we could and brought them deep into the dragon cave. Once the wizards poured themselves into their dragon crystals, I transformed myself into their dragon caretaker. Since then, I've dedicated myself to locating the Dragonstone."

Dane could not mask his pain. "It's hard to believe so much time has passed. For me, it's been a matter of days."

"I feel the same way," Manny said. "But Shimmer's face tells a different story."

Shimmer pretended to take offense. "I beg your pardon. I look pretty good for someone two hundred and eighty years old."

"I wish we could go back in time and set things right," Heather said.

"Sadly, that's impossible. We must try to make the best of it," Shimmer said. He unfurled a rudimentary map. "No one has managed to completely map Boravagg due to the hostile conditions—"

"The geography or the natives?" interrupted Joe.

"Both," Shimmer replied.

Joe studied the map. "It must be near five hundred miles from Ormaria to Boravagg! Can a dragon really fly that far without stopping to rest?"

"I've flown it before, although that was when I was younger. Our boat cannot sail as fast as a dragon flies, so it will probably take us three days to make the crossing," Shimmer said.

"And then what?" Heather asked.

"That's where things get a little murky," Shimmer said.

He refused to say more.

DAWN BROUGHT clear skies and a calm sea to Port Providence. Heather, Joe, and the Ormvalders trooped down to the docks to wait while provisions were loaded onto their newly purchased, single-masted packet ship. The vessel was about one hundred yards long and twenty-five feet across. Although the ship might have been considered small, to Heather it was enormous. "It's very nice," she said.

"Nice?" Manny echoed in dismay. "I daresay she's better than *nice.*"

"I apologize, Manny. It's just that I don't know the first thing about sailing ships. I grew up in the mountains, and I've never even been on a rowboat."

Joe swallowed hard. "It makes me ill just to look at it. Perhaps I should have mentioned I get seasick."

Manny rubbed his hands together. "A new ship must have a new name. What shall it be?"

"The *Ormaria?*" Heather suggested.

"The *Court Annoyance?*" Joe offered.

"Let's name her the *Bonny Heather,*" Dane said.

Heather blushed, but Manny's face lit up. "That's perfect."

With a wave of his hand, Dane magically changed the name of the boat to read the *Bonny Heather* in fancy letters. Shimmer, Manny, and Joe hastened on board to explore, but Heather hung back to speak with Dane. "I truly appreciate your kindnesses, but please understand you don't have to make up for anything anymore."

"You like me better rude?"

"No, of course not."

Dane flashed his straight white teeth and held out his arm toward the gangplank in invitation. "After you, Lady Heather."

"Oh...no, I have no title. I refused it, you know. Coming from King Chance, it would have been an insult."

"Would you have accepted it from the King of Ormaria?"

"Why...yes, I suppose I would."

"Then I shall make it a priority once the kingdom has been restored." He paused. "We will need to rebuild the kingdom quickly, and there will be many wizards in want of a suitable wife. A title will assist you in making a good match."

Her smile froze on her lips. *So Prince Dane wishes to foist me onto one of his friends, does he?* She couched her reply in the most civil tone she could muster. "Thank you for the compliment, Prince Dane, but I must decline. The cause is an excellent one, but I simply have no interest in becoming an Ormarian brood mare."

Heather boarded the ship, leaving the prince standing on the dock, speechless. Although she kept a serene countenance as Shimmer showed her into the modest captain's quarters, she seethed with anger—and hurt pride. Ustin and Obie's friends had often said ribald, insensitive, or outright rude things to her, and they'd provoked only a laugh. *So why should I care what Dane Ormvalder thinks—or doesn't think—about me?*

"I don't care," she muttered out loud.

"What was that?" Shimmer asked.

"Oh, I mean only that I don't care about having the captain's quarters. You should take them."

"The men will be sharing the crew quarters."

"That doesn't seem right. I don't mind sleeping in the cargo hold."

"Thank you for your concern, my dear, but I wouldn't dream of it. Our sleeping quarters will be more than adequate," Shimmer replied.

USING LONG POLES, Manny, Joe, and Dane pushed the *Bonny Heather* away from the dock. Manny barked out orders to his minimal crew and shortly thereafter the wind filled the sails. The *Bonny Heather* tacked parallel to shore a few times before she headed due west.

The prince spoke little, and eventually Manny noticed the troubled expression on his cousin's face. "Are you perfectly well, Dane? You look as if you have a nagging ache somewhere."

"It's that girl. I've been trying to be cordial but nothing I say pleases her. I even offered to give her a title, and she turned me down."

"That's odd. Receiving a title is an honor."

"Exactly. I explained that a title would assist her in finding an Ormarian husband once the kingdom is restored, and she practically accused me of trying to auction her off to the highest bidder."

Manny chuckled and shook his head. "I'm hardly a ladies' man, Dane, but you're far clumsier than I would have given you credit for."

"What did I say?"

"You as much as told her that you find her unattractive."

"I did no such thing," Dane said, indignant. "And I don't, in point of fact."

Manny made an exasperated noise. "You're a good-looking fellow, as much as it pains me to admit it. No woman wishes to hear you say she'd make a nice wife for someone *else*."

"Heather has no interest in me, nor I in her," Dane sputtered. "You're quite mistaken."

"Really? If that's true, why was she insulted?"

"Apparently she has an unfortunate tendency toward peevishness."

"If so, it's a tendency that emerges only around you, Cousin."

"No, I'm sure you're wrong."

"Then you don't mind if I borrow your razor?"

"Whatever for?"

"I just might shave off my beard." Manny stroked his chin. "I'd like to put my best foot forward as far as she's concerned—unless you object."

"You're joking."

"Not at all. Heather is very pretty, exceptionally brave, and quite amiable. I'm not near as handsome as you are, but I've been told I can make a girl laugh. Some girls prefer a man with a sense of humor."

Dane scowled. "That's an empty threat, Manny."

His cousin roared with laughter. "So I'm a threat now, am I? I'll take that as an objection, then. You don't know your own mind, Dane."

Joe ran past, green-faced and retching. He hung over the railing, in misery. Manny and Dane grinned as they hauled him back onto the deck by the seat of his pants.

"Let's get you below deck, young Jovander," Dane said.

ALTHOUGH HIS STOMACH had long since been emptied, Joe continued to moan in his hammock with a moist cloth on his forehead. Heather sat with him, murmuring the occasional supportive word.

"Are you sure you wouldn't be better off topside, Joe?"

"Ungh."

When Dane entered the crew's sleeping quarters, Heather stood so abruptly she hit her head on a low ceiling beam. "Ow."

Dane's hand shot out keep her steady. "Are you all right?"

"More or less." Heather rubbed her new bruise. "I forgot that beam was there. Excuse me, I was just leaving."

"Actually, I need your help. Now that the ship is safely underway, I can finally attend to poor Joe here."

He produced a leather apothecary case from a locker and set it down on a small table. Inside were various bottles full of dried plants and herbs and some rounded pebbles. He plucked the moist cloth off Joe's forehead.

"I didn't have much time to get supplies in Port Providence, but I can at least alleviate Joe's symptoms."

"You're a physician?"

"A magical healer," he replied. "I work—I mean worked—alongside physicians in the royal hospital. There's a bit of over-lap, but magical healers and physicians can accomplish far different things."

As the *Bonny Heather* rode a large swell, a labored sigh escaped Joe's lips. "Somebody kill me," he begged.

"Can you sit up, Jovander? We need to remove your shirt." Dane said.

Joe opened his eyes just wide enough to give Dane a baleful glare. "Shove off."

"Come on now, Joe, he's trying to help," Heather said.

After some jostling and aborted maneuvers, Dane propped Joe up so Heather could remove his tunic. Joe fell back into his hammock, limp. Selecting four of the pebbles from the apothe-cary case, Dane blew gently over the stones. At the same time, his dragon crystal gave off a gentle glow.

"Is that some kind of healing spell?" she asked.

"No, it's just to warm them up." Dane gave her one of the pebbles. "Can you put that one on Joe's stomach and make sure it doesn't slip off?"

Heather laid the warm pebble on Joe's abdomen. "Is this the right spot?"

"Perfect."

Dane placed a pebble on each of Joe's shoulders and his forehead. He spoke some strange words that made the pebbles rise in the air and turn in unison.

"What's happening?" she asked.

"The pebbles are aligning themselves, like a compass," Dane explained. "The spell allows Joe to achieve equilibrium so he won't be seasick anymore."

The color in Joe's face began to return almost immediately and before long he was snoring. Dane picked the stones out of the air and returned them to the apothecary case.

"When Joe wakes up, he'll feel much better," he said. "Now let's tend to you. I can see the bruising on your forehead from here."

"It's fine," Heather lied, edging toward the door.

The ship's sudden swooping motion caused Heather to stagger forward into Dane's arms. "What in blazes is going on?" she exclaimed.

"Shimmer said we'd be using a little magical assistance on our voyage. I believe we are flying."

"What?"

"If Shimmer's magic was fully restored, this vessel would be flying up above the clouds. As it is, we'll skim the surface of the water on our voyage to Boravagg."

After a few moments, the ship leveled out. Heather became aware she was still holding on to Dane. "Oh, do forgive me," she said, pulling away.

But Dane continued to hold her fast. "Stand still while I heal your bruise."

The delicate touch of his fingertips on her forehead sent ripples of pleasure down her spine. She closed her eyes and wished the moment would continue.

"Your bruising is much better now," he murmured finally.

Her eyelids popped open. When Heather felt her forehead, the knot raised by the wooden beam had disappeared.

"Thank you."

Dane frowned slightly as he peered at her. She wondered if she had a smudge on the end of her nose. "Is there something wrong?"

"No. I-I should see if Manny needs me."

Brushing past Heather on his way out of the crew quarters, Dane paused before he stepped through the door. "I didn't mean to offend you with what I said this morning. Any man would be lucky to win your favor."

Heather was glad he left without waiting for her reply. Had he glanced back, he would have seen a slow smile light her face.

WHEN HE AWOKE, Joe was quite recovered from his seasickness. Since the ship's movements were eerily smooth as it flew through the air, his illness was unlikely to return. In addition, Joe's appetite had rebounded. To his delight, Manny proved himself to be an adept cook. He prepared a delicious meal of roast chicken, fresh vegetables, and biscuits. The atmosphere on board was optimistic, and after a few sips of wine Heather felt her shoulders relax. Even a somewhat taciturn Dane began to laugh at Manny's jokes.

After dinner, Manny produced a piccolo, and everyone climbed topside to listen to him play under the stars. Sunset was a glorious mix of deep blue sky streaked with purplish clouds. Standing at the prow of the ship, Heather lifted her face toward the gentle warm breeze that filled the sails. When Manny began to play a waltz, Joe jumped to his feet.

"Finally, those wretched dancing lessons will prove themselves useful." He extended a hand to Heather. "Shall we dance?"

Heather waved him away, laughing. "I don't know anything other than a jig."

After several cups of wine, Joe was in high spirits. He insisted on teaching Heather how to waltz. When they had danced around the deck of the ship twice without stumbling, Dane finally climbed down from his perch on the railing.

"May I?" he asked Heather.

"I-I don't know if that's such a good idea. I'll likely trample your feet."

"I'll take my chances." When his hand slid around her waist, Heather flinched. "Relax," he murmured. "I'm not going to bite."

Heather found Dane to be an assured partner. To her surprise, they moved well together. When he gave her a sudden twirl, she giggled.

"You see? I'm not so terribly frightening," he said.

"I'm not scared of you."

"Ah, too bad," he murmured, pulling her closer. "I must be losing my touch."

At that, a rosy blush stained her cheeks. "You've a high opinion of yourself."

He pouted with mock pique. "Must you speak that way? I may be royalty, but I'm still a human being with feelings, you know."

When a peal of mirth escaped her lips, Dane's eyes crinkled at the edges. He gave her waist a squeeze. "It's good to hear you laugh."

When their waltz ended, Shimmer bade Manny to play a jig. He and Heather danced together in a riotous fashion that had everyone clapping with the beat. Then Heather tried to teach Joe how to jig. Although he did the best he could, Shimmer's jig put Joe to shame. He became particularly irked by Dane's merriment.

"I suppose dancing the jig is too undignified for you, Prince Dane?" he asked.

"Not at all."

"Let's see it, then," Joe said.

"Try to keep up, Manfred," Dane said, with a wink at his cousin.

Manny played a fast number that would have challenged the most agile of dancers. Heather expected Dane to be no better than Joe, but he tapped out a treble jig that took her aback. Although Heather and Shimmer applauded at the end, Joe's enthusiasm was muted.

"Is there anything he can't do?" Joe muttered to Heather.

"Being accomplished is only part of the equation." Heather patted his arm. "A gentleman should also endeavor to be charming, even-tempered, and friendly. You are that and a great deal more, Joe."

"Thank you, Heather. I'm glad you think so."

Joe's eyes lingered on her profile. Although Heather was oblivious to his interest, Dane was not.

BORAVAGG

*T*he *Bonny Heather* navigated through intermittent
rainstorms the next day. A skillful captain, Manny
managed to keep the ship on course. Dane conjured a sword
and armor for Joe, and the two of them practiced swordplay
above deck when the sun shone. Joe was well trained, but he
lacked discipline and focus. Heather was impressed with Dane's
ability as an instructor. She also noted how quick Dane was to
give Joe the encouragement and praise he sorely needed.

"Not too bad that time, Jovander. I thought you had me once
or twice."

"I learned from the head of the king's guards," Joe boasted.

"I *was* the head of the king's guards," Dane replied, winking
at Heather. "Let's work on that disarming move. You've almost
got it down."

The third morning dawned wonderfully clear and bright.
Heather soaked in the sunshine while enjoying Joe and Dane's
latest match. She was glad for a ready excuse to gaze at Dane,
admiring not only his quick reflexes and finesse, but also his
athletic frame and handsome face. When she'd first met him,
she thought his looks were arresting—despite his disdainful

and arrogant attitude. Now, she acknowledged privately he was the most handsome man she'd ever seen. After he caught her staring a few times, however, she tried to be more discreet. She had no wish to give Dane the false impression she was besotted with him. *One can admire a thing of beauty, such as a stallion or a dragon, without desiring to possess it*, she told herself firmly.

Joe's sword clattered to the deck as Dane disarmed him once again. Heather was brought out from her reverie.

"Say, how do I know you're not using magic against me?" Joe asked, retrieving his sword.

"Fair enough." Dane lifted the pendant from around his neck and handed it to Heather. "If you don't mind holding this for me, Joe and I will go again." He paused to brush a lock of hair back from her face. "Your hair has returned to its original color, did you know?"

As before, a ripple of pleasure went down her spine at his touch.

"That's good. I wouldn't know how to be anything other than a redhead."

Shimmer and Manny cheered Dane and Joe as they squared off in a fast and furious bout, but Heather's attention shifted to Dane's crystal. The slim dark pendant, strung on a silken black cord, was fragile and precious in the palm of her hand. *It's almost like a beating heart.* She slipped the cord around her neck for safekeeping, allowing the cool and smooth crystal to rest against her skin. A thrill of euphoria spread through her body, raising goose bumps. All at once, Heather was filled with the same confidence she had when sighting a target with her bow and arrow.

She closed her eyes and pictured an arrow speeding toward a bull's eye. *I am the arrow, and I will find my mark.* The ship suddenly flew out from underneath her feet, and she slammed onto the wooden deck. The wind whistled overhead, threatening to rip the sails from their rigging. Manny held onto the creaking mast as he tried desperately to stay upright.

"Please, Shimmer, stop it," he bellowed. "We'll be de-masted!"

Frightened, Heather raised herself onto her bruised elbows. Shimmer, Joe, and Dane had also been thrown to the deck when the ship shot forward. She could see from Shimmer's face that he was as bewildered as she was.

"It is not my magic," he yelled. "Dane?"

"It must be Heather. She has my crystal," he shouted.

"Heather, slow the ship." Shimmer exclaimed.

"But I'm not *doing* anything." she cried.

"Yes, you are," Dane said. "What were you thinking about, right before it happened?"

The image of the speeding arrow popped into Heather's mind. She squeezed her eyes closed as she imagined the arrow slowing. The wind eased, and the creaks and groans from the ship lessened. The crisis was over, but suddenly she was hauled roughly to her feet. Dane snatched his dragon crystal from around her neck.

"Idiot child. You could have killed us all."

"That's enough, Dane. She didn't know what she was doing," Shimmer said.

Heather muttered something under her breath as Dane turned away. An expression of utter incredulity came over his face. "What did you just call me?"

This time, Heather made an effort to articulate every syllable. "A…horse's…*arse.*"

Joe and Manny nearly fell to the deck again, helpless with laughter. Even Shimmer had difficulty keeping his countenance.

"Why you cheeky monkey!" Dane sputtered. "I ought to spank you for that."

"Try it, and you'll feel the sting of my blade," Heather spat.

Shimmer quickly stepped between the two. "Settle down, children. We have work to do. Heather's mistake was unorthodox, but it has had an unintended benefit. Boravagg is dead ahead. We have arrived ahead of schedule."

Nursing bruises to more than her elbows, Heather hastened to the bow of the ship. Her first glimpse of Boravagg's eastern coastline was sobering. A dark granite cliff face stretched north and south, taller than Destiny Castle. Waterfalls spilled to the ocean below in several spots. Green foliage rimmed the top of the cliff in an explosion of color. Beyond that, a mountain range thrust skyward, dark and forbidding, with a long-dormant volcano at the far north end. Boravagg was an incredibly lush and beautiful island, but the danger of their quest suddenly registered in the pit of Heather's stomach. When Joe joined her, she glanced over to catch his reaction to the view. Surprised, she found him gaping at her.

"What's wrong?" she asked.

"You can work magic!"

Heather pondered that a moment. "I suppose you're right."

"That wasn't magic," Dane muttered, a few feet away. "It was a debacle."

To SHIELD their vessel from view, Manny navigated *The Bonny Heather* inside an inlet of tall volcanic rocks, halfway up the coast of Boravagg. Shimmer unfurled his map and marked the ship's location. He made a second mark in the crater of the volcanic mountain. "The Dragonstone sits here. We can fly most of the way."

"Most of the way?" Joe echoed. "Can't we fly there directly?"

"The Dragonstone is not unguarded. If we are seen as a threat, it will be defended," Shimmer replied.

They split up several days' provisions into five knapsacks. Heather tucked her few other belongings into her knapsack as well, picked up her bow and quiver, and went to find Shimmer.

"I saw Dane perform a duplication spell in Port Providence. Could you do the same for my last few arrows?" she asked.

"I can do better than that. I shall enchant your quiver to replenish itself."

He held the quiver in his hands and performed a spell—but nothing happened.

"Didn't it work?" Heather asked, confused.

"Of course it did. Pour your arrows out onto the floor."

Heather emptied her quiver of its handful of arrows. As soon as she righted it, the quiver refilled with arrows identical to the ones at her feet. In awe, she bent to retrieve the originals.

"My father made these arrows by hand. He would be dismayed to see you have copied them with so little effort."

"You will never be defenseless. I daresay that will please him very much."

"Indeed it would."

Heather followed Shimmer above deck, where Joe was waiting. Dane and Manny had already transformed into dragons. Heather gave Dane a wide berth and headed over to Manny.

"Where is your knapsack?" she asked him.

"Anything we are wearing when we transform gets folded into the magic," Manny replied. "Otherwise, it would be quite awkward—"

"And chilly," Dane interjected.

"Definitely chilly—when we return to our human shapes," Manny said.

Joe snorted with laughter, and Heather stifled a smile. As Shimmer rolled up his map to tuck into his knapsack, Dane swiveled his blue-scaled head toward Heather.

"Get on."

"Thank you, no. I'd rather ride a shark."

"I'm sorry I lost my temper with you, Heather. I was wrong to do so. I was actually angry with myself for assuming you weren't magical. Get on, *please*."

Manny gave Heather a droll glance. "It's not often I hear my cousin admit that he's wrong. You'd best accept his apology, or we'll have no peace."

Although she still harbored some resentment, Heather settled onto Dane's back. She didn't understand him at all. At times the prince was nasty and superior, but then he could be gentle and kind. Why couldn't Dane be more like Joe, who was always in a good humor? She wasn't sure why she cared one way or the other. When the revolution was over, she'd probably never see the prince again.

Before Shimmer took his dragon form, he placed a magical spell of protection around the ship. Moments later, a seagull flew toward the tall mast and attempted to land. Squawking, the bird bounced off the spell and was forced to land on one of the rocks instead.

"What does that spell do besides repel seagulls?" Joe asked.

"As long as it's anchored here, the *Bonny Heather* will be shielded from the elements. A spell of protection also guards against magical attacks, but I hardly think we need fear that on Boravagg," Shimmer replied.

He morphed into a black dragon, and Joe climbed onto his back. The three Ormvalders took flight, with Shimmer in the lead. They angled upward to clear the steep cliff face and then skimmed the treetops toward the mountain range.

Heather marveled at the scenery below. Everything in Boravagg was larger than normal. The trees reached skyward, the leaves were the size of blankets, and many of the boulders were larger than houses. As they flew north along the crest of the mountain, they passed over a troll encampment. Gathered around an enormous fire pit, the trolls were roasting a huge animal that might have been an ox. When the dragons passed overhead, the trio of shadows caused some consternation. One troll picked up a firebrand and swung it around in a display of aggression. Heather had the impression he probably did that fairly frequently.

"I hope you're not still angry with me," Dane said.

Heather jumped, slightly startled. They'd been aloft for nearly an hour, and Dane hadn't made any attempt at conversation. Of course, she hadn't either.

"You puzzle me, Dane Ormvalder."

For some reason, Heather found it easier to converse with him in his dragon form—perhaps because she didn't have to gaze into his azure blue eyes.

"You confound me as well," he replied.

"How so?"

"Other girls I've known were all about dresses, ribbons, and gossip. You're different. I suppose a lot has changed in two hundred thirty-six years."

"Not as much as you might think. Since my focus was always on training for the tournament, I never really had time for those other things."

"What will you do after the revolution?"

"I imagine I'll become a hunter or craftsperson and work with my father. I want to travel a little first, like my Uncle Latimar."

"Nothing else?"

"Well...I would have liked to study magic properly, but after the Dragonstone is destroyed, having a dragon crystal of my own will be impossible. Does a dragon crystal's power ever fade?"

"I cannot say if it will continue forever, but the power has lasted since the founding of Ormaria."

"How did King Liam discover the Dragonstone enabled him to work magic?"

"Nobody knows, unfortunately. That part of our history predates recordation."

"Some mysteries will never be solved, I suppose, while

others take an amazing turn. Imagine my surprise when I learned so many young men in my village were Dragon Rebels!"

"Um...that fellow Ustin seems fond of you."

"And I of him. He's a fine man and a good leader. His sister is my dearest friend."

"Then you two are to be married?"

Heather giggled. "No, I love Ustin like a brother. Besides, I'm not inclined to marry. If I ever do consider matrimony, it would have to be with a gentleman who is jolly and even-tempered."

That last part was aimed at Dane, and he shook his head in amusement. "Should I happen to meet such an extraordinary specimen, I'll be sure to send him your way."

As the sun kissed the treetops in the west, Heather estimated the volcano was still an hour off. "We ought to find somewhere to camp while we still have light. Search for a place with access to water, and make sure it's defensible," she told Dane.

"Are you sure you're only eighteen? You remind me of an Ormarian general."

"I'm nineteen tomorrow."

"Is that so? Many happy returns." Dane sped up until he was flying in between Shimmer and Manny. "General Heather has advised us to make camp."

"None too soon," Joe said. "I'm starving."

"Yes, it's an excellent idea. Perhaps we should rest by that lake up ahead?" Shimmer suggested.

"No, that's too open," Heather replied. "I would look for a stream or—"

A flock of birds suddenly rose from a rocky shelf down below and streaked toward the dragons in a hostile mass. As the birds drew closer, Heather gasped. "Those aren't birds, they're flying reptiles!"

"Uh-oh," Manny said.

"Boratures. They are very dangerous," Shimmer said.

"Those must be nesting grounds," Joe called out. "Go *faster*."

The boratures were the size of sheep, with a tough hide covering their impressive wingspan. Their long and narrow heads ended with pointed beaks that appeared unpleasantly sharp. Heather guessed their talons were equally lethal. She shuddered to think what they would do to her skin. Although the creatures were far smaller than dragons, they numbered in the hundreds. Even worse was the incredible speed with which the boratures were closing in from behind. Forced to split apart, Shimmer and Manny headed straight up, and Dane angled lower.

"Hold very tight, Heather. I'll lose them in the trees."

She flattened herself against Dane's neck as he hurtled through the forest. Unfortunately, the boratures overtook him and began to claw at his wings. As their vicious talons opened gash after gash in Dane's hide, he flinched. With a keening cry and a barrel roll, he shot upward once more. Heather's grip loosened, and then she could hold on no longer.

Thick foliage slapped her in the face as she descended through the trees. A vine briefly broke her fall, but she continued downward when it snapped. Finally, her desperate fingers found purchase on a leafy branch. She dropped down to the next branch, and so on, until she managed to reach the ground underneath a heavy canopy of trees.

Stunned and dazed, a sharp pain in her midsection made it difficult for her to breathe. Cuts and scratches marked her flesh everywhere, and something warm and wet was trickling down her neck. Shaking badly, her knees finally gave way. Several minutes passed before she calmed down enough to assess her situation. Of one thing she was absolutely certain; Dane wasn't coming back, and she was on her own.

MANY HAPPY RETURNS

*J*oe stood frozen on the lip of a rocky outcropping, as if carved from the granite himself. He stared out over the treetops, the view becoming ever more obscure in the deepening twilight. His expression was uncharacteristically stiff, and his posture radiated resentment. Kneeling on the far end of the ledge was Dane, silent and brooding. His face, arms, and legs were covered with bloody gouges and bite marks. In between the two, Shimmer and Manny paced, their faces drawn with anxiety.

"Please, Dane, let me treat your wounds," Shimmer said, finally. "Allowing them to fester won't help."

But Dane would only shake his head.

"We search for her at first light," Joe said. His voice was choked and raspy. "No matter what we find, I have to know."

Dane's face was a study in anguish. "I can't even tell you where she fell. I was so busy fighting those creatures; I didn't even notice she was gone until it was too late."

"Is there a chance she could have survived the fall?" Manny asked Shimmer.

"Anything is possible. But Boravagg isn't an easy place for a human to stay alive—with or without magic," Shimmer replied.

"Heather is tough," Dane said. "If anyone can make it, she can."

But even to Dane, his words sounded empty.

FUMBLING in her boot for her hunting knife, Heather was relieved to find it safe in its sheath. *At least that's something. And my quiver is still attached to my belt.* Although vertigo almost overwhelmed her, she forced herself to her feet. Arrows had slipped out of her quiver as she fell and were scattered throughout the surrounding forest. She counted herself fortunate none had pierced her skin. Scanning the area for her belongings, she spotted her knapsack. One of the straps had ripped off completely, but she was grateful nevertheless. Although her bow wasn't visible, she guessed it might have become snagged on a tree branch overhead. Because the sky was growing darker by the minute, retrieving the bow would have to wait until the next day. She managed to fashion a pallet from some of the thick oversized leaves knocked down with her. A single leaf could have lined the bed of her father's cart. She pulled the foliage over her to form a sheltering cocoon. Then, mercifully, she passed out.

WHEN HEATHER AWOKE, early morning light was beginning to filter through the trees. Tears squeezed from the corner of her eyes as pain wracked her body. Bruises rendered every inch of her skin tender and sore. A cut on her scalp had bled copiously, matting her hair, face, and the inside of her left ear with dried blood. Any movement from the waist up became a knife in her side due to a broken rib. She cried quietly for a few minutes until she forced herself to get angry.

Saltimar's words echoed in her ears...*always make sure you're in a position to survive.*

"Quit sniveling, Heather," she gasped. "You're alive for now, and that's all that matters."

When she managed to stand, she was relieved to discover the vertigo from the night before had passed. A dry biscuit from her knapsack became breakfast, along with a few swallows from her waterskin. Because of her blood loss, Heather was horribly thirsty. Finding more water would be her top priority, right after she retrieved her bow.

Heather peered up at the tree that had broken her fall, finally spotting her bow hanging from a branch about thirty feet up. Dismayed at the distance, she burst into sobs once more. She would have given anything to leave her bow there, but unless she wanted to die on Boravagg, she had to have the means to hunt and defend herself.

A sturdy vine enabled her to shimmy up the side of the tree. She took a long rest at the first branch she reached, trying to muster the strength to go on. A long, excruciating hour later, she finally reached the bow. She slung it across her back, noticing with dismay that her brown scarf was snagged on a branch—out of reach. Since she'd already expended all her energy retrieving the bow, the scarf would have to remain behind. Heather climbed down the tree as a torrent of warm rain began to fall.

Heather cut a piece off a waxy leaf and twisted it into a funnel to collect the rain. After replenishing the water in her waterskin, she drank directly from the small end of the funnel. The rain was so heavy that she managed to quench her thirst and wash most of the dried blood from her hair and skin. Slightly more hopeful, Heather draped another leaf over her as a makeshift shelter and formulated a plan. She'd come to

Boravagg to release Ormaria's magic, and that's what she would do.

~

WITH JOE on Shimmer's back, the Ormvalder dragons skimmed the treetops searching for any sign of Heather. Joe clenched his fists in frustration.

"This is no good. The foliage is too thick. I can't see anything."

A fruitless hour later, Shimmer, Manny, and Dane were forced to agree. They landed in a clearing and retook their human forms.

"Can you use some kind of magic spell to find Heather, or perhaps let her know where we are?" Joe asked.

Shimmer shook his head. "Anything we do to draw her attention to us would also bring trolls or other predators. I'm not sure we could survive another clash with those boratures."

"Let's spread out and search from the ground as we walk north," Dane suggested.

"Why north?" Manny asked.

"If she's alive, she'll head for the crater," Dane said.

"I agree," Joe said, without glancing at Dane. "Heather is incredibly focused. She'll find a way to complete her mission if she possibly can."

"What if she gets turned around? I didn't put a compass in her knapsack," Manny said.

"Her father's a hunter. She'll know how to get her bearings," Dane said.

With rainclouds gathering overhead, Shimmer, Joe, Manny, and Dane spread out and began to search.

~

THE RAIN STOPPED AS QUICKLY as it had begun. When the sun came out, an eerie mist rose from the forest floor. Heather rolled several waxy leaves into a tight tube to take with her. She observed the shifting shadow of a tree for a few minutes to determine east and west. Drawing a line perpendicular to that showed her which direction was north. Before she left her impromptu campsite, she gathered rocks together and placed them in a large arrow formation, pointing north. She was fairly certain trolls wouldn't understand what the symbol signified, but anyone else searching for her would know which direction she'd gone.

Her injuries, coupled with the dense underbrush, hampered her from making rapid progress. Fortunately, she found several trees heavy with exotic, unfamiliar fruit to sustain her. She bit into a soft, tangy fruit similar to a pear and peeled the skin off a long fruit that resembled a blue banana. A bit of dried meat from her knapsack completed her meal.

In the afternoon, Heather found a small waterfall-fed pool where she took a cool bath. She washed the rest of the blood from her hair and clothes with the cake of soap in her pack. Afterwards she laid the garments on a rock in the sun. Her skin was mottled with bruises and scratches, and her midsection appeared to have been struck with a whip where she'd fallen across that vine. *I wish Mother were here to bind up my ribs!* Eating lunch and bathing had been a welcome respite, even though her injuries curtailed her movements. When her clothes were dry, she dressed and braided her hair. She used the tree shadows to get her bearings again. Once she'd laid out another arrow formation in pebbles, Heather headed north.

A VICAR RODE into the town of Merrymouth, a sheaf of leaflets under his arm. He tacked the leaflets on the side of buildings, on trees, and even on the church bulletin board. He spent the rest of the day in the tavern, nursing a tankard of ale, handing out leaflets, and talking to anyone who would listen to him about the evils of King Chance.

"Is it true King Chance intends to raise our taxes again?" asked a local farmer, in shock. "I can't afford it."

"Your tax burden will double," the vicar replied. "I, for one, am sick of it. Meet me in the schoolhouse at sundown if you are too. Bring your friends."

Word of the meeting spread quickly and as darkness descended, the schoolhouse was bursting with people. Whole families had driven in from outlying farms to hear the vicar speak. Just after sunset, he strolled up to the front of the schoolhouse and held up his hands for quiet.

"King Chance is a tyrant!" he bellowed. "We do the hard work while he has an easy life in his pretty seaside castle. He has no regard for his subjects, and it's time to do something about it. Are you with me?"

Cheers and whistles of agreement rang out.

"The Dragon Rebels have the right idea. They've been quietly organizing to depose the monarchy. With new taxes coming, revolution couldn't come too soon," the vicar continued.

A few men shuffled toward the exit. They tried to be casual, but the vicar wasn't having it. "Go then, spineless dogs! We need real men, men of conviction and fortitude. Do we have any rebels here? Stand up for what you believe in. We will lend our support."

Gasps and murmurs erupted when the baker stood, along with the schoolteacher. The vicar rubbed his hands together. "Come forward, gentlemen, and make your plans known. And forgive me, ladies, but I must ask you to escort your young ones outside for a little while. There's likely to be some harsh language."

Since a vicar was asking, the ladies obediently took their children from the schoolhouse. The two Dragon Rebels related the tale of Heather's escape from the castle, and of her quest to Boravagg. As the two men answered questions, the vicar stepped outside and shut the door behind him.

His eyes grew wide. A retinue of the king's guards had surrounded the schoolhouse with crossbows and torches in hand. Two of the soldiers took the vicar into custody and hustled him away. Women and children were sitting on the ground, whimpering, at the point of a sword.

"Bless you, vicar," one of them managed.

"You as well, my child," he replied.

The guards dragged the vicar out of sight and into the stables. Once they were alone, the man dug in his heels and shook off his captors.

"Have a care. I bruise easily, you know."

"Many apologies, Lord Embrue."

The vicar stripped off his costume, revealing the military uniform underneath.

"Commoners are simpletons. Saddle my horse. Our next target is Jagged Peaks."

Screams rang out a few blocks away as the king's guards set fire to the schoolhouse. The purge of Destiny had begun.

HEATHER LAID the gutted fish on a flat rock nestled in glowing embers. As she waited for it to bake, she counted her blessings. She'd managed to extract the sizeable fish from a stream, using one of her arrows as a spear. Then, just before dark, she'd stumbled across the remnants of a troll fire pit. She'd stoked the embers and found a clean rock suitable for cooking. Luck had certainly been on her side tonight, but such luck could not hold forever.

After she'd eaten her fill of the tender white fish, Heather piled wood into the fire pit and retreated into the shadows. Pulling her tube of leaves from her knapsack, she fashioned a cocoon underneath the overhang of a boulder several yards off. She would have preferred to stay next to the warmth of the fire but sleeping out in the open with predators around wasn't appealing.

As Heather lay there waiting for sleep to come, she wondered if Dane was all right, and whether Joe, Shimmer, and Manny had managed to evade the boratures. Most of the flock had followed her and Dane into the forest. His scales had given him some protection from the creatures, but he'd still been bitten and scratched badly. A pang of remorse went through her—if she hadn't been on his back, he probably would have been able to escape injury altogether. The prince had put his life in jeopardy trying to keep her safe, and Heather prayed that he'd managed to get away safely. She closed her eyes and tried to remember the wondrous sensations of his healing fingertips on her skin, but her aches and pains wouldn't let her.

Her thoughts turned to her parents. Would she ever see them again? At least Obie and Ustin would tell Saltimar and Rose about her quest. Even if she never returned, they could be proud of what she had tried to accomplish. Suddenly she laughed.

"Happy birthday, Heather," she murmured.

She was nineteen.

ALTHOUGH HE WAS EXHAUSTED, Dane took the first watch that night. Shimmer and Manny transformed into their dragon forms to sleep under a stand of trees, and Joe curled up between them on a conjured bed of sheep's wool. As the others slept,

Dane sat on a boulder and stared out into the blackness, tormented by Heather's absence.

I should be the one who is lost, not her. He'd asked her to ride with him out of some arrogant notion he was the best person to protect her. *If only I'd followed Shimmer and Manny, she would have been safe.* He'd made the wrong decision to fly into the forest—and Heather had paid the price for his miscalculation. His father had often cautioned him about his headstrong tendencies. How right Ansgar had been.

Everything about Heather had forced Dane to reexamine the world, and his role in it. For one thing, he'd been quite comfortable with his feelings about women before he met her. He'd been perfectly truthful when he'd told Heather she was different. Her manner of speaking was direct and confident, without any of the coy flirtation he'd come to expect. Conversing with her was almost like talking with one of his friends—although Heather stirred his senses in ways they never could. He could almost envision debating with her on many topics as an equal, even though she was female...and a commoner.

Because of Heather, his views on commoners had also been challenged. Her lowly station in life had been dictated by an accident of birth. By entering the Tournament of Chance, she'd attempted to earn a title, but he'd done nothing to earn his. Was it fair that he should have so much privilege because he'd been born a royal? Her ability to work magic was quite an unusual trait for someone not of noble birth—or was it? Occasionally a member of Ormarian royalty would be unable to work magic, like the royal surgeon Sir Icarus, for example. But no one had ever considered whether or not commoners might have the ability. How unjust to condemn a wizard to a non-magical life merely because he or she had been lowborn!

Truth be told, the girl haunted him in other, more personal ways. Almost from the beginning, he had sensed an inexplicable connection with Heather. When he used his healing spell on her in the crew quarters, his body had reacted to her physical proximity. She seemed so familiar, as if he'd somehow known her before. Since he'd been in crystal stasis for well over two centuries, any prior acquaintance was impossible. Yet, the strange, unsettling feeling when they'd touched had been almost overwhelming. In that moment, he had almost kissed her. How would she have reacted if he had? Dane grinned. She probably would have slapped him or dumped the contents of his apothecary case over his head.

He was glad he'd controlled the urge. Heather was maddening, rebellious, opinionated, and far from being his ideal. No, his perfect woman would engage his eye only when he chose to look at her, and not demand his attention with the face of an angel, or fiery hair that could not be ignored. If Heather was alive, she was probably cursing his name about now. His feelings for her were likely the strange residual effect of his crystal stasis, and he would do well to remember that. Nevertheless, he would not rest until he found her again—not ever.

AN EARTHQUAKE SHOOK HEATHER AWAKE. At least that was what she assumed until the grunts of an unintelligible language assailed her ears. Though a narrow opening in her leaf covering, she watched a group of five trolls lumber past. She blinked in amazement. The creatures were gigantic, draped in animal skins, and possessed such misshapen heads and bodies that Heather could not decide which, if any, were female. Her decision to sleep under cover had been a shrewd one, since the trolls most certainly would have stepped on her without breaking stride.

The youngest troll paused at the long-cold fire pit and sniffed the air. When he took a step in Heather's direction, her heart began to race. Fortunately, the fish head she'd discarded from the night before distracted him. He scooped it up, popped it into his mouth, and chewed with loud satisfaction. When his companions yelled, he strode off to rejoin them. Heather breathed a sigh of relief.

After she'd eased herself from her hiding place, she rolled up her leaf bedding and tucked it in her knapsack. In the daylight, a well-trodden path through the forest became obvious.

"It's a troll road," Heather said with a giggle.

Avoiding trolls was critical, but if she didn't have to battle the underbrush mile after mile, she might be able to reach the crater before nightfall. After she'd eaten a biscuit from her provisions, she made a stone marker by the side of the road in the shape of an arrow. Shouldering her pack, Heather took the trail north.

Although Shimmer and Dane were still out hunting for breakfast, Manny returned to drop a dead beast at Joe's feet. Joe recoiled from the carcass in horror. "It's *raw*. That's all right for a dragon, but I'm human."

"Stand back," Manny said.

Joe scrambled away. Manny inhaled a lungful of air, and then roasted the carcass with dragonfire. A few moments later, the sight of the blackened, smoking dead animal made Joe swallow hard. "Thanks, but I'm not that hungry. I think I'll take a swim."

As he turned toward the waterfall-fed pool, he stubbed his toe on some stones.

"Blast it! Who put these rocks here?"

Joe stared at the rocks for a moment. Except for the ones he'd kicked out of place, they formed an arrow. A broad smile lit his face, and with a whooping holler, he turned a handspring.

"She's alive!" he shouted. "Heather's alive!"

THE TROLL ROAD

*O*bie ran into the smithy, a leaflet in hand. He paced while Ustin finished pounding out the edge of a blade. As Ustin lowered the steel sword into a vat of cooling water, Obie waved the leaflet in front of his friend's face. Ustin stepped back to give Obie a level look.

"Was there something you wanted?"

"A vicar rode into town this morning with this," Obie exclaimed.

Ustin took the leaflet and walked out into the direct sunlight to read. Afterwards, he crumpled the parchment into a ball.

"King Chance intends to raise taxes again. What of it?"

"The vicar wants to organize against him. He's holding a meeting tonight at the schoolhouse, at sundown. This is exciting, Ustin. Everybody is talking about it."

"Tell the Dragon Rebels to ready themselves. You shouldn't be so quick to trust a stranger."

"I don't understand. He's a vicar."

"Anyone can don a cassock, Obie. It doesn't make him a vicar."

Obie slumped in disappointment. "Are we not going to the meeting then?"

"Aye, we're going. And afterwards we'll have ourselves a bonfire."

~

THE LAST LINGERING rays of twilight were fading as the residents of Jagged Peaks crammed themselves into the schoolhouse. Their earnest faces tilted up toward the vicar as he spoke.

"King Chance is a despot. Each and every one of us works hard to survive while he skims off the fruits of our labor. If there are any Dragon Rebels among us, show yourselves. We must be prepared to fight for the cause."

Ustin jumped to his feet and advanced on the vicar. "Scoundrel! Knave! The residents of Jagged Peaks are all loyal to King Chance. Be gone with you and take your rabble-rousing elsewhere."

Ustin grabbed the vicar by his arm and marched him out of the schoolhouse. When they emerged, there were a dozen or more soldiers waiting outside. Most were armed with drawn swords and still others had burning torches in their hands. Ustin surveyed them with a wry smile.

"The king's soldiers. How fortuitous. Take this trouble-maker into custody."

He shoved the vicar down the stairs. Soldiers rushed to grab the vicar before he sprawled in the mud. One of the soldiers pointed his sword at Ustin.

"You're under arrest."

"What's the charge? Assaulting a royal spy?" Ustin sneered.

As the soldiers moved to take Ustin into custody, arrows began to fly from the darkness. Dragon Rebels emerged from every direction and set upon the king's men. In the melee, the vicar edged toward the forest, but Saltimar blocked his path. He ripped the front of the vicar's cassock and Lord Embrue's military uniform was revealed.

"You'd see us burned alive?" Saltimar growled. "To the devil with you."

Saltimar clocked Embrue in the head with his hammer-like fist, and the man dropped to the ground. As rebels dragged the man off by the heels, Ustin caught Saltimar's eye.

"Well done."

Saltimar made a sound of frustration deep in his throat. "I've been praying for more time—at least until Heather returns."

"We're out of time, my friend. The revolution has begun without her."

"So be it."

THE SKIES BURST forth with one of the fast and fierce rainstorms Heather had come to expect on Boravagg. Instead of being annoyed, she waited out the storm in a shallow cave and took the opportunity to collect drinking water with the help of her improvised leaf funnel. So far, her decision to use the troll road had justified the risks. The peak of the volcano loomed closer, and she was making good progress. Every few miles she arranged a rock marker just in case one of her friends might see it.

When the rain slowed to a gentle mist, Heather resumed her journey. After a short distance, she came across a tree with some ripe, reddish-orange fruit. The flesh inside was sweet, firm, and juicy, and she picked several to take with her. As she walked, she licked the sweet scarlet juice running down her fingers. The path curved around a big boulder, and she glanced up to see a snarling female tiger in the clearing to her left, pacing back and forth. On her right, five trolls cowered underneath a rocky overhang. Heather dropped her fruit, slowly unhooked her bow and reached for an arrow.

The tiger attacked. Heather shot three arrows in rapid succession, but the tiger leaped into the air and knocked her flat. Her arm pinned to the ground, Heather was unable to reach her knife. She closed her eyes and braced herself for death. When the tiger moved, she screamed. But the tiger was dead, and the movement was because one of the trolls was lifting it away. Frozen in fear, she willed her body to get up and run, but it refused to respond. Surrounded by trolls, Heather sprawled in the mud, trembling.

To her astonishment, the trolls left her alone. The tallest one broke off the arrow shafts protruding from the dead tiger and draped the carcass over his shoulders. The group resumed their trek north, but the youngest troll paused before he left. He pointed a thick finger in her direction. "Good shot," he grunted, pantomiming shooting an arrow.

"Thanks," she squeaked.

The troll followed the others on the trail. Covered with tiger blood and mud, Heather got to her feet gingerly. Her encounter with the tiger had wrenched her ribs, and when she bent to retrieve her knapsack and bow, she groaned with pain at the movements. A grunting noise nearby nearly sent her into a panic. For some reason, the young troll had returned. Did he plan to squish her into human residue? He gestured at her midsection and again mimicked the way she had groaned.

She held her hands over her ribs and then pantomimed a breaking motion. The troll shuddered, his ugly face distending in a sympathetic grimace. He showed her a gash in his elbow. Heather reciprocated by grimacing too. "Ow," she said.

In the distance one of the trolls yelled, "Gumm!"

"Goodbye, Gumm." She tapped her chest. "Heather."

"He'er," the troll repeated. "Friend of anger."

Gumm wheeled around and loped off. In the blink of an eye he was out of sight—but Heather remained taken aback.

~

SHIMMER EXAMINED the stone marker on the ground. "Clever girl. I'm becoming more and more impressed with Heather with each passing moment."

"Not only is she alive, but she's told us where she's going," Joe said.

A muscle in Dane's jaw rippled. "We must move faster. The longer she's alone, the more likely it is she'll encounter something dangerous."

"She's done well enough so far, no thanks to you," Joe muttered.

Dane peered at Joe with narrowed eyes. "What's *that* supposed to mean?"

"You've shown your distaste for Heather upon more than one occasion."

"I would never let my personal feelings interfere with my duty to protect the child," Dane exploded.

"Really? Then why is she lost?"

Dane hands formed fists at his side. As the two men squared off, Shimmer stepped in between. "Jovander, I've known Dane much longer than you have. You accuse him unjustly."

"That is so," Manny concurred.

"No, no. Don't bother to defend me. It won't make a difference. Jovander Chance has a deep-seated resentment toward the royal class and doesn't believe we could ever act unselfishly," Dane scoffed.

"Forgive me for saying so, but this whole quest is selfish!" Joe yelled. "If it succeeds, you Ormvalders resume ruling the kingdom. Heather gets nothing except for a pat on the back. She's the only one of us here who has acted in an unselfish manner."

"You've acted unselfishly too, Joe," Manny said.

Dane smirked. "No, he hasn't. Haven't you noticed? Young Joe is quite taken with the lass."

Joe flushed bright red. "Don't act so smug, *Your Highness*. I've seen the way you look at her."

"First you practically accuse me of doing her in, and now you accuse me of having designs on the woman?" Dane thundered. "Make up your mind."

"First you call her a child, and now a woman?" Joe pointed out. "You should make up your own mind."

A long, smoldering silence followed in which nobody spoke.

"Well, now that we've poked that particular stick in the anthill, I suggest we put these little squabbles behind us and concentrate on recovering Heather," Shimmer said.

Dane stomped off.

"Er...before we go, does anyone mind if I finish eating my breakfast?" Manny asked.

A VAST CHESSBOARD spread out on the lawn next to the castle gardens. The king sipped a glass of chilled white wine as he finished his move. "Ponder *that*, my dear Lord Survill," he crowed.

"My word, Your Majesty, you've got me on the run," Survill exclaimed.

Various young pages stood on the checkered lawn, in chess piece costumes. Although a shady canopy had been set up for the king and his opponent so they could play their game in comfort, the pages waited in the fierce sunlight. As sweat dripped from underneath their hot and heavy paper-maché headdresses, the boys struggled to stand at attention.

Minister Uspy hastened from the castle toward the chessboard. "Please forgive the interruption, Your Majesty, but I have news."

King Chance's brow creased in annoyance. "Has Jovander or that wretched girl been located? Hester, wasn't it?"

"Heather is the name. They both have vanished, Your Majesty. And I'm afraid that Lord Embrue has not returned from Jagged Peaks, nor the soldiers that accompanied him," Uspy said.

King Chance waved his fingers, dismissively. "No doubt they have fallen into a game of cards or a bit of debauchery somewhere. Embrue's success at Merrymouth may have gone to his head."

"That's entirely possible, Your Majesty; however Embrue's steed was found wandering the countryside yesterday. Several mounts from the king's army have turned up as well," Uspy said.

"Send Lord Tether with the cavalry to question the villagers about Embrue. If you get no answers, burn Jagged Peaks down."

"And if the villagers cooperate?"

"Burn it anyway. The commoners must understand I am in charge."

Uspy left. King Chance returned his attention toward the chessboard, where his bishop had just keeled over from sunstroke. "I'm going to need a new bishop. Drag that boy to the dungeon and beat him for having spoiled the game."

AS THE PATH snaked up the side of the volcano, the slope of the trail became far steeper. With her broken rib on fire, Heather could only manage a snail's pace. Finally she reached a clear, flat area where a large indentation in the volcano formed a wide lookout point. A turtle-shape rock formed a natural barrier between the lookout and the valley below. Several almost perfectly round tunnels led into the mountain's interior, as if something had burned through the granite. Heather guessed the tunnels were created from the flow of lava long ago, and marveled that anything could be hot enough to melt solid rock.

From the unappetizing quantity of fur and gore on the turtle rock, it appeared the trolls had gutted and skinned the tiger there, and cooked some of the meat over the still-glowing fire pit nearby. Although Heather longed to rest, the smell of the place turned her stomach. Leaving the campsite, she continued to climb up the trail. The rank odor of the slaughtered animal followed her.

A few minutes later, a blue dragon appeared from the north. With her heart in her throat, she yelled as loud as she could, waving her arms to get Dane's attention. When he veered in her direction, she was overjoyed. After six other dragons joined him during his descent, however, Heather's ebullience turned to horror. The dragon was not Dane, a flock of wild dragons was headed straight for her, and on the open trail there was nowhere to hide.

Gritting her teeth against the pain in her side, she hurtled down the trail, past the turtle rock. At random, she picked one of the lava tunnels and darted inside. Heather hoped the dragons would leave once they lost their prey. Unfortunately, the smell of blood at the campsite sent the animals into a frenzy. The dragons' piercing, trumpeting cries echoed down the tunnel, forcing Heather to cover her ears. The creatures attacked the rock face with their claws, chipping off bits and pieces of granite. Heather backed further into the darkness, but when she heard one of the dragons inhale, she ran. A fireball followed her up the tunnel, coming so close that she felt the heat at her back. She paused long enough to nock an arrow. When the dragon inhaled a second time, the arrow flew down the tunnel and into its gullet. Roaring in agony, the dragon fell. To Heather's dismay, its fellows took up the task of trying to tear into the tunnel.

She tried to move further away from the danger, but the dragonfire had burned up so much oxygen that she became faint. She staggered forward a few more paces before she sank down onto the cool stone floor and passed out.

WHEN HEATHER OPENED HER EYES, only the sound of her own breathing pierced the darkness. Disoriented, she couldn't decide which direction would return her to the lookout. Soft curses gave way to tears of panic.

"Get on your feet, you useless lump," she said finally. She wiped her eyes on the sleeve of her jacket. "Wouldn't your father be disappointed to see you lurking in a hole like some kind of rodent?"

After she'd fumbled in the dark to gather her belongings, Heather picked a direction and began to walk. When glowing light became visible in the distance, she laughed with relief. *Daylight!* To her surprise, however, she emerged from the tunnel into a large cavern, glowing with illumination. A serene pool of water spread out before her, surrounded by a treasure trove of colorful, luminescent crystals.

Dragonstones.

Some of the Dragonstones were in huge blocks, larger than crates. Others had crumbled into piles of smaller dragon crystals. When Heather ran her hand along a wall made completely of Dragonstones, the magic inside was palpable. She marveled at how the radiance followed her fingertips, as if it could sense the magic within her as well.

The lake itself was splendidly beautiful. The water gleamed from the luminous Dragonstones at the bottom of the pool, and gentle curls of mist rose from the surface. Covered with mud and tiger blood as she was, Heather could not resist going for a swim. She shed her clothes as quickly as her broken rib would allow, and then lowered herself into the soothing, warm liquid. The serene water around her was soon floating with fragrant bubbles as she scrubbed her skin with the bar of soap from her knapsack. Heather lingered in the pool until she was completely refreshed. When she finally emerged, she was pleasantly surprised to discover her bruises and cuts had faded, and the soreness in her muscles had diminished. Even the pain in her ribs was minimal.

"Thank you," she said out loud.

The dragon crystals at her feet suddenly flared with light, as if in response. One particular dragon crystal with a reddish glow caught her eye. When she picked it up, the amber crystal filled her with a sense of personal power, wonder...and hope.

ASHES OF DESTINY

The Ormvalders flew north. As Joe rode on Shimmer, he scoured the ground for another stone marker. His heart lifted when he spotted one near a large fire pit. "Look," he cried, pointing. "Follow that path. We must be getting closer."

Dane flew as near to the ground as possible. A few minutes later, he angled sharply downward. Shimmer and Manny followed his lead when he landed on the trail. Morphing into human form, Dane knelt next to a dark stain.

"What is it?" Manny asked.

Dane touched the brown stain with his fingertips. "Blood." Enormous footprints were visible in the soil softened by the recent rain. "And trolls."

Joe gulped as he gathered up three broken arrows. "These are Heather's."

"Was she attacked, do you suppose?" Manny said.

"I don't know, but at least she got off a few shots," Joe said.

"Something left a trail of blood," Dane said. "We should see where it leads."

A dark cloud passed overhead, casting a ragged shadow on the ground.

"Gah! Does it never stop raining on Boravagg?" Manny groused.

Shimmer gasped. "That's not rain; it's a flock of wild dragons. Get under cover."

They sought refuge under the nearest tree, peeking through the leaves toward the sky. The six dragons flew south without a pause.

"Er...you didn't mention wild dragons, Shimmer," Joe said.

"I saw but one when I was here before. A lone dragon guards the crystal," Shimmer said.

Dane gave his uncle a sidelong glance. "That's a wrinkle upon which you failed to elaborate."

Shimmer smiled sheepishly. "Perhaps I was not entirely forthcoming on that point."

The four men continued up the trail on foot, hoping to find some further signs of Heather. As time went on, however, they became increasingly discouraged.

COR AND LANE burst into Jagged Peaks Tavern, which was packed with rebels and villagers. "Soldiers approach. At least a hundred strong and all mounted on horseback," Cor gasped.

The room erupted in an excited, anxiety-laced hubbub. Ustin climbed onto a table and raised his hands as he called for calm. "We knew this would happen, and we have a plan. Obie, take some of the boys and close the gate at the bridge. That'll slow them down. Saltimar, make sure the women and children have been evacuated to the mine. Then everyone take your places and wait."

The tavern exploded with nervous energy as people rushed out to prepare. Rose turned to her husband in anguish. "We're going to lose our home. The whole village will be destroyed."

"We were going to lose it anyway, Rose." He kissed his wife

on the forehead and held her close. "Never mind, dearest. Human life is more important."

"I pray Heather's mission succeeds quickly. Otherwise, there will be no country left for the Ormvalders to rule."

"It won't come to that," Saltimar said. But as he turned away, his smile slipped.

JOE and the Ormvalders arrived at the lookout. Manny shied away from the distinctive turtle-shaped rock covered with the slaughtered remains of an animal. "How droll—if you like gore."

But Dane, Shimmer, and Joe were gaping at the nearby carcass of a dead dragon. When Dane knelt to examine the creature, he discovered Heather's arrow protruding from its mouth.

"How astonishing," he said. "It's dreadfully difficult to slay a dragon under the best of circumstances."

"Heather is a remarkable shot," Joe said. "Haven't you been listening to me?"

Shimmer ran his hands across the granite wall. Fierce claw marks scored the surface and chunks of rock had broken off. Furthermore, the scorched surface indicated dragonfire so hot that some of the rocks had actually melted together. "I've never seen anything like this."

"A single dragon could not be responsible," Manny said.

"It may have been the flock that passed us earlier," Shimmer replied.

"I bet they were trying to get at Heather. She has to be inside," Joe said, trying unsuccessfully to move the largest rock aside.

Dane rolled the rock away from the entrance with a surge of magic. "Let us hope she is not mortally wounded."

"Why are you always so quick to give her up for dead?" Joe snapped.

"Why are you so eager to take offense?" Dane retorted.

"And why must you two constantly bicker?" Manny asked.

"Gentlemen, please," Shimmer said. "These lava tunnels frequently intersect. I suggest we each take one and search. Joe, come with me."

THE ILLUMINATION PROVIDED by Dane's dragon crystal revealed the lava tunnel to be a marvel of nature. As he sped along the passageway at a fast clip, however, the prince took no time to admire the perfect symmetry of the walls. His annoyance with Jovander spurred his pace. *I shouldn't let him get under my skin.* He used to wish for a younger brother, but not anymore. The lad was like a gnat…or a guilty conscience that wouldn't stop nagging at him. The last thing Dane needed was another helping of guilt. But as he pressed forward, he was forced to admit his haste was motivated by something else entirely. If Heather was inside this tunnel, he wanted to be the one to find her. And if she was alive, he needed to tell her how sorry he was for losing her. His feet faltered. Was it a trick of his eyes, or was there a glow up ahead? Dane bolted toward the light, running as if his very salvation hung in the balance.

PERCHED on a rock next to the pool, Heather had dressed and was nearly finished combing the tangles out of her hair. When Dane suddenly burst into the chamber, the comb slipped from her fingers.

"Dane!"

He strode over and pulled Heather to her feet in the same manner as he'd done on the ship. This time, however, he wrapped her in his arms and held her tight.

"I've been out of my mind with worry," he murmured. "Thank God you're alive."

"I'm so glad you're all right. I can't believe you found me."

A feeble voice inside her mind said *Dane Ormvalder is royalty...he's everything you despise.* But the delicious sensations flowing through her body as it pressed against him sapped her willpower completely. Dane's lips hovered over hers—and then a voice rang out.

"Heather!" Manfred exclaimed. "How marvelous."

Dane and Heather sprang apart.

"Manny!" she cried.

Joe and Shimmer emerged from their tunnel moments later, and she embraced each of them in turn. With Joe, she added a kiss on the cheek. Joe shot Dane a triumphant glance, but the prince was frowning at an innocuous boulder as if it had done him a mischief. Shimmer knelt at the side of the lake and brushed his fingers across the crystals at its edge.

"My word."

"These are Dragonstones, aren't they, Shimmer?" Heather asked.

"Indeed, yes...and a pool of liquid magic. I've never seen such a thing before."

Heather gasped. "I swam in liquid magic? That explains why the water was so soothing. My cuts and scratches are gone, and my broken rib is healed."

"Broken rib? Tell us what happened, Heather," Joe urged.

"Yes, do. How did you manage to survive?" Manny said.

Heather related everything that had unfolded since she fell in the forest. While she spoke, Dane sat on a rock nearby and silently fiddled with a piece of crystal.

"Bad luck to have been spotted by those wild dragons," Manny said. "They were a nasty lot."

Heather frowned. "It's my fault. I accidentally attracted the first dragon's attention when I thought it was...well, when I thought it was one of you."

Suddenly Joe stood, kicked his boots off and dove into the pool with his clothes on. He came up sputtering. "I couldn't help myself. It's absolutely fantastic."

Heather giggled. "It is, isn't it?"

As Joe tossed his clothes out on the pool and onto the rocks, a smile tugged at the corner of Shimmer's lips. He exchanged a mischievous glance with his son. "Last one in?"

They shed their shirts and boots and dove in alongside Joe.

"Come on, Dane," Manny called out from the middle of the pool. "How often do you have the opportunity to swim in liquid magic?"

Heather rose. "I'll give you gentlemen some privacy."

She wandered through the cavern, glancing back in time to see Dane pull his shirt off. He was almost as muscular as Ustin, but in a more streamlined way. Sadly, he dove into the pool before she caught much more than a glimpse of anything else.

SOLDIERS KICKED in the front door of Saltimar's home, unannounced. They found the modest dwelling empty, as expected. None of the houses they'd gone to had been occupied. Jagged Peaks was seemingly a ghost town. After they ransacked Saltimar's abode for trinkets, they set the roof on fire. The air was already thick with smoke and raining ash from their earlier handiwork.

Lord Tether yawned through the handkerchief pressed to his nose and mouth. His ride from the castle had been long, made even tedious when they had to saw through a barricade erected across the bridge. Did the village idiots of Jagged Peaks really imagine any fence could keep the king's soldiers at bay?

Soldiers emerged from the workshop Saltimar kept in the

stables, carrying several of Saltimar's artisan bows, arrows, and quivers. Lord Tether snapped his fingers. "Let me see those."

Somewhat reluctantly, the soldiers complied. An archer himself, Lord Tether examined the workmanship. "Find a blanket to wrap these in and store them in my cart," he ordered. "Then scour the countryside. The rats of Jagged Peaks are hiding somewhere. I intend to find them."

Soldiers dragged Vicar Jenns into view. His hands were tied, and his face was bloodied and bruised. One of the more brutish men kicked the vicar's legs out from under him, causing the vicar to sprawl in the dirt.

"This one tried to keep us from entering the church."

"It's the house of God!" cried the vicar.

"It's a house of ashes now."

Laughter accompanied the words.

"Have mercy on your souls," the vicar said.

"Where are the villagers hiding?" Lord Tether asked.

Vicar Jenns shook his head, his lips clamped in a line.

"Captain Mansur, take him away and persuade him to talk," Lord Tether said.

A half hour later, Mansur returned. He was covered with spatters of blood, and his knuckles were raw, but he wore a smile. "They're all in the mine, Lord Tether. The vicar will lead us there."

Lord Tether laughed. "I thought he might."

THE SOLDIERS ASSEMBLED in front of the entrance to the mine. The vicar wrung his hands in anxiety. "Please don't do this. Young women are in there."

A murmur rippled across the company of soldiers. "Women."

"My own two beautiful daughters are hiding in the mine.

SUZANNE G. ROGERS

They are young, and unfamiliar with the ways of men," the vicar lamented.

Even as his words were met with snickers and derisive laughter, Vicar Jenns made one last plea. "I beg you to leave now."

Lord Tether nodded to his Lieutenant. Soldiers began to pour into the mine with their swords at the ready. As they surged forward, Vicar Jenns backed away. Then he turned and staggered off toward the trees.

"Coward," muttered Lord Tether.

Moments later, the mine exploded with the force of two crates of the mining compound, geyser cake. His horse reared up in panic, and Lord Tether was thrown to the ground. Dragon Rebels, perched in the surrounding trees with their bows and arrows, emptied their quivers. Afterwards, the residents of Jagged Peaks ran into the melee with pitchforks and blade-tipped poles. Any soldier with the use of his limbs ran for his life. Few made it very far. Cursing at the top of his lungs, Lord Tether was stripped naked, hogtied, and thrown sideways over the back of his horse. The horse was led across the bridge, and a swat to its hindquarters sent it off down the road.

As a huge bonfire blazed outside the mine, Saltimar went to shake Vicar Jenns' hand. The poor vicar was barely able to stand, even with the help of his proud daughters.

"Good work, Vicar. We all appreciate your sacrifice," Saltimar said.

Vicar Jenns nodded. "My family and I are heading to Clarry Falls tonight. My sister will take us in. If you have anywhere to go, I suggest you leave, too—and quickly. We are enemies of the king now."

Saltimar bade him and his daughters a safe journey. Most of the town had already packed up wagons and carts with their household goods and hid them in the woods, in anticipation of this eventuality. He planned to take Rose to his brother's family in Crescent Creek. As their wagon joined the long queue heading through the embers of Jagged Peaks, they said another prayer for their daughter's safety. Then, Rose wept.

HEATHER PACED near the opening of an oversized lava tunnel in the back of the cavern. Since her embrace with Dane, she'd been unable to stop the fluttering in her stomach or the sweating of her palms. *Kitty would laugh if I told her Dane Ormvalder's blue eyes and handsome face made my heart pound.* She'd clung to him like a silly schoolgirl, and to think she'd almost let him kiss her! Only her happiness at being found could account for her behavior, or perhaps she was merely confused by his healing energy. Certainly the sensations of the healing spell he'd used on her before were remarkably similar to the feelings she'd had in his arms. No doubt she was confused and disoriented by her recent ordeal. Nevertheless, she was resolved to put the unfortunate moment of weakness behind her and treat the crown prince with the same polite disinterest as before. Since he probably regretted his actions as well, it shouldn't prove too difficult.

When Heather returned to the pool, she staunchly refused to even look at Dane—even though he had not yet put his shirt on.

"Shimmer, there's a huge lava tunnel in the back of the cavern. Do you suppose it leads to the crater?"

"If it's very large, there's a strong probability that it does," Shimmer replied.

"Wouldn't such a tunnel bring us right to the Dragonstone?" Joe asked.

"I like the sound of that. No more worries about being eaten by wild animals," Manny said with a shudder.

"Taking a tunnel to the crater would mask our approach," Dane said.

"That's an excellent idea," Shimmer said. "And by doing so we will likely shorten our journey."

As Dane stood, the two dragon crystals around his neck brushed up against one another with a bright spark. He was taken aback.

"How odd," Shimmer said. "I've never seen *that* happen between crystals before."

Dane cleared his throat. "Heather, I noticed you left an amber dragon crystal on top of your knapsack. I took the liberty of forming it into a pendant." He lifted the amber pendant over his head and proffered it to her. "I hope you like it."

She gasped with delight. "Oh, thank you, Dane. It's absolutely beautiful."

Joe waggled the green dragon crystal resting in the hollow of his throat. "See? Shimmer made one for me too."

Shimmer patted his shoulder. "You're an Ormvalder and a wizard. Why shouldn't you have one?"

"A wizard? I could have guessed as much, but when did you find out?" Heather asked.

"Just now, when Manny showed me some magic. Watch this." Joe held out his palm and made a little flame dance over it. When it began to burn his skin, however, he couldn't put it out. "Uh-oh. Ow! A little help, someone?"

Dane quickly extinguished it with a wave of his fingers. "A bit of power in untrained hands can lead to disaster. You might want to dip that thumb in liquid magic, Jovander. You've raised a blister."

"This cavern is an absolutely marvelous find, Heather. I've been wondering how Ormaria would furnish new wizards with dragon crystals once the Ormarian Dragonstone is destroyed," Shimmer said.

"Ormaria now has a source for all the dragon crystals it will ever need," Manny said.

"Er...that's great, but aren't we pressed for time? There's a revolution waiting for us," Joe said.

"Just so. There's no time to harvest the crystals now. Perhaps when Ormaria is restored, we can return to select another Dragonstone," Manny said.

Dane knelt and lowered his waterskin into the pool. Joe was puzzled. "What are you doing?"

"This liquid magic has healing properties that might come in useful. I want to take some with me."

Shimmer clapped Dane on the shoulder. "You're a gifted healer. I'm certain the discovery of liquid magic will assist you in your work."

Dane shook his head. "Apparently not gifted enough. I was unable to help my father."

"There are some illnesses for which there is no cure, Dane," Shimmer said. "Blame yourself no longer."

RED HILLS FOR KING CHANCE

*H*eather led the group to a lava tunnel high and wide enough to accommodate three trolls walking abreast. A myriad of smaller channels and caves branched off the main passageway, where ancient drips of lava formed fantastic configurations. Not only were the walls of the central lava tunnel not as smooth as in the smaller conduits, but the slope of the floor was far steeper. After a short while, it became difficult to talk without gasping for breath.

When they stopped to rest, Shimmer stretched out in one of the alcoves and was soon snoring lightly. Joe, Heather, Manny, and Dane sat in the passageway and chewed on a few pieces of beef jerky.

"I've been thinking," Joe said, struggling to get the words out past a particularly dry piece of meat. "If we're successful in our quest, the Ormvalders expect the people of Destiny to support them in a revolution. The people's distaste for King Chance only goes so far. How do you intend to win their hearts and minds?"

"The commoners must know what they are fighting for.

They must believe their lives will improve as Ormarians," Heather said.

"It has always been the duty of the Ormvalders to serve the people. We are obligated to use our magic for the greater good," Manny said.

"We don't judge people on their titles, but on their talents," Dane added. "We had an open court. Unlike the Tournament of Chance, any citizen was allowed to issue a challenge. The winner was welcome at the castle at any time."

"So, a blacksmith and a knight had the same opportunity to dine with royalty?" Heather asked.

"If he were an excellent blacksmith, I daresay we would have much to learn from him," said Dane.

Heather had a sudden vision of Ustin taking tea with members of the Ormarian court. She couldn't suppress a giggle. "Now *that* is something I would like very much to see. I expect it would prove quite entertaining."

"Entertainment was always my specialty," Manny said.

He got to his feet, conjured several sparkling horseshoes, and proceeded to juggle them. Joe was entranced.

"Manny...you wouldn't be able to teach me how to do that, would you?"

Catching the horseshoes handily, Manny took Joe down the tunnel to practice. Heather and Dane were left to themselves. A long, pregnant silence followed.

"We must speak in private," Dane told Heather finally. "Will you walk with me?"

The prince escorted her up the tunnel and into one of the small caves. The glowing crystals around their necks alleviated the darkness and lent a warm glow. Dane glanced at Heather briefly and then took a deep breath.

"First, I want to apologize for having dropped you in the forest. I've gone over it again and again wishing I'd done things differently."

"It was an unavoidable accident, Dane. I didn't blame you in the least."

"That you're still alive is a testament to your fortitude. I admire that very much." He paused a moment and then cleared his throat. "Nevertheless, I may have, er, allowed my emotions to get the better of me a little while ago. We—you and I—aren't suited to each other at all."

Heather let out her breath in a gust. "Oh, I'm so glad you feel that way, Dane. I completely agree."

"Good."

The tension broken, they shared a relieved laugh.

"I really don't know what happened," he said. "I just saw you there and…lost control for a moment."

"It's one of those silly things. We should forget it entirely."

"Absolutely." He gripped her upper arms, gazing into her eyes as if searching for something. "So we're friends, nothing more. Agreed?"

"I'm not sure we're even friends, really. Not in the truest sense of the word." She rested her hand on his chest. "Acquaintances, perhaps, on a quest together."

"Yes, I like that. Acquaintances with a common goal."

As they stared at each other in the dusky light, their smiles faded along with their pretenses. Heather reached out to caress the contours of his face.

"Dane—"

"Blast it," he cursed.

Pulling Heather close, he kissed her with unleashed passion. She pressed her body against his, answering his passion with joy. As they gave themselves to one another, their dragon crystals flared with the strength of their emotions. Dane suddenly buried his face in her neck.

"Don't leave me again."

"I won't. Not ever."

"I love you, Heather of the Jagged Peaks."

"And for some strange and marvelous reason I love you, too, Dane Ormvalder."

He cradled her in his arms. "Well, now that we've got that settled, perhaps I can finally think straight."

As she closed her eyes, a peaceful sort of happiness filled her up inside. "This doesn't make any sense at all."

"The universe has a way of arranging things. Perhaps it makes perfect sense but we just can't see it yet."

He scooped her up and twirled her around as if they were dancing. She giggled. "That liquid magic has gone to your head."

"It's not the liquid magic, it's you, Heather. You've healed my soul."

"What a beautiful thing to say."

He kissed her until Joe and Manny began to call out their names.

"Time to come back to reality," Dane groaned.

"I'm not sure I will ever have my feet on the ground again."

When Heather and Dane emerged from the cave, her hand was held firmly in his and they were both smiling. Awake from his nap, Shimmer laughed. "So we've worked out our differences, have we?"

"What differences?" Dane said with a wink.

Manny grinned, but Joe had a scowl on his face. Dane released Heather long enough to put Joe in a good-natured headlock. "Come on, Jovander, let's declare a truce. After the Ormarians are restored, I'll introduce you to Manny's sister."

"Hey! Leave my sister out of it," Manny protested.

"What's her name?" Joe asked, unconvinced.

"Wren. She's exceptionally pretty, wonderfully congenial, and I guarantee you'll like her," Dane said.

Shimmer cleared his throat. "Not *too* much, I trust, Jovander. My daughter is only sixteen."

LORD TETHER WAS GREETED with raucous, mocking laughter whenever his horse wandered through a town or village. To add insult to injury, the blazing hot sun raised blisters on his back and the milky white skin of his exposed buttocks. No one would lend a hand to untie the man, although several people gave his horse water and a bucket of oats. Unbeknownst to Lord Tether, a sign hung around the horse's neck that read: "Delivery for King Chance." The whole episode sparked the imagination of poets and minstrels alike. The song *Red Hills for King Chance* became an instant favorite.

When the king's guards found him, Lord Tether was unconscious. The guards covered him with a blanket and led his horse to the castle. Unfortunately, King Chance was on a weeklong hunting trip with Lady Felicia and could not be informed. The royal physician treated Lord Tether's wounds with cut aloe leaves and cold compresses. Queen Chelsea sat with Lord Tether after he awoke. She listened sympathetically as he told her how the little village of Jagged Peaks had soundly trounced one hundred of King Chance's finest men. The queen thereafter gave the royal physician an enormous sum to ensure Lord Tether would succumb to his injuries. After taking a sharp knife to King Chance's mattress and clothes, Queen Chelsea packed a huge chest with gold coins and jewels and fled with it to South Umberlin. She'd met the king of South Umberlin once. Although she'd found King Grago a bit dull, he was in need of a wife—and she would most likely be available soon.

KING CHANCE and Lady Felicia returned from their trip slightly ahead of schedule. Even though they had been hunting, they hadn't managed to bring back so much as a pheasant. After he was apprised of recent events, the king's afterglow disappeared.

He fumed in his throne room for a half hour before he finally calling for his head of guards.

"Take the army to each town and torture people until they surrender any Dragon Rebels in the area."

"As you wish, Your Majesty."

"The queen is a traitor. Send tracking dogs after her. When you find her, bring back only her head."

"At once, Your Majesty."

"And fill the castle grounds with commoner children," the king said. "The rebels won't attack if there are innocent lives at stake."

"Very clever, Your Majesty."

"Until these Dragon Rebels are crushed, I will bring this kingdom to its knees."

ALMOST TWO HOURS AFTER HEATHER, Joe, and the Ormvalders left the Dragonstone cavern, the lava tunnel roof became noticeably thinner. Tree roots poked through and twisted downward in spots. Shafts of daylight streamed through completely open holes, and rainwater had formed large puddles here and there. Manny spotted a young troll sprawled on the tunnel floor, where he'd fallen through a caved-in section of roof.

"Stand clear," Manny said. "These trolls can be unpredictable."

Surrounded by broken pieces of lava, dirt, and rocks, the troll was scraped, bleeding, and dazed. Joe and Dane unsheathed their swords nevertheless. Suddenly Heather recognized the troll. "Gumm!"

"You know this troll?" Joe asked, bewildered.

"We met before. He's not dangerous."

"Ow," moaned Gumm.

After handing off his sword to Manny, Dane quickly checked the troll for injuries. "No broken bones, but it looks like he hit his head when he fell into the tunnel."

He removed several pieces of deeply embedded lava shards from Gumm's legs and arms. Blood gushed from one wound until Dane muttered a spell to check it. He unstopped his waterskin. "Can you drink?" he asked the troll.

"But that's liquid magic," Heather protested.

"Exactly," Dane said. "What better way to test the effects?"

Heather gasped. "Dane, he might be a troll, but nevertheless—"

"It's all right, Heather. I accidentally drank some when I was swimming in it. It did me no harm. In fact, the liquid magic healed the blisters on my heels," Joe said.

Manny nodded his agreement. "I had a terrible heat rash. Cleared it right up."

"I feel eighty years younger," Shimmer said, his beard twitching in mirth.

Gumm didn't reply, but his mouth popped open. After swallowing some of the liquid, he belched. They recoiled. The troll managed to focus on Heather. "He'er?"

"Yes, Gumm, it's Heather," she replied. "I brought some friends with me."

Gumm sat up and rubbed his head.

"You fell," Heather said.

She indicated the opening overhead and grimaced. Gumm patted his ribs and grimaced.

"Oh, I'm much better. So are you, see?" Heather brought Gumm's attention to the rapidly healing cuts and bruises on his arms, legs, and elbow.

"Impressive," Dane murmured.

"Gumm, this is Dane. He helped you," Heather said.

"You'll be fine," Dane told the troll. "Although you should probably rest a while."

Gumm gurgled at him, and then reached into an animal skin pouch to produce a bloody pair of tiger fangs. He proffered them to Dane, who took the fangs only after Heather gave him a sharp nudge in the ribs. "Take them."

"Er, thanks," Dane said. "These are splendid."

Manny and Joe stifled a laugh.

The crystal around Shimmer's neck caught Gumm's attention. "Dragonman anger."

Shimmer's brows raised in surprise. "No, no, I'm not angry. Not at all."

"Dragon. Man. *Anger*," Gumm tried again.

Shimmer smiled in an exaggerated fashion. "I'm really very cheerful most of the time."

"Anger," Gumm repeated, before he dozed off.

"I wish I knew what he was talking about," Shimmer said. "Do you have any ideas, Heather?"

"He said 'friend of anger' to me before, but I didn't understand," Heather said.

"How curious," Shimmer said. "A tame troll who speaks of anger."

"A rather unique contradiction," Manny said.

"Can you guess why he gave me these teeth?" Dane asked Heather.

"I expect Gumm wanted to repay you for healing him, Dane."

"Maybe that's why they call him Gumm," Manny joked.

"They're tiger fangs, silly," Heather said. "The tiger was about to attack Gumm and his family when I stumbled in between."

"That's right, we found your arrows on the trail. You killed a tiger?" Manny exclaimed.

"I had no choice. At least the trolls ate him afterwards and not me."

"That explains the blood on the ground," Joe said. "We were worried it might be *your* blood, Heather."

"I'm surprised it wasn't, honestly. I was convinced the trolls would attack me afterwards, but they were more interested in the tiger carcass. Only Gumm was friendly."

"What do you make of that, Shimmer?" asked Dane. "It certainly goes against anything we ever knew about trolls."

"Perhaps our information is outdated," Shimmer said.

"Maybe they've had contact with humans recently," Manny said.

"Gumm has definitely spoken with humans before. He knows actual words. The other trolls mostly just grunt," Heather said.

Joe's brows knit together. "How did he know you are a dragon man, Shimmer, unless he'd seen you transform?"

"I cannot say, Jovander," Shimmer replied. "Ask the troll when he wakes."

"Perhaps now would be a good time to tell Heather about the guardian dragon," Manny said.

One of Heather's eyebrows lifted. "I suppose this is a bit more incredible information you planned to mention at some point?"

"Indeed, yes," Shimmer said. "The Dragonstone is closely guarded by a large male dragon. That's why we must shatter the stone from afar."

"Once the magic is released, what happens then, exactly?" Dane asked.

"Our crystals should have their full power restored immediately. That's how we'll know if our plan has worked," Shimmer said. "I expect the magic will continue to flow across the ocean like a mighty wave. Eventually, all Ormarian crystals will reabsorb their original power."

"You don't sound entirely certain," Joe said.

"I'm not," Shimmer admitted. "It will be rather exciting to find out."

Manny gave a little laugh, but he wasn't amused. "More like terrifying, old boy."

"This must lead to the crater," Shimmer said, peering at the cave-in overhead. A mass of tree roots and vines poked through the opening to form a ladder. "We've come far enough."

Dane began to climb. "Stay here while I have a look around first."

Not to be outdone, Joe grabbed a handful of vines. "I'm going too."

Dane glared at him, but Joe merely returned the stare with one of his own. The prince finally relented. "All right, Jovander, but keep quiet."

The two climbed through the opening and disappeared.

"Now we wait," Shimmer said.

"Will the Ormvalders in crystal stasis wake automatically when the magic is restored?" Heather asked.

"No. I must touch my crystal to theirs and speak their name to break the spell," Shimmer said.

Joe stuck his head through the opening. "Come on."

The lava tunnel opened halfway up the inner slope of volcanic crater. Heather, Manny, and Shimmer joined Dane and Joe as they peeked out from behind a tree. An impressively large brown dragon sat on a dais of white granite on the crater floor some distance below. A multifaceted Dragonstone rested next to the creature, its obsidian surface glowing with an intense inner light.

"I've never seen the Dragonstone shine like that before. It must be fairly bursting with magic," Dane murmured.

"What say you, Heather?" Shimmer asked. "Can you destroy the Dragonstone from here?"

"We should get closer, old boy. Not even Sir Bast could have made that shot," Manny said.

"Heather can do it," Joe said.

Dane gave her an encouraging smile. "I know she can."

Heather let a little silt drift through her fingertips to check the wind. She glanced at Shimmer and nodded. Nocking an arrow in her bowstring, she sighted her target. "Just say the word."

An enormous troll suddenly emerged from the stand of trees ringing the lake, with a flaming spear in his fist. He ran toward the dais, roaring. The brown dragon yawned.

"He's bored," Manny chuckled.

As the troll threw his spear, the dragon morphed into an elderly man. With a wave of his hand, the spear splintered into a shower of sparks. With another gesture, the graybeard turned the troll into a dragon. The creature twisted into the air and then sped off into the sky.

"That man is a wizard!" Joe exclaimed.

After a long pause, Heather spoke. "Shimmer? Do I take the shot?"

But Shimmer was silent. Heather finally lowered her bow and glanced over. He and Manny were stunned beyond measure, and the color had completely drained from Dane's face. She glanced at Joe, but he shrugged in bewilderment.

"Will somebody tell us what's going on?" she asked.

"That's my father," Dane managed.

Gumm had crept up from behind, his animal skin bag bulging with some hidden treasure. "Dragonman Anger."

"He's trying to say *Ansgar*," Manny murmured.

Heather peered at the wizard on the dais. Even at a great distance, the man bore a strong resemblance to Shimmer. "That's impossible," she sputtered. "King Ansgar died two hundred thirty-six years ago."

"You saw his body, didn't you?" Joe asked.

"My brother disappeared with the crystal and didn't return. Because Ansgar was so ill, we didn't believe he had much longer to live. We just assumed..." Shimmer's voice trailed off.

"He must have sustained himself in his dragon form all this time, like you, old boy," Manny said.

"Shatter the crystal, Heather," Dane said. "Then we'll bring my father back home."

Heather put the Dragonstone in her sights once more. *I am the arrow, and I will find my mark.* Her missile arced through the air—dead on target.

"You've got it," Joe muttered.

"She really does," Manny said, astonished.

Mere inches away from the surface of the Dragonstone, however, the arrow skittered to one side.

"What was that?" Heather exclaimed.

"*Blazes*," Shimmer cursed. "Ansgar put a spell of protection on the Dragonstone."

King Ansgar stared at Heather's spent arrow a moment before picking it up. "It seems we have a visitor." His voice reverberated throughout the crater. "Show yourself."

"Stay out of sight," Dane said. "I'll go speak with him."

"Manfred and I are coming with you," Shimmer said.

"So am I," Heather and Joe said at the same time.

Dane made an exasperated noise. "Heather, won't you *ever* let me protect you?"

"By all means, protect me," she replied. "And I'll protect you in turn."

Joe stifled a smile. When the group began the trek down the side of the crater, Gumm followed.

DRAGONMAN ANGER

"*F*ive humans and a troll," exclaimed Ansgar. He peered down at the group from the raised dais. "Hello, Gumm. It's been a long time since I've seen you. I've missed our conversations."

"Dragonman Anger...friends," Gumm said.

The king suddenly noticed the bow in Heather's hand. "Somebody has been very naughty," he said, waggling the arrow at her. "You'll be turned into a dragon first—a very pretty red one."

Dane stepped in front of Heather. "Don't you know me, Father? It's Dane. We're here to help you."

"Do you think you're the first to try? Look at all those other people over there," Ansgar said. He gestured toward an empty grove of trees. "They've been waiting for an audience longer than you have."

"He's barking mad," Joe whispered into Heather's ear.

Shimmer stepped forward. "Ansgar, it's Shimmeris, your brother. You could always trounce me at cards, do you remember?"

Manny waved. "And I'm your nephew Manfred. We used to go fishing together."

Ansgar frowned and stroked his sparse, gray beard. "Who sent you? Come back again tomorrow and I may grant you an audience." The king swayed, and perspiration was beading up on his brow.

"Would His Majesty care for some water?" Dane asked.

As Dane offered his father the waterskin, Ansgar licked his lips. Suddenly he recoiled. "Poison. You must take me for a fool."

"No poison, Dragonman," Gumm said. "Good."

"Oh, if a troll says so, it must be true," Ansgar scoffed.

"I no lie," Gumm retorted, stung.

"Prove it's not poison," Ansgar said.

Dane drank a long swallow and then handed the waterskin to his father. After a moment Ansgar took a sip. "What an interesting flavor." He drained the skin and dropped it. "Now be gone, the lot of you. It's tea time, and I don't believe in ghosts."

The king lost consciousness and fell off the dais. Dane caught him and eased his father to the ground.

"What have I done?" Dane cried out in anguish.

Shimmer knelt by his brother's side and took his hand. Suddenly a band of trolls came crashing down the sides of the crater, with all manner of spears, clubs, and firebrands.

"Uh-oh," Gumm said.

"We're under siege!" Manny exclaimed.

Dane and Joe drew their swords, and Heather readied her bow. Manny transformed into a dragon and blew a warning gust of dragonfire, but the trolls were undeterred. Heather leaped on top of the dais and began to drop trolls as fast as she could. Even Gumm tried to help by flinging boulders with gusto.

"Where did they come from?" Heather cried.

Ansgar let out a big belch and sat up. "What the devil is

going on here? I turn my back for one minute, and the island devolves into complete chaos."

With a wave of his hand, the king transformed the hostile trolls into large, misshapen butterflies. The insects fluttered in confused circles for a moment before they flew off into the forest. Ansgar noticed his family for the first time. "Dane? Shimmeris…and is that Manfred?"

Manny morphed into human form. "Hello, Uncle Ansgar."

"What are the three of you doing here?"

Emotions ran high among the Ormvalders at this unexpected reunion. Joe and Heather beckoned Gumm, and the three moved away several yards to allow the royal family privacy.

"Thank you for your help, Gumm," Heather said.

He nodded, somewhat bashfully. "Scary."

Joe and Heather laughed.

"With dozens of trolls on a rampage, yes, it was fairly scary," Joe agreed.

Gumm held his animal skin bag carefully.

"What do you have, Gumm?" Heather asked.

"Eggies," he said, proudly.

"Mmm, I like eggs," Joe said. "Especially with sausage and toast."

The troll peered at Joe and frowned. "No eat my eggies."

Joe held up his hands. "I wouldn't dream of it."

Heather glanced back at the Ormvalders, who were exchanging hugs and talking over one another in a cascade of excitement. "Finding King Ansgar alive is a dream come true. And it seems the liquid magic has even brought him to his senses."

"I suppose all that's left to do is to release the magic, go home, and depose my dear father," Joe said.

"Home? Not live here?" the troll asked.

"No, Gumm, we live across the ocean a long way off. No trolls live there," Heather replied.

"Me come, too. Me no like trolls."

"You don't understand, Gumm," Joe said.

As he tried to explain to the troll where Destiny was in relation to Boravagg, Dane appeared at Heather's elbow.

"My father has removed the spell of protection on the Dragonstone, so we can release the magic. After you do the honors, will you allow me to present you to the King of Ormaria?"

Heather beamed. "Dane, I'm truly happy you found him again, and I would love to be presented to your father."

He lifted her hand to his lips and kissed it. "I look forward to spending a lifetime with you, Heather of the Jagged Peaks. Even if that means I must be jolly all day long."

"I'm content with you exactly as you are, Dane."

He grinned briefly, but then his expression became sober.

"Listen, Heather, Shimmer says he's unsure what will follow when the Dragonstone breaks. I want you to promise whatever happens, you'll get yourself home. Find my mother's crystal in the Dragon cave and awaken her. She'll wake the others."

"But Dane—"

"Promise me, Heather. Her name is Mara Daniella Ansgar, and her crystal is embedded in the alcove shaped like a steeple."

"All right, I promise."

Dane gave her a lingering kiss before he rejoined his family. They moved several yards away from the dais and watched as Heather nocked an arrow. With Joe and Gumm safely behind her, Heather raised her bow and released her arrow. When the arrow found its mark, the Dragonstone shattered into crystals at last. Nothing happened for a long heartbeat. Heather and Dane locked eyes—just before a strange black bubble exploded out of the shards.

"That doesn't look good!" Joe cried.

The Ormvalders instantly transformed into dragons and

darted into the sky. Dane flew toward Heather, but the spreading darkness quickly enveloped him. Joe and Heather began to run. Gumm grabbed them both, one under each arm, and bounded toward the opening in the lava tunnel. He jumped down into the hole, landing on his feet as the wave passed over. Suddenly dizzy, the troll sank to his knees, retching. Heather and Joe slipped from his grip and landed with a thud. Something reached down Heather's throat and turned her inside out.

"I'm going to be sick," Joe moaned.

Heather leaned against the wall of the cave, breathing deeply, until the nausea eased. Unfortunately, the air was becoming increasingly permeated with fumes.

"Are you all right Joe? Gumm?" she asked finally. The troll grunted in response.

Joe pushed himself into a sitting position. "I'm better now, but it's a little hard to breathe. You?"

Heather nodded. "That was horribly unpleasant."

"What in blazes happened?" Joe exclaimed.

"The pent-up magic was released from the Dragonstone," Heather replied.

"It's safe to say I don't think Shimmer expected the magic to explode," Joe said.

"It probably came as a bit of a shock."

Heather and Joe shared a laugh, made jagged by nerves. Even Gumm joined in. Perspiration began to roll down Joe's face, and he unlaced the ties on his tunic.

"It's bloody hot in here. I need air."

"Let's climb out of the tunnel and find the others," she said.

Heather willed more light from her crystal. She discovered the opening overhead had closed, and there were no vines or tree roots like before.

"How very strange. We're sealed in," she said.

A tremor shook the ground underneath their feet.

"Uh-oh. Bad," Gumm said.

"Is that my imagination, or is this volcano going to erupt?" Joe asked.

"It *can't*. It's dormant," Heather said. "Maybe the explosion of magic caused the earth to shift?"

The tremors continued. Gumm stood as best he could, considering the space had somehow shrunk. He punched through the tunnel ceiling until daylight filtered through once more. After giving Joe and Heather a boost up, he crawled out himself.

The three of them gaped at the desolate landscape. The lake had disappeared, and no vegetation was growing in the crater at all. Steam was rising from cracks in the floor of the lava dome. In the center of the crater was the Dragonstone, now swollen to five times its former size. The Ormvalders were nowhere to be seen.

"Dane?" Heather called out.

Joe cupped his hands around his mouth. "Shimmer! Manny?"

Gumm joined in. "Dragonman Anger?"

Their voices were met by an eerie silence. Perhaps even more ominous, the tremors were becoming increasingly violent. Joe, Heather, and Gumm were nearly knocked to the ground.

"It's no use; we can't wait here. We must take the Dragonstone to the ship. I expect the others will meet us there," Heather said.

"How are we supposed to do that?" Joe asked.

"We'll morph into dragons."

"What!"

"You're an Ormvalder, aren't you? You can do it, Joe. I'll carry the Dragonstone, and you take Gumm."

"Outside of burning my thumb, I've never done any magic."

"Nor I, except by accident. But this volcano is going to blow, and we can't run fast enough to escape. We must transform or die."

Heather sped toward the Dragonstone, visualizing herself as

a dragon—and then she became one. She darted into the sky, exhilarated. The sensation of freedom was intoxicating, but she forced herself to focus. After a few clumsy attempts, she finally managed to seize the huge crystal block in her claws. The Dragonstone was almost too big to carry, but Heather circled higher, determined to hold on.

"Come on, Joe!"

Even though he was desperate to transform, Joe could not master the concept. He spread his arms and flapped them like the wings of a bird, but nothing happened. As pieces of the crater floor began to fall away, however, Joe suddenly expanded into an enormous bronze dragon. After Gumm jumped onto his back, Joe barely managed to take flight. Heather held her breath when Joe's belly accidentally brushed the top of the crater. But he seemed to gain confidence with his increased altitude, and soon he joined her in the skies over Boravagg.

"You scared me for a minute, Joe."

"You're not the only one who's scared. The troll is nearly strangling me."

Gumm had his eyes screwed shut, and his beefy arms were wrapped around Joe's neck as if he indeed meant to strangle him. Since the troll wasn't dragon apt, neither Heather nor Joe could tell him to relax. When the two dragons angled toward the water, Gumm screamed with fright. Joe leveled out, but then the volcano exploded behind them, spewing hot gas and black ash into the air. As debris began to rain down, Heather and Joe put on a burst of speed.

When they reached the inlet off the coast, the rocky shapes appeared to be larger than before. Nevertheless, the *Bonny Heather* was safely anchored inside the inlet. Heather set the Dragonstone down on the deck and morphed into human form just as Joe landed beside her with a loud thump. Gumm slid off, doing his best to protect his animal skin full of eggs. Panic twisted his grotesque face when lava began to spew from the volcano.

"Go!" he exclaimed, pointing to sea. "*Go!*"

"It's all right, Gumm. The ship is safe," Heather said.

Joe finally managed to morph into his human form—although his skin was still a little scaly in a few places. He ducked below deck to see if anyone else was aboard, but rejoined Heather and Gumm on deck almost right away.

"We're alone. I can't believe the Ormvalders would leave us to fend for ourselves," he said, bewildered. "I'm worried. You don't suppose they were burned up in the explosion, do you?"

"No, of course not. They probably flew on ahead when we were sealed up in the tunnel," Heather said, fixing her gaze on the tips of her boots.

"Uh-oh," Gumm yelled.

A large mass of falling lava narrowly missed the ship. A plume of steam rose from the ocean where the molten rock hit the water.

Joe gulped. "Maybe we should go."

"We're fine here. The ship has a spell of protection on it."

A hot flaming rock soared though the air, burning a hole in one of the sails. Heather gulped. "On the other hand, perhaps the magical explosion stripped it away."

Joe and Gumm pulled up the anchor while Heather tried to magically lift the *Bonny Heather* from the water. The vessel lurched to the side, nearly breaching the hull on one of the rocks.

"Steady!" Joe yelled.

Even though fear was numbing her brain, Heather tried to visualize the ship as one of Dane's floating stones. To her surprise, the ship responded by rising into the air. A few more burning bits of debris perforated the sail before Heather managed to nudge the vessel out to sea. Shortly thereafter, they'd left Boravagg behind. More relaxed now, Gumm patted his stomach.

"Food?"

"Why don't you take Gumm below deck and see what we've got for dinner?" Heather suggested to Joe.

His eyes slid toward the hatchway. "Um…I don't think he'll fit."

"Good point."

Joe brought food up from the galley for Gumm to eat. Whatever he fed the troll went into his gullet like an appetizer. As a result, Heather went below deck to survey their meager food stores. *If we don't fly faster, we may run out of food before reaching Destiny.* She increased the ship's speed, making it difficult to walk above deck without holding on to the railings. Gumm stuck out his tongue and made faces into the wind.

The *Bonny Heather* continued to move east. When the sunlight faded, the red glow of lava lit the nighttime sky like a perpetual sunset—visible even after they'd been flying for hours. The troll slept under a tarp that night, his regular snores rising even over the sound of the rushing wind. Heather found sleep impossible. She kept reliving the horror of the black wave as it overtook Dane. Despite her reassurances to Joe, she knew none of the Ormvalders would have abandoned them unless they had had no choice. She buried her face in her pillow and dissolved into helpless, silent tears.

PREDESTINED

*D*espite Heather's best efforts, the return journey took almost four days. The ship arrived off the coast of Destiny late at night, so they dropped anchor until morning. Joe and Heather stayed up late, stargazing, but Gumm went to sleep on his pallet. He slept cuddled with his eggs, which Joe had discovered were dragon eggs.

"I guess he means to hatch them as pets," Joe said.

"Oh, no! The dragons I met on Boravagg wouldn't have made good pets at all," Heather said. "Ormarian dragons are much more civilized."

"Gumm seems determined to tame his clutch. He's actually quite tender-hearted."

"He's a good fighter too," Heather said. "Did you see the way he can hurl boulders?"

"The Ormvalders are supposed to make the revolution bloodless. But if not, I've got a troll to unloose."

"How is Gumm going to react when he realizes he's the only one of his kind here, I wonder?"

"From what I've seen, I think he'll like it."

~

JOE AWAKENED HEATHER AT DAWN. "Heather, get up. There's something very wrong."

"What is it?" she asked, still groggy.

"According to the map and all of our instruments, we're off the coast of Destiny. But I don't see the castle."

"That can't be right. Let me have a look."

She followed Joe topside. To her surprise, the coastline appeared to be desolate.

"There's the dragon cave at the bottom of that cliff," he said, pointing. "The triangular opening is unmistakable. But the castle should be right above it."

A faint glimmer of hope began to burn in her heart. "Maybe the Ormvalders vanished it for some reason."

Gumm staggered over, rubbing his eyes. "Home?"

"Yes, we are home," she replied.

After Heather ate a small breakfast, she transformed into a dragon and carried the Dragonstone from the deck of the ship into the cave. The cave was larger and more extensive than she'd imagined. After she deposited the Dragonstone deep inside, where no casual intruder would find it, she morphed into human form.

"Shimmer?" she called out. "Dane?"

Her only reply was the sound of her own voice, echoing off the cave walls. Joe and Gumm arrived moments later. While the troll busied himself with his clutch of eggs, Joe and Heather explored the cave. They could find no evidence any humans had ever been there.

"Shimmer said the Ormvalder wizards were here, in crystal stasis form," Heather said, bewildered. "Dane specifically asked me to wake his mother, but I don't see any crystals at all. Do you suppose they've already been wakened?"

Joe frowned. "This can't be the right cave. It looks the same, but that rusty old anchor is missing from the entrance."

"You've spent a lot more time here than I have," Heather said. "Do you really think this isn't the right place?"

Joe stared at her, something close to fear in his eyes.

"No. But it's different." He put his hand on one of the mineral formations. "You see this stalagmite? I broke it off at the base when I was a young lad. Now it's whole."

"I don't understand this. Let's see what's happening at the castle."

Gumm bounded over, pleased with himself. He had arranged all seven of his eggs next to the Dragonstone. "Eggies happy. Where dragon men?"

Heather gulped. "We're not certain, Gumm."

Joe led the way as they climbed up the cliff. He peeked over the top.

"Be careful," whispered Heather. "Don't let any guards see you."

"Don't worry; there aren't any."

He stood up in plain sight. When Heather joined him, she discovered Destiny Castle was gone without a trace. Tall trees grew where the foundation had once been. The groomed lawns, gardens, and carefully constructed stone fences had been replaced by underbrush and forest. While Gumm loped off after a wild turkey, Heather and Joe wandered through the trees, stunned.

"Do you remember the enormous, gnarled oak tree that was right here?" Joe asked. "It's now a sapling. Heather, I think we've gone back in time."

At that, her heartbeat hammered in her ears. Her knees grew

weak, and she had to find a rock to sit on. She wanted to tell Joe he was crazy, but the evidence was incontrovertible.

"Joe, you could be right," she said finally.

He sat down on a lump of grass. "Well...what should we do?"

"I suppose we should be prepared to make the best of it."

~

WHILE JOE BUILT A CAMPFIRE, Heather went off to hunt for food. A small herd of wild boar was grazing in an open field not far away. To her relief, Gumm went off to hunt for himself. The troll might not mind eating his food raw, but she didn't want to be around while he did so. They dined well that night, eating roasted boar, crabapples, and the last of the stale biscuits from the *Bonny Heather*. Gumm was full from his own hunting foray, but he enjoyed eating the bits of boar Joe and Heather didn't want.

"I just don't understand," Joe kept repeating. "We saw the Dragonstone shatter, but now it's bigger than ever—without a mark on it."

"It's the original Dragonstone, Joe. I suppose there was so much magic pent up in the smaller stone that its destruction reset time."

"How is that even possible?"

"There's evidently a lot about magic we don't know. We got lucky we weren't stuck on Boravagg. That spell of protection Shimmer put on the ship left it unaffected."

"And why are *we* here—or Gumm for that matter? There was no spell of protection on us."

"Huh?" Gumm said.

Heather fingered the dragon crystal around her neck. "Maybe it's because our dragon crystals are different. Gumm was holding us both when the wave passed over, so he came with us to whatever time we're at now."

Gumm was bored at the conversation, and his eyelids began to droop. He stretched out next to the campfire, and before long he was snoring.

"Lucky fellow," Joe said. "He doesn't much care one way or the other."

"Probably not," Heather agreed. "Do you realize we are living in a time before Destiny or even Ormaria came into existence? Nobody we knew will be born for centuries."

"At least we solved one mystery," Joe said.

"Which mystery is that?"

"How a troll came to bring the Dragonstone to this continent."

Heather gasped. "I hadn't thought of that."

They both stared at Gumm as he slept.

"This is really weird," Joe said. "Really, *really* weird."

"My head hurts just thinking about it."

THE NEXT DAY was spent foraging for food. Finding water wasn't too difficult since there was a creek not too far away. Heather, Joe, and Gumm stained their fingers eating the fruit from a wild blueberry patch. The troll enjoyed the blueberries so much that he stripped the patch bare. The three of them sat in the sunshine and dangled their feet in the water.

"I found my first peacock feather here," Heather said. "I thought the colors were so beautiful, the feather must have come from a magical bird."

"But that hasn't happened yet."

She winced. "A person could go crazy thinking about what hasn't happened yet."

"Gumm, why don't you like trolls?" Joe asked.

Gumm wrinkled his nose. "Always 'Gumm come here' or 'Gumm do that.' Gumm wants to live free."

"You don't mind being alone?" Joe asked.

Gumm grinned. "See birds? Fishies? Bugs? Me not alone."

Heather peered skyward. The dark clouds and flashes of lightning on the horizon signaled a rainstorm. "I suppose we should build some kind of shelter if we're going to be here awhile."

"How about we weather the storm on the *Bonny Heather?*" suggested Joe. "Just for tonight."

"I like cave," Gumm said.

Despite their best efforts, neither Heather nor Joe could convince Gumm to come with them. Heather and Joe flew to the ship as a light rain began to fall. They headed below deck and played a half-hearted game of cards throughout the afternoon. Finally, Joe tossed his cards aside and jumped to his feet.

"Is this what it's going to be like the rest of our lives?" he asked in exasperation. "Never knowing where our next meal is coming from or where we're going to sleep for the night?"

Heather bit her lip as she watched him pace. His upbringing had been completely different from hers—a fact that was never more clear than now. Joe had been raised in Destiny Castle, and although his life had been unhappy, he'd never had to deal with physical discomfort or hunger in the same way she had. There were times, particularly in the winter, when she and her parents hadn't had enough to eat. And even with the fireplace blazing, the freezing cold always cut right through the walls of their dwelling. No, Heather was no stranger to deprivation, but she could not say the same for her friend.

"Let's find a village," she suggested. "Maybe we can trade with the villagers for things we need."

Joe brightened. "Maybe so. I miss griddlecakes."

"Hot bread and butter," Heather said. "Cobs of corn."

"Salt. I'd love a little salt on my food."

"This is making me hungry. Let's fly out tomorrow morning and see if there's a settlement anywhere near here."

A hugely loud crack of thunder made them both jump. At the same time, rain began to pelt down in earnest. As the sea roiled in response to the incoming storm, Joe turned green.

"The cave doesn't sound like such a bad idea right about now," he murmured.

Heather scooped up the cards. "Let's bundle up our bedding and fly over."

"I won't argue with you."

Another rolling peal of thunder galvanized them into action. They raced into their sleeping quarters and emerged a few moments later with armfuls of bedding and pillows. Joe used a length of rope to tie them into two bundles. The *Bonny Heather* began to list from side to side, and he clapped his hand over his mouth to keep from vomiting. Heather practically hauled Joe up the stairs. Moments later they'd morphed into dragons and were airborne.

Lightning was lacing the sky as they flew toward the cave, and huge waves were pounding against the cliff. Gumm gaped at their arrival, surprised to see them. Joe cocked a thumb toward the ocean. "Scary," he explained.

Gumm's face split into a smile. Joe and Heather arranged their bedding and sat down. She noticed a little depression in the center of the cave that would make a nice fire pit.

"It's a shame we don't have any wood," Heather said, blowing on her cold fingers. "I long to have a fire."

"When we were on Boravagg, the Ormvalders sometimes made fire without any fuel at all," Joe said.

"Gah! I wish we knew more about magic," Heather said. "We're both wearing crystals, with no idea how to use them."

They experimented for a few minutes and finally got a rock to glow. It radiated an impressive amount of heat.

"That's not bad," Joe said.

Entranced, Gumm picked up his dragon eggs and clustered them next to the rock for warmth. The storm outside continued to rage, as if the elements had a personal vendetta. When the tide began to rise, moisture crept deeper and deeper into the cave. Heather managed to conjure piles of sand, which Gumm had a great deal of fun arranging into a berm. A tremendous crashing noise suddenly reverberated throughout the cave. Heather leaped over the berm and climbed over wet rocks to find out what had happened.

"Oh, no," she groaned.

The *Bonny Heather* had been picked up by the ocean and hurled into the mouth of the cave. A huge hole had been torn into her hull from the rocks at the base of the cliff, and the ship had been de-masted. Joe and Gumm appeared at Heather's elbow. As they watched, the surf continued to pull the vessel apart.

"Uh-oh," said Gumm.

"Well, that's that," Joe said.

A wave washed over Heather's boots, and she scrambled backward.

"I guess it's a good thing you get seasick, Joe. Otherwise, we would have been on that ship when it ran aground."

"Now we know how a ship came to be wrecked here," Joe said. "It was ours."

PART OF HISTORY

*T*he next morning dawned clear, and the seas were calm. While Gumm went out to get his breakfast, Joe and Heather sat on the cliff and ate crabapples.

"Gumm is an independent sort of a troll," Joe observed.

"I'm glad he hunts for himself," Heather replied. "He eats so much; I was worried how we were going to keep him fed."

After they ate, Joe and Heather salvaged the sails from the *Bonny Heather*. They also managed to save the table and several of the chairs from below deck. The location of the future castle became their campsite. One of the oilcloth sails formed a roomy tent, complete with a waterproof floor. They angled another sail to form a roof over a dining area. With the table and chairs underneath, it resembled an outdoor room. Heather and Joe looked over their handiwork, pleased.

"It's not a castle or anything, but it'll keep the rain off. And if it's not too cold, we can sleep here tonight," Heather said.

"That would be a relief," Joe said. "Gumm snores too loud."

"Now that that's done, shall we fly? I'm rather keen to enjoy myself for a while."

For the first time, the two were able to savor the sensation of flight without the threat of imminent danger. As they soared over the treetops, Heather forgot her troubles. Joe began to show off, flying upside down and making looping swirls in the air like a dolphin. Heather was laughing so hard, that she almost flew past a village without noticing it.

JOE AND HEATHER landed in a field, morphed into human form, and walked to the village on foot.

"This is roughly the same place Destiny Village will be," Joe said. "I used to go there in the summertime to buy candy."

"You couldn't get sweets at the castle?"

"Of course I could. But since it bothered my father to have me mix with commoners, I took every opportunity to annoy him."

"It's strange to think we're part of history now."

"I wish we'd been put closer to our own time so we could alter events. I would have liked to save my mother."

"There are lots of things I'd change if I could."

The walk through the village, called Runningdale, took about five minutes. The houses were made of mud, wood and stones, and were rudely thatched with straw. They stopped by a domed oven and negotiated with the baker to trade a wild boar for bread and some salt. The baker's son came out of the cottage to stare at the visitors. He was about ten years old, with a curious, intelligent face surrounded by a thick brown mane.

"You have red hair like a fox," he said to Heather.

"Indeed I do," she replied. "And your hair is like that of a minx."

While Joe juggled several pinecones to amuse the boy, Heather finished making arrangements with the baker to deliver the boar the next day. She signaled to Joe when she was ready to go.

"Perhaps we will see you tomorrow," Joe told the child.

Several of the villagers came out of their cottages to stare as they left. Heather and Joe nodded and tried to act friendly.

"They must not get many strangers here," Heather whispered to Joe.

"It's a good thing we didn't bring Gumm," Joe murmured. "We would probably have been stoned to death."

When they reached the open field, Heather and Joe morphed into their dragon forms. They flew off, unaware that Liam had followed them and was gaping in amazement.

HEATHER TOOK the rest of the morning to hunt while Joe brought his knapsack into the woods to forage for nuts, berries, or fruit. When he returned to the campsite, Joe was riding on Gumm's shoulders, and his knapsack was bulging. Heather was roasting a couple of rabbits over an open fire, and a small wild boar hung from a sturdy branch a short distance away.

"Gumm found a walnut tree," Joe said. "He lifted me up so I could pick a whole bag full."

The troll set Joe down with a giggle. "I like here. Good food." He paused a moment. "Who young friend?"

Puzzled, Joe, and Heather turned to see the baker's son hiding behind a tree.

"Hello there," Heather said. "Did you follow us?"

The boy nodded without speaking. Heather and Joe were both impressed. The child was peering at the troll, but he hadn't run away.

"Would you like to meet Gumm?" Heather asked.

The troll sat down so he wouldn't appear quite so intimidating. The boy came out to have a closer look.

"I've never seen a giant before," he said. He turned his solemn gaze on Joe and Heather. "Or magical people."

"You don't seem afraid," Joe said.

"I'm not."

"What's your name?" Heather asked.

"Liam," the boy replied. "Liam Ormvalder."

When Heather and Joe delivered the boar to Runningdale the next morning, Liam appeared with a basket and a fishing pole. As Heather and Joe left with bags of warm bread and a quantity of salt, Liam told his father he was going with them to fish. To Liam's delight, Joe allowed the boy to ride on his back after he'd transformed. Heather and Joe flew directly into the cave, where Gumm was holed up with his eggs. The troll's eyes were shining.

"Eggies hatching."

Liam slid off Joe and came running. Sure enough, several of the eggs were cracked and quivering with animals struggling to emerge.

"What kind of birds are those?" Liam asked.

"No birds. Dragons," said Gumm.

As Joe and Heather clustered around, Liam shook his head in confusion. "Dragons? Did you hatch from eggs too?"

They laughed.

"We're as human as you are, Liam," Heather replied. "It's our crystals that allow us to transform."

Heather took out her hunting knife and used it to chisel off a piece from the Dragonstone. She handed the dragon crystal to Liam. When his fingers closed around the magical object, it gave off a flare of light.

"Not everybody can do magic. But I have a feeling you've got a gift, Liam."

Her eyes met Joe's. They both shared the same wonderment in this event. Just as the newly hatched dragons would one day roam free across the countryside, the child sitting before them would one day be a king—the future ruler of Ormaria.

~

JOE TRADED with one of the villagers for a fishing pole of his own. The dragon hatchlings adored fish, so he and Gumm spent a great deal of time catching perch to feed the rapidly growing brood. Liam came around as frequently as he could, to help with the dragons or demonstrate his latest magical trick. He'd asked the village smithy to make a clasp for his crystal so he could wear it around his neck like Heather and Joe wore theirs.

One morning, about two weeks after the hatching, Liam arrived at the campsite with a delivery of bread. Joe had brought one of the male dragons from the cave to keep him company while Heather went hunting. Pan had become everyone's favorite dragon, with his playful personality and distinctive silvery forelock. While Joe whittled a bowl from a wedge of cedar, the baby dragon snuffled through the underbrush, searching for grubs and insects.

"Hello, Pan," Liam called out. The little creature bounded over like a puppy, and the lad scratched him under his chin. "When I talk to dragons, I could swear sometimes they talk back."

"You're dragon-apt. The first time a dragon spoke to me I thought I was going mad."

The memory suddenly made Joe long for Shimmer. He'd even begun to miss Manny—and to a far lesser extent, Dane.

"I used to imagine dragons and giants as monsters," Liam said. "I'm beginning to understand there's a lot more to the world than I can possibly imagine."

"You're right, Liam. My advice to you is to dream big."

"Someday I'm going to build a beautiful castle overlooking

the ocean, right over there," he said, pointing. "You and Heather can live in it, if you want."

"That sounds terrific. We'd like that a lot."

Pan sneezed and accidentally scorched a bed of leaves. As Joe and Liam scrambled to put out the fire, the dragon hung his head in shame. "Oops," he said.

Liam laughed. "If that's your first word, Pan, I hope it does not predict your future."

THAT NIGHT, a fierce lightning storm once again caused Heather and Joe to seek shelter in the cave. They cooked bits of venison on the glowing rock, and fed some of the meat to the dragons. There was one other male dragon besides Pan, and five females. Like Pan, all the hatchlings were starting to talk—and argue—amongst themselves. Although Gumm couldn't understand the dragon chatter, Heather and Joe were glad when the little dragons had eaten their fill and nodded off to sleep.

They left Gumm gnawing on venison bones and went to the entrance of the cave to watch the electrical storm light the sky.

"I really miss Shimmer," Joe said.

"He was like a father to you," Heather replied.

"You miss Dane a lot, don't you?" A crimson stain crept over Joe's cheekbones. "I hear you calling him in your sleep sometimes."

Heather picked up a pebble and tossed it into the churning water. "It doesn't matter. I'm never going to see him again."

Gumm appeared, a troubled expression on his face.

"Is something wrong, Gumm?" Heather asked.

"I think you leave soon."

"Why do you say that?" Joe asked, mystified.

He pointed to the surf, which curled up as it came in off the ocean and crashed against the cliff. "Wave come and stop at rock. What happen if no rock?"

"The wave keeps going, I suppose," Heather said. "It loses momentum eventually. Why?"

"On Boravagg, Dragonstone break. Black wave make big problem and then keep going," Gumm asked. "Come back and take you—like dragonmen."

Heather and Joe stared at Gumm, startled. He was a troll, but apparently he'd understood more about their situation than they'd given him credit for.

"I hadn't thought of that," she said. "Maybe it lost its energy and it won't."

"I don't know, Heather," Joe said. "Perhaps the wave takes a while to circle the globe."

A long, sober pause ensued as she digested that idea.

"What do you think that release of magic really did to Shimmer and the other Ormvalders?" asked Joe. "Do you think they're dead?"

"How can they be dead if they've not been born yet?" Heather mused.

Gumm scratched his head. "I'm confused."

ALTHOUGH GUMM'S warning seemed to hang in the air like a vulture, Heather managed to push it from conscious thought. She filled her days with hunting. One afternoon, she had a pheasant in her sights. Before she could loose her arrow, her eyes focused on a black wall on the horizon, rolling her way. Her heart jumped into her throat.

"Joe!" she gasped.

Her bow slung across her back, Heather morphed into a dragon and flew toward the campsite at breakneck speed. Gumm was playing hide and seek with Liam in the trees.

Heather raised a cloud of dust as she landed abruptly and morphed into human form.

"Gumm, the wave is coming. Where is Joe?" she blurted out.

"Walnut tree."

"Protect Liam from harm. He's going to be a great leader someday," Heather said. "Goodbye, Gumm."

With tears streaming down her face, she sprung into the sky once more.

"He'er!" Gumm bawled.

She sped through an open field toward the walnut tree, where Joe had amassed a large bag of nuts. He was just knotting the top closed when she arrived. Heather morphed into human form as she landed and gripped his hand.

"It's here."

She pointed over his shoulder. Joe gulped as he stared at the oncoming rush of magic.

"I'm scared, Heather."

"It will be all right as long as we're together."

As Heather and Joe clung to each other, the wave engulfed them. The world rotated so fast she wasn't sure if she was alive, dead, or somewhere in between. The only thing that gave her comfort was Joe's hand in hers. She squeezed her eyes shut as she fought to stay conscious. Then the ground rose up to meet her, and everything went black.

HIDDEN AGENDAS

*H*eather had a dim awareness of someone carrying her in his muscular arms. The nightmare was over, and Dane was taking her to safety.

"Thank you, Dane," she murmured.

The prince paused mid-stride. Then he deposited her unceremoniously on a hard stone surface. Heather was jarred wide-awake. "Hey, that hurt! What's wrong with you?"

Dane glared at her, unrepentant, without a trace of recognition in his blue eyes. The lower half of his face was now covered with a silky, dark blond beard, and he wore the sword and uniform of a guardsman.

"That's how we treat poachers in Ormaria. And you're to address me as 'Your Highness.'"

He turned on his heel and strode past two guardsmen who were dragging Joe in by his arms. When they released him, Joe flopped to the floor. He moaned when his head banged against the stone. The door of their cell slammed shut. Joe sat up and stared at it, aghast.

"Welcome to Ormaria," he muttered.

Heather discovered she was missing her bow, quiver, and the

knife in her boot. Her fingers moved to grasp her dragon crystal, but that was gone too. Joe's crystal had also been taken, as well as the carved dragon pendant he always wore around his neck. Heather ran to the window, but the bars precluded escape, and the bushes outside obscured the view.

"We're in the castle, but not in the dungeon. It's too light and clean," she said.

"I think we're in a detention cell," Joe said.

"I suppose so. Are you all right?"

Joe rubbed the back of his head. "I'm alive, but why does time travel have to be so painful? Do you have any idea *when* we are?"

"Dane doesn't know us and he's wearing a beard, so I'm guessing we've traveled to a time before his father becomes ill."

"Why is the good prince out of sorts?"

"He thinks we're poachers. They've taken our weapons. I expect we'll be brought before a hearing."

"In Destiny, the penalty for poaching was death."

"Well, I don't intend to go quietly to the gallows," Heather said. "You wanted to be somewhere in time where you could change events. This is our perfect opportunity."

Despite her brave words, she slumped onto the stone bench, forlorn. Dane had regarded her with the same cool contempt as he had when they first met. He didn't remember her or anything they'd shared. Grief threatened to engulf her, but she pushed it away. She couldn't afford the luxury of emotions right now. If she could devise the right plan, she and Joe might just be able to prevent the fall of Ormaria.

DANE LAID HEATHER'S BOW, quiver, and hunting knife on the table in the king's sitting room. While Manny picked up the bow to admire its workmanship, Dane handed the two crystal pendants and Joe's Ormarian carving to his uncle. Shimmer examined them carefully, a shock of dark hair falling over his forehead as he did so.

"These crystals are not the same as ours," he declared, glancing at the Dragonstone, glowing softly in the corner. "They are from a different source altogether. But this carving is identical to yours, Ansgar."

Shimmer passed the crystals and carving to his older brother. King Ansgar, whose face was only slightly lined, regarded the artifacts with equal fascination. Manny upended the quiver, and its contents fell out with a loud clatter. Arrows spilled to the floor.

"Sorry about that," Manny said. He gasped with pleasure when he righted the quiver. "Oh, look! The quiver is spelled to refill itself. How clever."

"Manfred, please," Dane said. "Now is not the time to play games."

"Sorry, but the bow and arrows are exquisite. They were obviously made by a master craftsman. I wonder how the lad came by them?"

"They were in the possession of the girl, along with the knife," Dane said. "She and the lad were unconscious next to the stump of that old walnut tree. I believe they may have collapsed from heat exhaustion or perhaps malnutrition. They are both quite thin."

"If they had no game in their possession, we can charge them only with trespassing," King Ansgar said. "I'm inclined to return their possessions, give them a meal, and send them on their way."

"I, for one, should like to see these trespassers. The guards told me the girl is extraordinarily beautiful," Manny said.

"I had not noticed," Dane said.

Manny's beard quivered with mirth. "No, of course not,

Cousin. Which is why you insisted on carrying her to the castle personally."

As Dane and Manny began to squabble, Shimmer held up his hands for quiet.

"That's enough! I would also like to ask these trespassers a few questions—with your permission, Ansgar."

"Have them brought here," the king said.

HEATHER AND JOE were ushered into the king's sitting room, where the Ormvalders were assembled. Heather and Joe exchanged a startled glance. The king and his brother were still in their prime. A broad smile spread over Joe's face.

"It's good to see you looking so well, Shimmer," he cried.

Joe clapped his hand over his mouth and gave Heather an apologetic glance. Shimmer peered at Joe. "Do I know you, lad?"

"Er…no, Your Highness. I beg your pardon," Joe mumbled.

"Explain yourselves," Shimmer said.

"We're not poachers," Heather said. "Jovander and I are from a kingdom called Destiny. We've traveled to Ormaria seeking asylum. Joe is the natural son of King Chance. He posed an embarrassment, and his father tried to have him killed."

"He drowned my mother," Joe burst out.

"And who are you?" Dane asked Heather.

"She's Heather," Joe replied. "My father tried to have her killed, too. We helped each other escape."

"I've never heard of Destiny, nor of King Chance," Dane said.

"The kingdom is a very long way off, Your Highness," Heather said.

King Ansgar held up the dragon crystals and the Ormarian pendant. "Where did you get these?" he asked.

"The Ormarian pendant was handed down to me by my mother," Joe replied. "She was an Ormvalder descendant."

"Our crystals are from Boravagg," Heather said.

Manny and Dane reacted with disbelief, but Ansgar and Shimmer exchanged a glance. The king pointed to his brother with an exultant expression.

"Ha. What have I been telling you?" Ansgar chortled. "I knew it all along."

"It is a fine tale, but impossible to disprove," Dane said. "And we cannot grant asylum to subjects from a mythical kingdom. I shall escort our visitors to the kitchen. After they've eaten, they will be shown the gates."

The crown prince reached for Heather's elbow, but she moved out of the way.

"I hereby issue a challenge to the most skillful archer in the realm. I will best him or her in a contest of accuracy," she said.

Dane laughed. "A contest with you will be an insult to our most skillful bowman."

Heather flinched.

"Now come quietly or I will have to call the guards," Dane said.

Joe's face was pale, with splotches of red over his cheekbones. "So the talk I've heard about Ormaria being a free and open society was a *lie*. Heather and I sacrificed everything to come here—just to find out you're no better than my father."

Although she wanted to shout as well, Heather was simply too stunned.

"Stop, Joe, that won't help," she said. "It seems you and I have been misled."

Joe closed his mouth, but his chest was heaving with righteous indignation. Heather could not bring herself to meet Dane's gaze, nor any of the Ormvalders for that matter. She fixed her eyes on the Dragonstone, nearly identical to the one she'd destroyed not too long ago, and summoned whatever dignity she still possessed.

"If we may have our belongings, we will remove ourselves from the grounds at once. Please forgive our trespass."

To her horror, her eyes began to fill with tears.

"Oh spare us the dramatics," Dane muttered.

Pushed too far, Heather snapped. "You really are a horse's arse, Dane Ormvalder."

Dane gaped in shock, but King Ansgar, Shimmer, and Manny burst out into laughter.

"How dare you address me so?" Dane sputtered.

"She said nothing we haven't been telling you for ages, Cousin," Manny chortled. "You take yourself far too seriously."

Still laughing, the king rose from his chair. He walked over to Heather and rested his hands on her shoulders.

"Well spoken, child. You are quite right about many matters. I invite you and Jovander to be my guests in the castle for a few days while we sort this out. Shimmer will take you to my private dining room for a meal, and then he will find living quarters for you. I accept your challenge, but it will take time to arrange."

Ansgar returned the dragon crystals and pendant to her.

"Thank you, Your Majesty," Heather replied. "*Your* kindness, at least, has not been exaggerated."

When Heather shot Dane a pointed glance, he at least had the grace to act abashed.

THE KING'S dining room was almost as big as Saltimar's entire cottage. While Joe waited for the servants to bring lunch, he wandered around the room. He pretended to be fascinated with the mirrors and carvings and such, but he was actually trying to give Heather a wide berth. As soon as they were alone, she'd burst into tears. He'd patted her on the back, but she was inconsolable. Finally, when the flood slowed to a trickle, Joe resumed his seat.

"I'm sorry about Dane. Are you all right?"

"Forgive me, Joe. This is more difficult than I had anticipated."

"I understand. Even though we won't be meeting them for another two hundred thirty-six years, it feels strange the Ormvalders don't recognize us. Shimmer, especially."

"I keep expecting one of them to burst out laughing and admit they've been having a joke at our expense."

"If we're meeting them now for the first time, how come they don't remember us in the future?"

"The future is unwritten as of this moment, Joe."

"Do you suppose the wave of magic will return to push us forward again?"

"I expect the waves will keep coming until we are returned to our own time, like birth pangs. We will have only a few weeks to prevent the fall of Ormaria."

"How do we *do* that exactly? We don't know the name of the traitor."

"The Ormvalders will think we're out of our senses if we tell them the truth. I thought the challenge might get their attention. If we can earn their respect, perhaps they'll listen."

"In the meantime, I suppose we should look for someone with a hidden agenda," Joe said.

"Exactly."

A middle-aged servant entered the dining room with a heavily laden rolling cart. The woman ladled out bowls full of fragrant onion soup. Joe grabbed his spoon but the servant clucked her tongue. "You'll want to be careful, lad, or you'll burn yourself."

Joe put his spoon down, but his eyes grew wide at the basket of freshly baked rolls and a large crock of butter she set on the table.

"My name is Bette," she said. "Enjoy your soup, and I'll be back with the second course in a twinkle."

"Thank you, Bette," Joe and Heather said at the same time.

After the woman left, Joe slathered a roll with a thick layer of butter and took a big bite.

"I want to stay here, Heather," he said with his mouth full. "They've got food."

By a peculiar trick of architecture, magically enhanced of course, any conversation in the king's dining room was audible in the adjacent listening closet—and a bewildered Shimmer was hanging on every word.

AFTER HEATHER and Joe finished their meal, Bette showed them to their rooms. Joe's chamber was light, spacious, and comfortable, and had a nice view of the ocean.

"Look, Heather, I have my own privy!" Joe ran his face over his scraggly beard. "Do you suppose I could get my hands on a razor, Bette?"

"Not too much call for razors around here, I'm afraid, but we'll manage. There are fresh clothes in the wardrobe, young gentleman. Have yourself a bath, and I'll send a manservant around in a half hour to give you a haircut and a shave," she replied.

Heather giggled. "You do look a trifle wild, Joe."

"If you need anything else, just ask," Bette said. "The king has directed the staff to extend you every courtesy."

Bette ushered Heather to a room at the end of the hallway. "There are fresh clothes in the wardrobe for you too, Miss."

"Thank you, Bette."

When Heather entered her room, she was startled to see a pretty girl about Joe's age bouncing up and down on the bed.

"I'm so sorry!" Heather exclaimed. "I was told this was my room." Red-faced, Heather started to back out.

"Wait! This *is* your room." The girl bounded to the floor and ran over to grab Heather's hand. "My name is Wren Ormvalder. My father asked me to help make you comfortable."

"You're Manfred's sister?"

"Some days I think Manny wishes otherwise. He's always telling me I talk too much."

The princess *was* a vivacious chatterbox. In the first few minutes of their acquaintance, Heather knew the name of every boy Wren had ever fancied and which subjects she liked in school. She played the piano and violin and loved to act. She was slightly plump, with a gorgeous complexion, dark brown hair, brown eyes, and a dainty rosebud mouth. She whirled around the room as she showed Heather the garden view, the gowns hanging in the wardrobe, and the chest of drawers full of fine linen undergarments. Heather was pleased to discover that her bow, quiver, and hunting knife had been placed on a table.

"You're ever so thin," Wren said, when she paused to catch her breath. "I wish I were slender like you."

"It's not exactly on purpose," Heather admitted. "I haven't been eating on a regular basis. And anyway, you're perfect just the way you are."

"That's a lovely thing to say. Oh, I'm to leave you alone for a little while, but I'll be back. And the flowers in the privy were Dane's idea. I heard he was beastly to you, so I wouldn't be so quick to forgive him. See you soon."

Wren pirouetted out like a tornado and shut the door behind her.

INCREDULITY ANIMATED King Ansgar's face as Shimmer finished speaking.

"What did you say?"

"Heather and Jovander believe they come from the future," Shimmer repeated.

Dane walked off a few paces, but Manny leaned forward. "Time travel?" he said. "They're barking mad, both of them."

"I'm not so sure," Shimmer said. "Their crystals are unlike anything we've ever seen before, and they behave as if we share an intimate acquaintance with them. Didn't you notice?"

Manny gaped in amazement. "I can't believe you're taking this seriously, old boy. What say you, Dane?"

Deep in thought, Dane didn't hear Manny's question. The way the girl had called him by name, and her expression of betrayal at his words had been rather unsettling. Her unhappiness was weighing heavily on him for some inexplicable reason —and despite his assertions to the contrary, the girl's beauty had made an instant and profound impression.

"Dane? What is your opinion?" Manny prompted.

The prince glanced at his cousin, startled. "Oh...I agree with Shimmer. That's not to say I believe in time travel, but Jovander and Heather are sincere."

"I'm particularly interested in this so-called 'downfall of Ormaria'. What in the world is supposed to happen?" Ansgard asked.

"Jovander mentioned a traitor of some kind," Shimmer said. "It's all very intriguing."

Manny threw up his hands. "So what are we supposed to do with them? They don't seem dangerous; I'll grant you that much."

"Let this play out for a few days at least," the king said. "Dane, invite Sir Icarus to dinner. Tell him only that I'd like his opinion on our guest's state of mind."

"And Heather's challenge?" Dane asked. "Sir Bast will not be amenable."

"Ask him to accept as a personal favor to me," the king said. After a pause, he laughed. "This is all rather fun, isn't it?"

"Father, your notions of what passes for fun have always escaped me," Dane replied.

A FLORAL FRAGRANCE drew Heather's attention. As she followed the scent, she discovered an enormous privy adjacent to her bedchamber. A resplendent vase of roses decorated the vanity table. The blooms displayed shades of dark purple, teal, and sapphire blue. Her gasp of delight echoed off the elegant tile on the walls, and she bent forward to breathe in the roses' intoxicating aroma.

To her delight, separate spigots let hot and cold water into the bathtub. At home, her parents used to heat kettles over the fire to fill a wooden barrel with a shallow layer of lukewarm water. As a consequence, bathing was never a terribly warm process and was always brief.

"What fantastic magic!"

After she stepped out of her clothes, she shuddered with disgust at the filthy garments. Even more upsetting was her undernourished reflection in the mirror. Her face was gaunt, and her ribs were showing. That explained why Dane had wanted her to leave. She resembled a stray cat and probably smelled far worse. As proof, the claw-footed tub crept over, nudging her leg to urge her in.

"All right, all right."

The hot, scented water was an uncommon luxury. Heather luxuriated in the bath as long as she dared, washing her hair and scrubbing every inch of her skin. She donned a dressing gown after she emerged from her bath, and then discovered another delightful bit of Ormarian magic. The hairbrush on the dressing table detangled and dried her hair instantly and left it with a marvelous shine. Her dark red locks surrounded her heart-shaped face and formed a wavy waterfall down her back. She left her hair unbound, hoping her tresses would serve to soften any overly angular lines. A creamy pomade soothed her dry lips, and a fragrant lotion restored the moisture in her tanned skin. She thought the lotion must be magic, too, because it made her freckles disappear.

The lightweight, olive green gown and silk slippers she found in the wardrobe fit perfectly—which seemed uncanny until it finally occurred to her that magic was at work. The dress and slippers were lovely, although there was no place to carry her hunting knife.

Wren burst into the room after the briefest of knocks.

"Oh, you're so beautiful! I wish my hair were red. Brown is so boring."

"Surely you jest. Your coloring is gorgeous."

Wren giggled. "You're nice." She grabbed Heather by the hand and pulled her out the door. "We're going to the garden now. We're having tea with my mum."

TOWCHEEZ AND ICKY

*a*s she and Wren passed through the castle gardens, Heather noticed the Ormvalder gardens were remarkably similar to those of King Chance. In the Ormvalder gardens, however, the topiary moved. The lion yawned and scratched himself as Heather passed, and the elephant stood on one foot and balanced there, albeit precariously.

"Does the elephant ever fall over?" asked Heather, wide-eyed.

"No, but it was spooked once by a snake and went on a stampede. That was a big mess, let me tell you," Wren replied. "The rose bushes had to scramble to get out of the way. Several flowers dropped their petals due to anxiety, and the groundskeepers were in tears trying to get them put back on afterwards."

Wren led Heather toward a large square gazebo in the middle of the garden. A stately woman smiled as they approached, fanning herself against the heat. Manny and Joe were on the lawn nearby, attempting to juggle skittle pins, but Dane was absent. Wren gasped at the sight of Joe. She clutched Heather's arm.

"Is *that* your friend? What's his name?"

"I'll introduce you," Heather replied. "Joe!"

He turned just as Manny launched a skittle pin at his head. Fortunately, Manny was able to magically stop the pin mid-air before it made contact. Joe was as handsome as Heather had ever seen him—clean-shaven, with a fresh haircut, wearing a crisp white shirt and a natty pair of trousers. He could easily have been mistaken for a prince. When his gaze settled on Wren, Joe trotted over with a smile on his face. As Heather introduced him to the princess, he picked up the girl's hand and brought it to his lips.

"Charmed to meet you," he said.

"Likewise," Wren said.

Heather could tell Joe and Wren were instantly besotted with one another. In the background, Manny scowled at Joe. Nevertheless, he came over to offer Heather his arm.

"You look very pretty, I must say. Come meet my mother."

The woman's resemblance to Wren was marked. She was plump and pretty, with rosy cheeks and a sense of merriment about her. She beckoned Heather to the chair next to hers.

"Get in out of the hot sun, child, before it does you a mischief. Such lovely hair you have. I could see you coming all the way through the garden."

"It's an honor to meet you, Your Highness. My name is Heather."

"Oh, 'Your Highness' is such a mouthful. Just call me Lady Parker."

Tea was a pleasant affair. Heather wasn't certain she would be hungry after eating such a big lunch, but she was surprised to find she had a healthy appetite. Even Manny stopped glaring at Joe after he had several custard-filled cakes under his belt. Lady Parker was every bit as talkative as her daughter. Heather learned that Queen Mara was traveling. She was due to return the day after tomorrow, and the king was planning a big welcome home celebration.

"Any excuse for a party to my way of thinking," Lady Parker said. "I do hope you and Jovander will attend."

"We're not—"

"Oh, there's my nephew," Lady Parker interrupted. "And he's with Sir Bast, the archery master."

As Dane drew near, Heather's insides melted. His close-fitting black trousers and white shirt accentuated his athletic figure, and the way he moved was not unlike a tiger. She did prefer him clean-shaven, but his well-kept beard had its own manly appeal. The archery master who accompanied him was a tall, barrel-chested man with an arrogant swagger. His hair was also red, but enough of it had turned gray that it gave the impression of pink tufts.

"Hello, Sir Bast. Please have some tea," Lady Parker said.

"No thank you, Mum," he said. "I came to clear up a misunderstanding."

He scowled at Heather. "I refuse to accept a challenge from this slip of a girl. It would be beneath me to do so."

Heather shot to her feet, her head held high. "Then you forfeit, sir?"

Bast's ruddy complexion turned even redder. "I will do no such thing."

Heather gave the archery master her steeliest glare. "The challenge has been issued. If you do not agree to the match, the victory is mine."

"Of all the ridiculous wastes of my time, this tops them all!"

"Now, Bast, the lady is right. We can't have you forfeit, can we? Let's agree to one little match and put it behind us," Dane said. "It's not as if we have people at the gates every other day issuing challenges left and right...and my father would consider it a personal favor."

At that last, a steely edge crept into Dane's tone that left Bast no choice.

"Fine. Have the child meet me at dawn at the practice field and be quick about it. I do not intend to be late for breakfast."

Bast turned on his heel and stalked off. Dane sighed and sat down to pour himself some tea. Manny passed Dane a plate of sandwiches.

"So Bast has his bow in a twist, eh?"

"I knew he would be difficult," Dane muttered. He gave Heather a rueful glance. "When I said a contest with you would be an insult to our most skillful bowman, you mistook my meaning. Sir Bast truly has the most volatile temperament in Ormaria."

Heather could feel the prince's eyes linger on her, and she was glad she'd spent the extra time on her hair and wardrobe.

"He'll be in worse humor after tomorrow," Joe said.

Manny laughed. "I don't know if that's possible."

"The way you stood up to Sir Bast was impressive, Heather, but winning your challenge is unlikely," Dane said.

"Upon what do you base this considered opinion, Your Highness?" she asked.

"Sir Bast is the finest archer in Ormaria."

"Then I shall savor my victory all the more," she said.

"You don't lack for confidence," Dane chuckled.

"I think confidence in a girl is a marvelous quality," Wren said.

Manny laughed. "That's because nobody could accuse you of being shy."

"Confidence is a very attractive quality indeed," Lady Parker said. "Would you agree, Dane?"

"I would, actually," Dane said. "Uncommonly so."

Heather blushed. "I've learned to fight for what I want—when the cause is just."

"Spoken like an Ormvalder," Manny said.

"If you're interested in Ormarian history, Heather, perhaps you'd like to see the mausoleum after tea?" Dane suggested.

"Cousin, you really know how to show a girl a good time," Manny said.

"On the contrary, Manny, the mausoleum is a national treasure," Lady Parker said. "The marble sculptures are simply incredible."

"I would like to see it very much," Heather said to Dane. "Thank you, Your Highness."

After tea, Dane escorted Heather down one of the paths leading away from the castle. She marveled at the magic at work all around her. They passed a stand of rainbow trees, with multi-hued arches spread out from the branches in dazzling displays of color. Sprays of bluebells splashed across the grass, tinkling gently in the breeze. Dane pointed out a dainty unicorn foal as it grazed on buttercups dripping with melted sweet butter.

Movement in an old, gnarled tree caught Heather's eye. Four small fairies were seated at a table in the roots, playing a game of cards. Heather had never seen fairies before, and she was fascinated. The fairies were not as enchanted with her, however. The oldest of the group had a face like a potato and wore a porkpie hat.

"Oi, what're ye lookin' at, Red?" he barked.

"Oh, sorry," she said, taken aback. "I've never seen a fairy before."

Dane stepped into view. "Now, Towcheez, is that any way to talk to a visitor?"

"Begging yer pardon, Yer Highness," he said, with a lift of his hat. "Didn't see ye standing there."

Dane gave him a disapproving glance. "Carry on."

As Heather and Dane continued along the path, the prince was chagrined. "I don't know what ill humor has infected the wee folk lately. Just the other day one of the stable boys ran afoul of a fairy. Poor lad had his ears turned into stalks of cauliflower for his trouble."

Heather couldn't stop laughing. Her merriment was infectious, and eventually Dane began to chuckle. "It's not really funny. It's devilishly tricky to reverse fairy magic."

"I'm lucky, then," she gasped. "Towcheez could have turned my nose into a turnip."

Finally, she managed to control her mirth.

"I haven't laughed like that in months, Dane—I mean, Your Highness."

"Mmm. That's a shame. You're quite lovely when you laugh."

Their eyes met, all too briefly, and Heather's breath caught in her throat. A short while later, a large marble structure loomed into view. The mausoleum was marked with the family name of Ormvalder. Heather stepped down into the beautiful place with hushed sense of awe. The burial niches, stacked four high, were unmarked at the entrance, but as she wandered toward the back, dates and names began to appear.

"The freestanding burial chambers up front are empty. They're reserved for future Ormarian monarchs," Dane said. "When a king or queen dies, they are laid to rest in the center of the mausoleum. The marble slab on the top of the sarcophagus is replaced by a life-sized sculpture."

"Which one is yours?" she teased.

Dane paused next to an unmarked sarcophagus. "This one, I suppose. It feels strange looking at my future."

You have no idea.

In the back of the mausoleum, Dane showed her the burial chamber for the first Ormarian monarch—King Liam. Tears stung her eyes, and her throat closed up. Her fingers traced his name, carved in the stone. *Hello, Liam. You did well.*

Picturing the little baker's boy as a king was difficult, but the proof was right in front of her eyes. Heather had an equally difficult time imagining hundreds of years had passed since she'd given Liam that first dragon crystal. According to the headstone, he had lived a long and fruitful life. He and his wife, Queen Gloria, had had seven children together. He'd built the Ormvalder castle and had laid the foundation for a long and enduring kingdom. Nevertheless, Heather was grieved the boy she knew was dead. She was sad for Gumm, too. He'd been a good troll and had evidently protected Liam well.

As Dane came to stand next to her, he noticed her distress. "Are you all right?"

Heather nodded. She closed her eyes for a moment and imagined a huge quantity of calla lilies. When she looked again, the sarcophagus was covered with the elegant blooms. Heather smiled; the tribute was fitting.

"Very nice," Dane said. "Had I'd known you liked calla lilies, I would have put some in your room."

"Oh, no, I love the roses. The beautiful colors remind me of peacock feathers. I used to carry the tip of a peacock feather with me for luck during competitions back at home."

Running footsteps echoed throughout the mausoleum. Wren skidded into view, clad in a pretty purple gown.

"There you are, Heather! It's time to get dressed for dinner."

"Won't this do?" Heather asked, glancing down.

"Of *course* not! Dane, you'd best hurry too. Icky's coming to dine."

As Wren and Heather hastened toward the castle, Dane followed a few paces behind.

"Who is Icky?" Heather asked.

Wren bent her head close to Heather's so Dane wouldn't overhear. "The royal physician, Sir Icarus. He's terribly handsome. Every girl in the castle is madly in love with him. He's unmarried, so you're going to want to look especially pretty tonight."

"I shall do my best."

"Icky shaves, too. Until I met Joe, I'd never seen another man without whiskers before. I do so love a man who shaves."

"I shave sometimes!" Dane called out.

"Oh, you're not a *man*, you're my cousin," Wren exclaimed, over her shoulder. "And quit listening to private conversations." She linked her arm with Heather's. "Tell me, do all the men shave their whiskers in your country, Heather?"

"Not all, but it's quite common."

"I think it's ever so dashing," Wren sighed.

"I do too."

WHEN THE BELL rang for dinner, Joe, Wren, and Heather made their way downstairs. Joe had added a jacket to his white shirt, and he was resplendent. At Wren's urging, Heather had dressed in a beige silk gown that complimented her coloring. Its whale-bone bodice also helped recreate the curves she'd lost over the last few weeks. She found a few tortoiseshell combs to hold her hair back from her face and made liberal use of the cosmetics on her vanity.

They joined the king, his immediate family, and Sir Icarus in the parlor. A shock went through Heather at the sight of Dane. Clean-shaven once more, his handsome face took her breath away. The prince gave her a rueful glance and rubbed his chin. As Heather nodded in return, her lips curved in a smile.

"Ah, there you are, Jovander and Heather," the king exclaimed. "Allow me to introduce Sir Icarus."

Wren had not exaggerated the man's classically handsome good looks. Perhaps a few years older than Dane, Icarus had dark wavy hair that he wore short and brushed back from his face. His eyes were an unusual light blue, and his full lips lent his face a sensual air. He gave Joe a little bow in greeting but took Heather's proffered hand and brought it to his lips.

"The rumors of your beauty don't do you justice."

"You're too kind, sir," Heather said.

Dane grinned as he clapped Icarus on the back. "Come, Icky, let's have a drink before dinner."

The royal physician allowed himself to be steered away, but his eyes lingered on Heather. Wren stuck an elbow in her ribs. "Lucky you," she whispered. "You've made a conquest—although I'm not certain if it's Icky or Dane."

When one of the servants rang the bell to signify dinnertime, King Ansgar offered his arm to Heather. "Will you sit next to me, my dear? I want to hear about Boravagg."

Dinner was festive. To begin, a retinue of fairies flew around the table with a basket of moist, hot towels. Heather held her towel, baffled as to its purpose, until she observed Joe clean his hands and return the towel to the basket. When one of the fairies accidentally dropped a hot towel in Manny's lap, the usually imperturbable prince erupted into some colorful language. Although the fairy apologized profusely, Heather could have sworn the creature smirked as he turned away.

Throughout the sumptuous meal, King Ansgar and Shimmer pressed her for details on Boravagg. Heather limited her narrative to describing the flora, fauna, and occasional troll. Joe interjected his enthusiasm into the conversation, unfortunately, and boasted how Heather had survived on her own for several days and had been set upon by a tiger and wild dragons. Embarrassed, she brushed off Joe's praise of her expertise.

"Could you not defend yourself with magic?" Icarus asked.

"I did not have a dragon crystal at that time," Heather replied. "And even now, I'm untrained in its use."

A line of confusion creased the physician's brow. "How is it possible for a wizarding member of the royal class to be untrained in the use of magic?"

"I wasn't born a member of the royal class," Heather replied. "Nor was I aware I could work magic until recently."

SUZANNE G. ROGERS

"That's fascinating. I'm a member of the royal class, but I cannot work magic at all," Icarus said. "I am somewhat unique in that way."

"It's a mystery why some people are able to use magic while others are not," Shimmer said. "The answer to that question has eluded me."

"You've done quite well without magic, Icky," Dane said. "I often think magic can be a crutch."

"How so?" Icarus asked.

"Wizards who rely too heavily on magic sometimes fail to fully develop all their talents," Dane said.

"You're a wizard, Your Highness, and yet you have many highly developed skills quite unrelated to magic," Heather said.

Joe chuckled. "Yes, there aren't too many men who can pull off a jig."

"I didn't know you could dance a jig, Dane," Icarus exclaimed.

Dane frowned. "Manfred, you've been telling tales about me."

Manny snickered. "I'm innocent, Cousin. I've not revealed your secrets. I will say, however, it was always terribly annoying when our dancing master rubbed my nose in your superlative abilities."

"Oh, I must have mentioned it, Dane," Shimmer said. "It's awfully difficult for me not to boast."

Joe and Heather exchanged a puzzled glance. Shimmer had just covered for Joe's blunder, but why?

"I'm looking forward to seeing what *you* can do tomorrow, Heather," Shimmer said, deftly changing the subject.

"As am I," the king added.

"I will be there to officiate," Dane said.

"Although I cannot promise to be entirely awake, I plan to attend," Lady Parker said.

Icarus raised his goblet as if in a toast to Heather. "I wouldn't miss it for the world."

"I don't wish to impose upon any of you," Heather said, taken aback. "Surely Sir Bast will relate the results of our contest faithfully."

Manny laughed. "Perhaps all the more faithfully under scrutiny, I expect."

SAFE AND UNSETTLED

eams of fairies reappeared toward the end of the meal to fly in dessert. Murmurs of delight greeted the cakes, which resembled beautifully decorated eggs. Towcheez donned a uniform to bring the king's dessert out personally.

"Yer Majesty," Towcheez said, with an exaggerated bow.

When Heather cut into her cake, delectable yellow custard ran out onto the plate. *If I were to dine this way on a regular basis, I would not need whalebones to fill out my gowns!* Sir Icarus eschewed dessert, instead preferring to enjoy another glass of wine.

"Say, Heather, would you care to accompany me to the onion run?" he asked.

"Oh, is it a full moon tonight?" Wren exclaimed. "I'd forgotten."

Heather laughed. "An *onion* run?"

"What in the world is an onion run?" Joe asked, equally baffled.

"The wee folk plant a whole bed of onions and let them ripen. They then hold an onion run on the first full moon," Icarus said.

"It's rather a lark," Manny said.

"I enjoy a good onion run," Dane said. "I'll tag along."

Icarus peered at Dane. "You hate onion runs."

"You must have caught me in a good mood," Dane replied.

Although the king, Shimmer, and Lady Parker begged off, everyone else traipsed down to the vegetable garden. The moon helped illuminate the path in the dark, in addition to the starflowers planted along the walkway. The twinkling starlight lent a festive, somewhat romantic atmosphere, not lost on the princess. Wren picked several starflowers and wove them into her hair. Joe even allowed her to tuck one of the sparkling blooms behind his ear.

"Tell me, Heather…how did you feel growing up without magic?" Icarus asked.

"I thought nothing of it, really. In Destiny, you see, nobody uses magic. The royals claim superiority as their birthright, without any merit whatsoever," Heather replied.

"No magic? I envy you. My brothers and sisters went to the Ormarian Royal Academy for Magic, whereas I was obliged to attend regular school. Many of my schoolmates felt the sting of a second-class status," Icarus replied.

"Oh, don't go on like that, Icky," Dane interjected. "You'll have Heather feeling sorry for you. Here you are, the royal physician. You're at the peak of your profession."

"I believe there is nothing you can't do, if you put your mind to it," Icarus said. "It just depends on the price to be paid."

"I admire your attitude, Sir Icarus," Heather said.

He gave her a dazzling smile. "All my friends call me Icky."

A short while later, the group arrived at a well-tended vegetable garden. Row upon row of rich abundance spread out before them. Fairy children, no bigger than Heather's hand, flew up and down the lanes playing tag. Adult fairies were gathered next to the onion bed, making wagers with one another. Several of the wee folk knelt in the soil, whispering last minute advice to their onion runners. A few of the fairies cast unfriendly glances at the humans, but most behaved as if they were not there at all.

Suddenly Icarus stopped cold, staring with horror at a bed of cabbages nearby. When she followed his gaze, Heather spotted a medium-sized snake.

"It's just a garter snake. Quite colorful, but perfectly harmless."

"Somebody kill it," he said through gritted teeth.

Dane conjured a sword, but Heather stepped in between the blade and the serpent. "That's not necessary, Your Highness. I'll be happy to remove the snake."

"I can't let you put yourself in danger," Dane said.

"Don't worry, Heather knows all about snakes," Joe said. "She saved me from one once."

Hastening over to the cabbages, she knelt in the dirt and grasped the foot-long snake behind its head. Walking several beds over, she deposited the snake gently in between rows of snap peas. After the snake slithered off unharmed, Heather returned to Icarus's side. He'd pulled a handkerchief from his pocket and was mopping his brow.

"Thank you," he murmured. "I had a rather bad experience with a snake when I was young, and I'm not fond of the creatures."

Towcheez flew onto Icarus's shoulder, startling him.

"What in blazes? Must you sneak up on a man like that!" Icarus exclaimed.

"Sorry, Sir Icky. Care to get in on the action?"

With a deep, calming breath, Icarus tucked his handkerchief from view. "I just might be persuaded to participate this evening."

Icarus produced a gold coin, which Towcheez promptly made disappear into the sack on his back.

"Pick a champion, Heather," Icarus said.

Heather knelt next to the bed of onions and pointed to a fat onion with a nice, full top. "What are the odds on this fellow?"

"Oh, that's Dim Bulb. He's even money," the fairy replied.

"That's a safe bet," Icarus said. "You can't lose."

Dane leaned over to brush the top of a scallion. "Go with this one, Heather. He's far leaner and can likely outrun them all."

"Three-to-one on Toothpick," Towcheez said.

"Toothpick it is, then," Heather said, exchanging a mischievous glance with Dane. "I enjoy long odds."

Neither Joe nor Wren had any money, so Manny had to cough up some gold for his sister. Wriggling with excitement, Wren bet on a leek named Puddle. Towcheez bit Manny's gold coin before tossing it into his sack.

"Good choice, Princess," Towcheez said to Wren. "Two-to-one odds on ole Puddle."

After the betting had concluded, the fairies readied their runners for the race. Heather marveled when each onion shrugged its roots free from the soil. An oniony fragrance scented the nighttime air as the runners took their mark. Towcheez flew overhead with a fairy candle in his hand. He held it high.

"Onions, yer running down to the water pump and back," he bellowed. "Fair warning...losers will be eaten. Ready, steady... yer off!"

The fairy candle punctuated his sentence with an explosion of sparks. Using their roots as legs, the onions peeled out. The runners with hairy roots moved along like millipedes, while the ones with longer roots stretched them forward like stilt-walkers. The fairies cheered with enthusiasm. Wren and Jovander jumped up and down as they rooted for their onion.

"Run, Puddle, run," Wren screamed.

At the outset, the onions were in a bunch. Heather couldn't begin to tell how Toothpick was faring. Halfway to the water pump, however, the race began to get choppier. Dim Bulb's roots gave out under his weight. He fell over and proceeded to roll toward the water pump like a cannon ball. He mowed several competitors down as he went, crushing their roots so badly they didn't get up again.

"That's cheating," Joe exclaimed.

"That's an onion run," Manny retorted.

As he neared the pump, Puddle was outdistancing his rivals. Toothpick ran a close second, and Dim Bulb rolled into third. After the runners rounded the pump, they put on the speed. The return journey quickly became brutal, as downed vegetables lay crushed and limp on the path. Dim Bulb shot forward and knocked Puddle over. Puddle retaliated by slapping at Dim Bulb with his dark green leaves. Toothpick took over the lead. Dim Bulb rolled free of Puddle and angled toward Toothpick. The last few feet, however, Dim Bulb became confused and began to roll in a circle. Heather screamed with laughter as Toothpick stumbled over the finish line and waved his leaves in victory. Puddle limped into second place, and Dim Bulb rolled into a pumpkin patch.

The race at an end, fairy children descended on the runners and began to eat them. In her excitement, Heather grabbed Dane's arm. "We won!" she exclaimed. When she realized what she'd done, she released her grip. "Oh...excuse me, Your Highness."

"No, that's all right," Dane replied. "Really. I'm glad you won."

Towcheez flew past. "Good night, then," he sang out.

The fairy stopped mid-air when Icarus snagged the bag on his back. "Now, Towcheez, one would think you didn't intend to honor your obligations."

Towcheez glowered, but he handed over three gold coins. "Been nice doin' business with ye," he muttered, with no trace of sincerity whatsoever.

Icarus dropped the coins into Heather's palm, but she

returned one. "That's for you, Icky, to repay you for my stake." The second coin she pressed into Dane's hand. "And that's for helping me pick the winner."

"Uncommonly generous of you," Icarus said.

"I'm not sure I deserve this, but I thank you all the same," Dane said, slipping the gold into his waistcoat pocket.

The festivities now concluded, the wee folk herded their children off to bed. Within moments, the vegetable garden was deserted. Wren yawned repeatedly on her way back to the castle. Dane hesitated at the door.

"Er...there's something I must attend to. Good night."

The prince loped into the darkness without another word.

"Hmm. Perhaps Dane needs to harvest a magical root or mystical berry by moonlight," Icarus said with a shrug.

The physician escorted Heather to the bottom of the main staircase. "Best of luck tomorrow. Sir Bast deserves his comeuppance."

"Thank you, Icky," she replied. "I shall do my very best."

Icarus took his leave, and Heather retired to her room. Although her eyelids were heavy, she examined her bow to make sure it remained sound. The arrows in her quiver were straight and sharp as only her father could make them. Truth be told, she could hardly wait until morning. Admittedly, Bast's arrogant and dismissive manner gave her pause, but she'd handled worse.

As she waited for sleep to claim her, Heather's thoughts settled on Dane. The prince was maddeningly difficult to read. The motivation for his attentiveness that evening was unclear. The only way to truly earn his respect would be to do the impossible. She must win her challenge tomorrow.

Even before dawn, Heather was up and dressed. She'd donned her hunting clothes, which fortunately had been magically cleaned and repaired while she was at dinner the previous evening. As was her habit, she concealed her hunting knife in her boot, and plaited her hair over one shoulder. When she was leaving, she noticed a handful of peacock feathers had been slipped under her door. Pleased Joe had remembered, Heather pinned one of the tips onto the lapel of her tunic. The colorful feather stuck out at a jaunty angle.

"I'm as ready as I'll ever be," she said to her reflection in the mirror.

Heather reached for her bow and quiver, and headed downstairs. A bleary servant pointed her toward the practice field. When she arrived, early morning light was glimmering on the horizon. Bast had busied himself placing a pair of targets at two hundred paces. A high wooden fence with horizontal slats surrounded the field. Benches for spectators bracketed one side, elevated to avoid errant arrows. As the sun rose, the Ormvalders began to trickle into the stands. Even some of the castle servants had come to watch the match. Joe climbed the fence and dropped into the field next to Heather.

"Good morning!"

Heather laughed. "There's an opening in the fence, right over there," she said, cocking her thumb over her shoulder.

"Oh, I know, but it's not as much fun coming in the normal way. How are you doing?"

"As long as nobody tries to poison me or lock me in the dungeon, I'll be fine. By the way, thank you for the peacock feather. That was very thoughtful."

"I wish I could take credit for the feather, but I can't," Joe said. "Wren kept me up half the night, talking. She's a terrific girl."

"Then it had to be Dane." Heather searched the small crowd

of people, but the prince wasn't there. "The prince can certainly be charming when it suits his purpose. Curse his blue eyes."

"I beg your pardon?" Dane asked.

Heather whirled around to discover Joe was gone, and Dane had taken his place. The prince could not have failed to hear her words, and she was certain the color of her face was indistinguishable from her hair at present.

"Oh, hello, Your Highness. Um, thank you for the peacock feathers."

"I may be officiating the match, but I'm allowed to wish you good luck. Those few plumes were all I could find in the dark and on such short notice."

"Truly, it was very kind."

Bast approached, a thundercloud over his head.

"Are we going to stand here yammering, or are we going to get on with this nonsense?" he snapped. "Begging your pardon, Your Highness."

Heather refused to let the archery master intimidate her. "Good morning, Sir Bast. It's amazingly unpleasant to see you again."

Swollen with indignation, Bast resembled a wet hen. "How dare you!"

Dane stifled a smile. "Crystals, please."

"Is that really necessary?" Bast exclaimed.

"In a contest of skill, the use of magic is not permitted, Sir Bast," Dane replied. "Protocol has not changed."

As Heather handed over her dragon crystal, she noticed Joe and Wren waving at her from the stands. Dane collected Bast's crystal next.

"Since you issued the challenge, Heather, Sir Bast may pick his target," Dane said.

The archery master selected the target furthest away from the spectators. Heather settled herself at the other.

"Whenever you are ready, Sir Bast," Dane said.

Bast's aim was true. His arrow landed on the bull's eye, but Heather had expected no less from an archery master. With a handful of soil, she reassured herself the wind was deadly calm.

"Heather?" Dane prompted.

"Yes, Your Highness."

Heather sighted the target. *I am the arrow, and I will find my mark.* Her release was good, and she was satisfied the arrow would hit the center exactly—but in the last few inches it skittered sideways and missed the target entirely. Stunned, Heather gasped, and a groan of disappointment went up from the stands. Joe shot to his feet.

"No," he yelled.

"Oh, too bad. Hard luck. Perhaps you should think twice about challenging a master," Bast sneered.

"I'm sorry Heather," Dane said. "You had excellent form. Maybe you're not on your game this morning."

While Bast slung his bow across his back, Heather managed to gather her wits. The last time her arrow had gone astray, it had been due to a spell of protection.

"Your Highness, my target has been tampered with," she said.

"Don't embarrass yourself any further with unfounded accusations. It's pathetic," Bast said with a withering glance.

"My target was tampered with," Heather repeated, loud enough for everyone to hear. "I'm quite certain."

To prove it, she stepped over to Bast's target and loosed an arrow that split his down the shaft. She quickly loosed two more, each arrow splitting the other. Joe jumped from the stands and ran across the field toward Heather's target.

"Archers, hold fast," Dane ordered.

Heather leaned her bow against the fence and watched while Joe passed his hand over the canvas.

"This target has a spell of protection on the front," he yelled. "I can't even touch it with my fingers."

Bast had grown paler than usual. "If it does, the spell can

have nothing to do with me. I've been back here the whole time. The girl probably cast the spell herself."

"You placed the targets, Sir Bast, and selected yours *after* I gave up my crystal. My accusations are neither unfounded nor pathetic."

Joe lifted Heather's target off its stand and brought it toward Dane for his examination. To Heather's shock, Bast aimed an arrow at Joe. Although she reached for her hunting knife and hurled it at the archery master, her actions came too late. The arrow whistled in the air and knocked Joe back. With her heart in her throat, Heather closed the distance between them. As he lay in the grass with the arrow protruding from his chest, Joe stared up at her in shock. "Ow." He gave her a little half smile before he slipped into unconsciousness.

QUEEN MARA

*B*oth Icarus and Dane tended to Joe's injury at the hospital. Heather paced in the hallway, utterly dazed. Wren had wanted to wait with Heather, but Manny had correctly guessed that she was in no mood for company. He'd taken his sister back to the castle, much to her displeasure. When Dane finally emerged from the surgery room, Heather stared at him with large, frightened eyes.

"I believe Jovander will survive, Heather. He lost an awful lot of blood, and he must rest while we make sure no infection sets in. I put an anti-sepsis spell on the wound, but you can't be too careful with these things."

Heather sank into a chair, her head swimming. Dane sat next to her and took her hand. "Are you unwell?"

"Just a little dizzy."

"I'm not surprised. You haven't eaten anything today."

Her hand tightened in his. "Thank you for helping him. I don't know what I would do if he died."

"You can see him for a few minutes while Icky attends Sir Bast. Your weapon pierced his left hand."

Dane led Heather into Joe's room. The lad was quite pale,

with a waxy appearance to his skin. Broad bandages swathed his bare chest and shoulder. Heather wiped tears away as she gazed down at him.

"He looks so young and vulnerable."

"I've put Jovander into a deep, healing sleep," Dane said. "The arrow was inches from causing a fatal injury."

"What will happen to Sir Bast?"

"His hand won't ever be the same. As soon as he's well enough to attend, Sir Bast will have a hearing. Since my father witnessed the whole, spiteful episode, the man is unlikely to be given leniency. He'll be stripped of his title and dragon crystal and expelled from the castle grounds."

Heather swayed, and Dane put a steadying arm around her waist.

"I'll take you back to the castle."

"Yes, please. Joe's accident has left me with no alternative. I must speak with you, Shimmer, Manfred, and the king at once, in utmost privacy."

HEATHER GATHERED with the Ormvalders in the king's sitting room.

"First off, I owe you an apology, Heather," Dane said. "Your ability with a bow and arrow is quite astounding."

"You can throw a knife well too," Manny added. "Remind me to keep things cordial between us, particularly in the dining room."

Sorrow etched King Ansgar's features. "I cannot say how grieved I am about Jovander. Sir Bast was my archery master, and I feel responsible for his behavior. I hope to make amends, Heather."

"Dane and Sir Icarus will work together to ensure that Jovander receives the best care," Shimmer said.

"That reminds me," Dane said, pulling Heather's dragon crystal from his pocket. "Your weapons were returned to your room, but I wanted to give this back to you personally." He pressed the crystal pendant into her waiting hand.

"Thank you." She slipped the pendant over her head. The cool crystal nestled against her skin like a caress. Several seconds passed while Heather struggled to frame her words carefully. "There is going to be an attempt on your life, Your Majesty."

Her shocking statement did not have the effect she'd intended. In fact, the Ormvalders were remarkably calm.

"Does this have something to do with the 'downfall of Ormaria' you mentioned before?" Dane asked.

Heather gasped. "How do you know about that?"

"It's my fault," Shimmer said. "I'm afraid I listened to your conversation with Jovander yesterday."

"And I'm afraid I'm having a little trouble believing you're from the future," Manny said. "No offense."

"You knew why we were here, and yet you let me carry on?" Heather cried. "Joe didn't need to get injured?"

"My dear, no one regrets that more than I," the king said.

"Please tell us your story," Shimmer said. "I assure you, Heather, you have our utmost attention."

Although Heather was trembling with emotion, she related the events from the Tournament of Chance onward. As she spoke, the mood in the room turned from disbelief to skepticism, and then to grudging acceptance—particularly when she knew details about how and where the Dragonstone had been discovered. At that part, Shimmer and Ansgar exchanged a startled glance.

"Joe and I are here to prevent the fall of Ormaria," Heather concluded. "If we can do so, it will prevent untold bloodshed and misery in the future."

"I'm particularly intrigued by the idea of a magical wave," Shimmer said.

"Why does it affect only you and Jovander?" Dane asked.

"Because their crystals are different from ours?" Manny suggested.

"I thought that was it too, at first. But now I realize there is another force at work. When most of the Ormarian magic was stopped up in the Dragonstone, events in the world went awry. I've come to believe the magic is trying to sort things out," Heather said.

"You make it sound like the magic is alive," Dane said.

"Perhaps it is," Heather said. "When I was in the Dragonstone cave on Boravagg, it felt that way."

The Dragonstone in the corner pulsed with light, as if to confirm her words.

"So what are we supposed to do now?" Manny scoffed.

"Look for traitors under every settee, I suppose," Dane said.

"Maybe you should conceal the Dragonstone, Shimmer," the king said with a laugh. "Just in case I get a strange notion."

Although Heather had marshaled the anger smoldering just beneath the surface, she could do so no longer.

"I cannot tell you how these events will unfold, and it's immaterial if you believe me. All I know is Joe is hurt, and it was for naught."

She turned on her heel and hastened from the room.

"Heather, please wait," Dane said, to no avail.

HEARTSICK, Heather climbed the steps leading to the top of a castle turret. When she was on the flat, open surface, she transformed into a dragon and soared into the sky. She headed for the one place where she could truly be alone for a while—the dragon cave under the castle. Low tide had rendered the anchor from the *Bonny Heather* fully visible. Heather landed on a rock and morphed into her human form, making sure not to disturb the wild dragons sleeping in the sun. As she headed deeper into the cave, memories surfaced like dolphins. She passed by the indentation where Gumm had originally set his clutch of dragon eggs and paused next to the large rock she and Joe had enchanted to glow hot centuries ago. When she touched it, she was surprised to find lingering warmth.

"Magic endures," she murmured. "Not so love, it seems."

You've healed my soul, Dane had told her—in a timeline that no longer existed. Tears slid down Heather's face. Her arrow had shattered the Dragonstone, but in doing so had also torn her heart asunder.

"I've done more than my duty," she said out loud—as if the magic were listening. "I've warned the Ormvalders, and that will have to be enough. I haven't anything left to give."

An ancient dragon stirred nearby, startling Heather. She'd mistaken him for a pile of rocks. A shock of recognition ran through her when she recognized the distinctive patch of silver on his forelock.

"Pan? Is it really you?"

The dragon snorted with laughter. "I've been waiting for you, Heather. Liam Ormvalder gave me the gift of prophecy. Listen well. There is treachery, deceit, and great loss ahead of you, but wherever you go, your heart will follow."

"My heart will follow?" Heather echoed. "What does that mean?"

But in the blink of an eye, Pan was gone, and the pile of rocks was just a pile of rocks. Bewildered, Heather was left to wonder if she'd imagined the whole thing.

~

HEATHER SNEAKED into the castle through the kitchen, only to find the staff in an uproar. Chefs were rushing about barking orders to harried servants.

"What has happened?" Heather asked one of the serving girls.

"Queen Mara's done returned a day ahead of time."

Heather took a back staircase to the second floor, where Bette was in a dither of her own. The woman's arms were full of sheets and pillowcases and strands of her hair had come loose from her usually tidy bun.

"You'd best be getting ready for tea, miss."

At the mention of food, Heather's stomach gurgled. She folded her arms over her midsection to stifle the noise.

"I'm afraid I won't be here for tea, Bette. I'm leaving right away."

"You can't leave before meeting the queen!"

"I must," Heather said, averting her eyes. "I need to be closer to the hospital while Joe recuperates. Thank you for all your kindness. I won't forget it. Oh, and please give my warmest regards to Wren and Lady Parker."

Heather retrieved her bow, quiver, and knife from her room. With a rising lump in her throat, she slipped through the kitchen the same way she'd come in. A baking sheet full of meat pasties had just been taken from the oven and left on the kitchen counter to cool. When the aroma reached Heather's nostrils, she stopped to stare.

"Well, go on then," said the chef with a wink. "Anyone who can put Sir Bast down is a friend of mine."

The man waved away her thanks and sent her along with a pasty in her hand and one warming her pocket. As she munched the first food she'd had that day, Heather walked down the road toward the castle gates. Although her departure was under unhappy circumstances, she couldn't help but marvel at the wonders that surrounded her. The castle grounds had been beautiful under King Chance, but their current glory put the memory to shame. At the same spot where she'd waved at Joe, she paused. A smile tugged her lips when she remembered the dead snake draped around his shoulders. She lifted her hand to wave goodbye to a ghost that would never exist.

ALTHOUGH WREN HAD NOT YET ARRIVED, Queen Mara and the Ormvalders were assembled in the parlor. Lady Parker and the queen were dumbfounded when Shimmer, Manny, and Ansgar related recent events regarding Heather and Jovander. As the narrative went on, Dane slumped deeper and deeper into a wingchair—his silence speaking volumes. Wren appeared, an expression of consternation on her face.

"I went to Heather's room just now, but she wasn't there. Bette told me she'd left with her things."

Dane groaned and dropped his head into his hands.

"The way you men treated her, I don't blame Heather for leaving," Queen Mara exclaimed.

The king sputtered in response. "But Mara—"

"What the four of you understand about women wouldn't fill a thimble," Lady Parker interrupted.

"Oh come now, Mother," Manny said. "Heather is delusional."

"Icky believed her mind to be sound," Shimmer said.

"He fancied her, couldn't you see that?" Manny retorted.

"What is everybody talking about?" Wren asked, confused.

"The girl is not delusional," Queen Mara said. "Whilst on my travels, I heard a rumor of Great Faturian soldiers massing near our northern border."

Shimmer, King Ansgar, and Manny gasped in surprise.

"I dismissed the rumor out of hand at first, but then decided to come home early to report it," Queen Mara continued. "If there is truly a plot against Ormaria, Heather's warning fits ominously well."

Dane lurched to his feet. "She can't have gone far. Not with Jovander still in the hospital. I'll go find her and bring her back."

"See that you do," his mother said. "I believe we owe her a debt of gratitude."

"Everyone must remain vigilant," King Ansgar said. "If we have a traitor in our midst, they must soon reveal themselves."

As Dane strode from the parlor, Wren stamped her foot in annoyance. "Isn't anyone going to tell me what's happening?"

At that moment, a servant pushed a teacart into the room. "Why, it's tea time, Your Highness."

WHEN HEATHER ARRIVED at Joe's hospital room, she was alarmed to see Sir Icarus at his bedside. She rushed inside just as the physician draped a cold compress across Joe's forehead.

"Is he all right?"

"He's been talking gibberish, poor boy. I'm afraid Joe's taken a turn for the worse."

Joe glanced up at Heather and giggled. "You were over there, and now you're over here. How'd you manage that?"

Icarus sighed. "See what I mean?"

"Is there anything you can do?"

"I've done all I can. Perhaps I should consult with Dane."

"Yes," Heather gasped. "Please hurry."

Her attention was so focused on Joe, that she barely noticed when Icarus left. Sweat poured from his face, and his skin had a waxy gray cast.

"I don't feel so good, Heather."

His words were slurred. Panic made it difficult for her to breathe. She leaned her bow and quiver in the corner and came to sit on the edge of Joe's bed.

"I'm sorry, Joe. Just hang on. Dane's coming."

Heather took his hand and began to pray. Only a few minutes later, Dane entered the room with Towcheez on his shoulder.

"Dane, Joe's in trouble," she cried. "Please help him."

"I'll do my best," Dane replied.

While the prince examined Joe's pupils, measured his temperature, and checked his pulse, Towcheez fixed his malevolent, unwavering gaze on Heather. She did her best to ignore the fairy.

"How did you get here so quickly Da—Your Highness?" she asked.

"Oh, Icky sent Towcheez with a message. I was already halfway to the hospital." He shook his head and frowned. "I'm afraid the only thing that will save Joe now is liquid magic."

"But Boravagg is *days* away." Heather cried. "Even if I left this instant, I wouldn't be able to return with the liquid magic for a week. Can Joe wait that long?"

"I should be able to put him into stasis," Dane said. "The question is, are you absolutely certain you know where to find the liquid magic?"

"Yes."

"Then I'll help you."

"Thank you." Heather bit her lip. "I'm sorry I called you a horse's arse before."

Dane's brows shot up. "Did you? I'd forgotten. Well, I can be a horse's arse every now and again."

As the prince took a stoppered bottle from a locked cabinet and brought it over to the basin, Towcheez cackled with laughter. Annoyed, Heather peered at the fairy.

"Why are you here?"

"Just come to pay me respects, Red. Ye got a problem with wee folk?"

Heather stepped away from Towcheez. "I'd prefer that you leave."

"Towcheez, wait in the hall," Dane said.

"Whatever ye say, Ick—er, Yer Highness."

The fairy lifted his porkpie hat and flew out the door. Dane crossed the room until he stood close enough to caress Heather's cheek. She gazed into his blue eyes, and her panic eased.

"You really are beautiful," he said.

Her heart began to pound in her chest as Dane slid his left arm around her waist and pulled her into an embrace. "Do you trust me?" he murmured.

"Yes, of course."

His right arm came up then, holding a gauze compress soaked with a sweet-smelling fluid. He pressed it to her nose and mouth. Heather tried to push him away, but his arms were like steel. A horrible buzzing began in her brain, and the last thing she remembered was Dane whispering in her ear, "You shouldn't trust anyone."

THE DRAGONSLAYER

"Good one, Icky," Towcheez chuckled.

The fairy snapped his fingers, and Dane transformed back into Icarus. Bast appeared in the doorway, dressed in a medical wagon driver uniform. One of his hands was heavily swathed in gauze bandages. The physician scooped Heather up in his arms, his eyes lingering on Heather's face. "I wish it hadn't come to this."

He transferred her to Bast, who gave Icarus a scowl.

"You're not going wobbly, are you, Icky?"

"No, of course not."

Icarus removed the crystal from around Heather's neck and offered it to Bast. The master archer shook his head. "I don't want anything of *hers*."

"The Ormvalders have confiscated your crystal. You need one to work magic, or you're no good to me," Icarus said.

Bast jerked his head toward Joe. "I'll take his, then."

"Have it your way."

Icarus tossed Heather's dragon crystal at the foot of the bed and removed Joe's from around his neck. Towcheez snatched the crystal from Icky's hand and dangled it in front of Bast.

"Here ye go, Bast. This'll make ye a big man again, eh?"

The man shot the fairy a foul glance. "That's *Sir* Bast, to you."

Another fairy appeared in the doorway just then. "Royal company's on its way from the castle. Better make tracks."

"The wagon is waiting outside. Let's go," Bast said.

DANE HASTENED into the hospital and went straight to Joe's room. To his disappointment, the visitor's chair was empty. Dane noted the sweat pouring down Joe's face. Alarmed, the prince checked Joe's pupils, pulse, and temperature.

"Jovander? Look at me."

Joe forced his eyes open. "Oh, it's you again. Where's your fairy?"

"What?"

The lad started to drift off, but Dane patted his cheek. "Stay with me, Joe."

"I'm like a holiday bird roasting on a spit." Joe giggled. "You keep checking me, over and over again. Am I cooked yet?"

"I haven't been here since this morning. Show me your tongue, Jovander."

At the sight of Joe's mottled tongue, Dane gasped. "You've been given Delirium root! How in blazes did that happen?"

Dane hastened to the medical cabinet, measured a powdered substance into a cup, and diluted it with water from a pitcher. Thereafter, he helped Joe to drink.

"You're going to have a troll-sized headache when your delirium wears off," Dane said.

One of the hospital nurses entered the room. "Is everything all right, Your Highness?"

"No. I must speak with Sir Icarus. This boy was given Delirium root."

The nurse gasped. "That's impossible. We don't even keep Delirium root in the hospital."

"Jovander's tongue says otherwise."

Joe stuck his tongue out at the nurse and giggled.

"Oh my," the nurse said. "Well, Sir Icarus left in one of the hospital wagons a while ago. He said he was transporting a patient home."

"Who?"

"He didn't say."

"Which patients have been discharged today?"

"Er...none that I know of, now you mention it."

"Please do a bed check," Dane said.

After the nurse left, the prince noticed a dragon crystal nearly hidden in the folds of Joe's bedspread. He picked it up to examine it more closely.

"My head hurts," Joe said. Then he jolted fully awake. "Heather?"

"She's not here, Jovander."

Joe trained his red-rimmed eyes on Dane. "What in blazes did you do to her? If you've hurt her in any way, so help me—"

He threw his covers off and swung his legs over the side of the bed. Dane grabbed his shoulders before he could stand.

"You're too weak to move, Jovander. I haven't seen Heather since she left my father's sitting room earlier. I was hoping to find her with you."

Joe tried unsuccessfully to shake him off. "You knocked her unconscious and took her away. I saw it with my own eyes."

"What? I did no such thing. I've been at the castle since I left you this morning. Whatever you think you saw, you were delirious. Somebody gave you a drug."

Joe sat back, his brow creased in confusion. Then he spotted Heather's bow and quiver in the corner of the room. "She *was* here. Look," he said, pointing. "I've never known Heather to go anywhere voluntarily without her bow and quiver."

"Maybe she accompanied Icky on an errand for some reason." He held the dragon crystal out to Joe. "Here, this is yours. I found it at the foot of your bed."

"That's not my crystal; it's Heather's." Joe put a hand up to his throat and gasped. "My crystal is gone!"

Joe and Dane stared at one another, mystified. The prince swallowed hard as a stab of fear shot through him. "Something is definitely not right, Jovander."

The nurse rushed in. "Your Highness, there were no patients discharged today, but Sir Bast is missing."

"What about the guard posted outside his room?"

"I found him on the floor of Sir Bast's room, unconscious."

"See if you can wake the man. We need to find out what happened."

The nurse left. When Dane tried to slide Heather's crystal in the pocket of his waistcoat, his fingers encountered a round, flat piece of wood. Confused, he examined it.

"Ah...Heather's gold coin. Damnable fairy magic. The wee folk can make one thing look like another long enough to fool..." His voice trailed off. "Wait a minute, Jovander, did you say something about a fairy?"

"When you were in here before, you had that nasty fairy on your shoulder."

"Do you mean Towcheez?"

"Yes, that's the fellow. I can't say that I like him."

Dane cursed under his breath.

"I'm going to have a word with the fairies, Joe. I'll tell the nurse to give you something for your headache."

As he moved toward the door, the prince slipped Heather's dragon crystal over his head. When her crystal touched his, a visible spark followed. Dane froze, mentally transported to another place and time. Memories of events not yet lived returned with nauseating speed. *"Shimmer, you were supposed to wake us for the revolution,"* he heard himself say. *"Don't do anything foolish. A little bit of power in untrained hands can lead to disaster.*" Dane relived his private conversation with Heather, underscored with a kiss. Thoughts and sensations flowed through his mind, lightning fast and with excruciating clarity. His emotions snatched him up and hurled him into a vortex of longing. In his mind's eye, he watched Heather's arrow shatter the Dragonstone, and then the ensuing exploding wave of magic ended the memories. He staggered backward, reeling.

"Dane? Whatever is the matter?"

The prince stared at Joe, his eyes moist. "I love her."

HEATHER WOKE in the cargo section of a ship, draped on a pallet of rice sacks. Her mouth tasted vile, and her head hurt as if split asunder. The creaking and listing of the ship meant she was at sea, which confused her muddled brain. *How did I get here?* Finally, she remembered Dane had kidnapped her. *Nothing is making sense...is he the traitor?*

When she tried to sit up, she discovered her feet were lashed together at the ankles. Her hands, fortunately, had been tied in front of her. Heather bent her knees and stretched her fingers toward the knife secreted in her boot.

"Lookin' for this, Red?"

Towcheez sat on a crate, balancing Heather's hunting knife on the tip of his finger. Since the blade was nearly as tall as he was, the spectacle was even more bizarre.

"Why are you doing this?" Heather croaked, her throat parched.

"I hate the royal wizards is why. They ain't the only magical creatures in Ormaria. It's high time for 'em to shove over, I says. After the new rulers come in, I'll be awarded me own title. Lord Towcheez sounds about right...or maybe Baron von Towcheez. Ooh, don't that have a grand ring to it?"

He flipped the knife in the air and caught it by the haft.

"But Dane *is* a royal wizard," Heather said. "I don't understand why he's part of this."

"His Royal Arrogance is an Ormvalder wizard, but Sir Icky ain't."

Towcheez snapped his fingers and turned the knife into a dripping icicle. His next snap morphed the icicle into a burning flame. One last snap returned the knife to its original form.

"See? My magic is right powerful," Towcheez bragged. "It was my spell what fooled ye into believing Icky was Dane Ormvalder. I made Jovander think he was talking to ye when it was actually Icky standing right there. It's my magic what's speeding this ship along. And I don't even need one of them stupid crystals for any of it."

The door to the cargo hold opened, and Icarus entered. He gave Heather a dazzling smile. "Good, you're awake. I thought I heard your voice."

He took the hunting knife from Towcheez and cut the ropes from Heather's ankles and wrists. As soon as the rope fell away, Heather's hand flew out and slapped Icarus's handsome face with all the strength she could muster. Towcheez hooted with amusement.

"That's for kidnapping me and for posing as Dane," she spat. "How *dare* you take advantage of my feelings!"

Icarus laughed as he rubbed his cheek. "I suppose I deserved that. Towcheez, can you go topside? Heather and I need a little privacy."

Icarus gave Heather's knife to Towcheez, and then the fairy zoomed out of the cargo hold. The physician closed the door. "Now we can speak more freely."

"Where are you taking me?"

"Boravagg, of course."

"No!"

"Joe told me all about your adventures, in amazing detail.

I've never met time travelers before. I was happy to learn that my plot to overthrow the Ormvalders will succeed beyond my wildest expectations. Now that I've met you, however, I want something more immediate for myself."

"There's no such thing as time travel," Heather bluffed.

"Oh, come now. You'd be surprised how a little powdered Delirium root loosened Jovander's tongue. I was especially intrigued to learn about liquid magic. The lad couldn't work magic before he'd bathed in it, and afterwards he could. I'm willing to bet liquid magic will have the same effect on me."

"You'd lose that bet. Liquid magic can't transform non-magical people into wizards."

"You can't know that for sure."

"It doesn't matter. I'm not going to help you."

"Oh, but I'm certain you will," Icarus said. "Otherwise, King Ansgar will die."

"Icky, a traitor?" exclaimed the king. "I simply don't believe it."

Dane had brought Joe back to the castle to meet with Shimmer, Manny, and King Ansgar. Although weak and pale, Joe rested on a chaise with his arm in a sling. Dane, on the other hand, could not remain still.

"Icky has been using fairy spies in the castle for some time, Father. He drugged Joe to get information about liquid magic," Dane said.

"Why? We've always had the highest regard for the man," King Ansgar said, bewildered.

"Apparently the feeling was not returned," the prince replied, bitterness tingeing every word. "Icky resents his lack of magical ability more than any of us could have imagined. He enlisted Towcheez and Sir Bast to kidnap Heather. I traced them to the harbor. They're sailing to Boravagg, and I'm going after them."

"I'm going with you," Joe said.

The prince shook his head. "You can barely sit upright, Joe. I'll transform into a dragon and fly."

"Boravagg's a big place," Joe replied. "You'll need my help to find the entrance to the cave."

"Shimmer and I will go as well, Cousin," Manny said. "You don't know how many men Icky has hired, or what they are capable of. We should take a ship of our own."

"I agree," Shimmer said. "Consider that Bast may not have the use of his hand, but he's a formidable wizard nonetheless. Towcheez is also a powerful fairy."

"That wicked *get*," Manny muttered.

"The two of them must be dealt with, and you will need more than one wizard to do so," Shimmer said.

"Outfitting a vessel will take too long!" Dane exploded. "Heather is in grave danger."

"Shimmer enchanted our ship last time," Joe said. "We flew through the air much faster than sailing. If you left off the mast, you could go faster still."

"A de-masted ship?" Shimmer mused. "That's brilliant. Manny, let's you and I go to the harbor right now and enchant something suitable."

Manny rubbed his hands together with enthusiasm. "We'll fly her right into the castle courtyard. That way we can leave as soon as she's loaded with supplies."

Shimmer and Manny strode toward the sitting room door. When Manny opened the door abruptly, the queen, Lady Parker, and Wren tumbled inward and to the floor with a collective shriek.

"There's no such thing as privacy in the castle these days." Ansgar drew a shirtsleeve across his face to wipe the perspiration that had suddenly appeared on his brow.

~

"Now if you can behave yourself, I'll let you move about the ship. I call her the *Dragonslayer*," Icarus said.

"The *Dragonslayer*? I'm sure you think that's very amusing."

"A bit. There's no reason our journey can't be pleasant. You and I have a remarkable lot in common, Heather. We're both single-minded in the pursuit of our goals, and we both detest royalty."

"I don't detest royalty."

"No?"

"Not especially. You see, I've discovered that malicious people hail from all walks of life, Sir Icarus."

"My friends call me Icky, don't you remember?"

"I've forgotten nothing."

Heather brushed past Icarus as she stepped out of the cargo hold and into the belly of the corvette ship. A one-eyed chef cursed and talked to himself in the galley kitchen. His language might have been rough, but she had to admit whatever he was cooking smelled appetizing.

"That's Piers Wellink," Icarus said. "He used to be a celebrated chef. He can't get a position anymore since he was half-blinded in a duel with Lord Gaston Ormvalder—a duel the wizard provoked."

While Icarus gave orders to one of his crew to string a hammock for Heather in the cargo hold, she slipped up the staircase and onto the deck. She emerged into twilight just as someone barked an order to a deck hand no older than eight years of age. To her shock, the unpleasant voice belonged to Sir Bast.

"I should have known you'd be involved in this wickedness," she exclaimed.

"If it were up to me, you'd be thrown overboard," he growled.

"Likewise," Heather retorted.

Icarus came up behind Heather. "Since she holds the key to restoring your hand, Bast, I would suggest you remain civil. The lass is the only one who can find the liquid magic."

"Gah!" Bast spat.

Heather recognized the pendant around Bast's neck. "That's Joe's dragon crystal!"

"Not anymore. The Ormvalders took mine, and you took my hand. I'm owed."

"Evil begets evil, Sir Bast. When you are repaid for your deeds, you will regret it."

Bast laughed. "That's an empty threat, little girl. You've no weapons, no dragon crystal, and no friends here. You won't be serving up revenge any time soon."

Heather scanned the faces of the remaining crewmembers, which numbered fewer than twenty. Various articles of Ormarian guard or naval uniforms marked the men as deserters.

"So you've cobbled together a crew of the discontented, disenfranchised, and crippled," she said to Icarus. "Why bring a young boy? Boravagg is a dangerous place."

"When I was eight, I would have done anything to work magic. So would Ariel."

"As an eight-year-old, I would have done anything to live at the castle and be a member of King Chance's court. It took ten years for me to realize I was wasting my time," Heather said.

"And yet you claim not to hate royalty?"

"I don't hate royalty as much as I dislike my envy of them. I have since learned that royalty are no better—or worse—than anyone else. In fact, the royal family of Ormaria is kind and deserving of loyalty. If you had grievances, you should have taken them to the king directly."

A knowing smile tugged at Icarus's lips. "You're besotted with Dane Ormvalder."

"And you are deranged. Your quest to gain magic did not have to involve deposing the Ormvalders. I consider your actions to be self-serving and despicable."

Icarus's pout mocked her with its exaggeration. "I am wounded, truly, but I don't require your good opinion—only your cooperation."

Piers stuck his head above deck, ringing a rusted triangle. "Dinner," he bellowed.

Icarus held back the men as they rushed forward. He smirked at Heather. "Ladies first."

Disgusted, Heather headed below deck. Although she had little appetite, she ate to keep up her strength. Without her dragon crystal or weapons, she had no choice but to go along with Icarus for the moment. As soon as they reached Boravagg, however, she intended to escape by any means necessary.

THE WEE FOLK

$\mathcal{M}$anny and Shimmer enchanted a small, sleek cutter to fly back to the castle. The vessel floated in the courtyard out front, its gangplank lowered to allow supplies to be loaded. Shimmer, Manny, and Dane worked through dinner using magic to de-mast the ship. They also removed the cannons to lighten the vessel as much as possible. When Joe was ready to board, Manny helped him up the gangplank.

"Without her mast and sails, the ship's not that attractive anymore, but she should fly like a falcon," Manny said. "What should we name her, Jovander?"

"The *Bonny Heather II.*"

Manny laughed. "Done."

Queen Mara and Lady Parker supervised the loading of foodstuffs. Fortunately, a great many dishes had already been prepared in anticipation of the queen's welcome home celebration. Those provisions were brought on board along with bedding, water, and other supplies. Notably absent from the proceedings was King Ansgar.

"Where is Father?" Dane asked the queen finally.

"He said he was a little tired, so I had dinner sent to his room. Perhaps—"

Dane bolted toward the castle, his jaw clenched with anxiety. Within moments he'd arrived at the king's bedside. His father's pallor and general weakness were alarming. Nevertheless, the king waved aside his son's concerns.

"It's just a cold or some such trifle. No need to be overly concerned." He paused. "I wish I were going with you. Travel by airship sounds delightful." A sudden fit of giggles left Ansgar gasping for breath. "We'll create a regular ferry to Boravagg and call it *Ansgar's Amiable Airship*."

Only the tension in Dane's shoulders revealed his distress. "After this nasty business is settled, that's just what we'll do."

The king threw off his covers. "Now is as good a time as any."

"No, Father, you're not going anywhere."

With an imperceptible movement of his fingers, Dane charmed his father into a restful slumber. As he left the king's bedchamber, he met his mother in the hallway.

"What Heather has warned us of has begun," he said, low.

"No!"

"I believe Father's malady may be of fairy origin...likely a parting gift from Towcheez."

A steely expression came over Queen Mara's beautiful face.

"I'll talk to the wee folk after you've left for Boravagg. It's time I gave the fairies a piece of my mind."

WREN WHIRLED ABOUT, exploring every last nook and cranny below deck on the *Bonny Heather II*. Joe rested on a hammock, grinning happily as he observed her movements. Finally satisfied that she'd discovered everything worth seeing, the princess gave Joe a teasing glance.

"I have something for you." She lifted her dragon crystal from around her neck and slipped it over Joe's head. "You'll need this more than I."

Joe sat up and budged over so that Wren could sit beside him. She looked exceptionally pretty in the lamplight.

"Thank you, Wren. I'll bring it back to you."

"That's not all I wanted you to have, though," she whispered, leaning into him.

"I was hoping it wasn't."

He kissed her, a sweet gentle caress that left them both smiling.

"I could stare at you for hours. You're the most beautiful girl I've ever met," he said.

"No, I'm not," Wren replied. "Heather is far more beautiful than I am...but I love you for saying so."

Manny came down the stairs just as Joe moved in for another kiss. "Whoa! That's enough of that. Wren, we're ready to depart. I suggest you do the same."

She giggled and slid off the hammock. She managed to give Joe another quick kiss before her brother grabbed her by the elbow and steered her up the stairs. Manny shook his head in exasperation. "*Children.*"

A short while later, Manny practically slid down the railings. To Joe's alarm, Manny advanced on him.

"Look, Jovander, I have the highest regard for you. But stay away from Wren. When the wave of magic comes next, you'll be gone, and she'll have a broken heart. Understand?"

Joe stared at Manny for a long moment as the words sank in. "I understand."

"So you'll keep your distance?"

Joe's temper flared. "I said I understand you, Manfred. Leave off."

In response to the raised voices, Shimmer came below deck to investigate. "Is everything all right down here?"

"Yes, Father," Manny said. "Young Jovander and I were just getting a few matters straight."

His son's unusually formal address took Shimmer aback. "Hmm. Well, we're about to set sail, so to speak. Jovander, do you need assistance climbing the stairs?"

"No, Shimmer, thank you. I'll manage."

Manny made a frustrated noise deep in his throat before extending Joe a hand. "Come on. I don't want you to fall on your head."

The gangplank had already been withdrawn by the time Manny and Joe joined Shimmer and Dane on deck. Queen Mara, Lady Parker, and Wren waved as the ship rose into the air, past the highest turret and beyond. Joe gulped when he could see the castle no longer.

"How high are we going, Shimmer?"

"Above the clouds."

The rising moon wasn't completely full but nearly so, and clouds were sparse. His pique with Joe forgotten, Manny sighed with happiness.

"It's almost like I could touch the stars."

The higher they went, however, the colder the air became. Dane passed around fur-lined cloaks.

"All right, gentlemen, we're about to pick up speed," Shimmer said.

"Thanks for the warning." Joe promptly sat down on the deck and braced his back against the stump where the mast used to be. The Ormvalders glanced at him in surprise.

"I've been through this once before," he muttered.

Shimmer, Manny, and Dane followed Joe's lead and grabbed onto the railings. Shimmer whispered a spell, and *The Bonny Heather II* shot forward into the night. Although the ship streaked through the sky, for Dane it couldn't move fast enough.

Because Heather was the object of much unwanted male scrutiny, her meal was extraordinarily unpleasant. Wedged in at the end of the table next to the bulkhead, she riveted her eyes on her food and ate quickly. Ariel sat across the table from her. Heather would have spoken to the lad, but his attention was fully focused on his plate as well. When the crew began to play drinking games, she picked up one of the lanterns and brought it with her into the cargo hold. After she'd closed the door, Heather cast about for some way to secure it. The door suddenly burst open, and Icarus stepped inside. He swayed from the effects of too much wine.

"Don't bother to block the door or tie it off," he said. "Towcheez will be checking on you every so often. If he cannot access the cargo hold, I'll have the door torn off its hinges for the duration of the voyage."

"Fairies are not what I'm afraid of."

She cringed when Icarus grabbed her around the waist and pulled her close. The stench of wine made her want to hold her breath.

"I wouldn't dream of imposing myself on you," he purred. "Although I wouldn't refuse an offer of companionship."

"No such invitation will spring from my lips, I assure you."

"I can have Towcheez work his magic. You can be with Dane, if you prefer."

Heather's eyes widened. "Get out. You disgust me."

Piers stumbled into the hold, his black eyepatch askew. "Oh, terribly sorry. I was wanting to get a bag of coffee for the morning." He hummed and went about his business of hunting down the coffee.

With a crooked grin, Icarus released Heather. He flicked a glance at a hammock strung between two pillars. "I see your sleeping accommodations are ready. Better watch yourself. I'm not sure the ship is free of vermin."

Heather lifted her chin to hide the quaking she felt inside.

"It's definitely not free of vermin, Sir Icarus. In fact, it's teeming with rats."

"I wasn't aware you were such a wit, Heather. Sleep well."

As soon as Icarus was gone, Piers stopped humming. The bag of coffee in his hands slid to the floor. "Are you all right, lass?"

"Yes, thanks to you."

The chef started to leave, empty-handed.

"You forgot the coffee," she said.

"I never needed any. Nobody told me when I signed on that I'd be a party to kidnapping. I just wanted you to know."

After Piers left, Heather pushed the door closed. Although she made no attempt to secure it, she searched the cargo hold for a weapon. How she would escape remained unclear, but when the opportunity presented itself, she intended to be ready. Working her way through the supplies, she stumbled across a small crate marked *EXPLOSIVES*. The lid was nailed shut, but Heather could smell the geyser cake inside. The stuff was used in the mines near Jagged Peaks, and she'd seen firsthand what it could do. Her friend Loman had smuggled a small piece of geyser cake out from the mine one night and ignited it in his father's garden. The resulting explosion was audible from miles around, and it left a crater the size of a cow. Poor Loman couldn't hear anything for days, and his father had been furious. Why would Sir Icarus have a whole case of geyser cake unless he meant to blow something up? Heather left the case untouched.

The hammock swinging from the bulkheads gave her an idea. The twine used to sew up the rice and flour sacks could be woven into a rock sling, if she could collect enough. She unraveled twine from three open sacks, knotted the ends and began to braid the strands together. When the sacks were emptied the next evening, she'd salvage the bottom lengths of twine and continue braiding until she had a narrow rope. Then she could fashion a sling—easily hidden in her boot. A smartly aimed rock slung at a man's head could knock him unconscious—or kill, if need be. As she worked, Heather smiled with grim satisfaction. Arrows and knives weren't the only weapons she could wield— and she wasn't Saltimar's daughter for nothing.

WHEN THE *BONNY HEATHER II* had reached a steady speed, Joe and the Ormvalders went below deck to finally eat a late dinner. Consumed with anxiety, Dane had difficulty choking down his meat pasty.

"At this rate we should arrive in two days, Dane," Shimmer said. "Can you not put your mind at ease?"

Dane shook his head. "I don't want to worry you, but Father has fallen ill. I believe it to be the result of a spell cast by Towcheez."

Shimmer, Manny, and Joe gasped.

"What Heather foretold is truly coming to pass," Manny said. "I'm sorry I doubted her—or you, Jovander."

"Mother said she would speak with the wee folk. If anyone can force them to undo Towcheez's enchantment, *she* can," Dane said.

Shimmer and Manny exchanged a glance.

"I would not wish to cross Mara," Shimmer said with a grimace.

"Nor I," Manny agreed.

"Nevertheless, we should be prepared to bring back a quantity of liquid magic." Dane lurched to his feet and grabbed his fur-lined wrap. "I'll check the weather and make sure our heading is unaltered."

After a few moments, they could hear the sound of Dane's boots on the deck above as he paced. Shimmer sighed. "Dane is a man consumed. I have never seen him like this before."

"He's a man in love," Joe replied.

"What? He has only just met Heather," Manny scoffed. "She *is* lovely, but my cousin isn't given to passing fancies."

"Have you not noticed Dane is wearing Heather's crystal along with his own? When their crystals touched several hours ago, it awakened memories of what happened—or what *will* happen—between them somehow."

"Memories of future events? I'm quite confused," Manny said.

Shimmer gaped. "How extraordinary! Heather suggested that magic is alive and trying to sort things out. I'm beginning to believe she's right about that as well as everything else."

"Trust me when I tell you Dane Ormvalder is completely in love with her and she with him," Joe said.

"Poor fellow," Manny murmured.

"I don't know how you can say that, Manfred," Shimmer said. "Heather is a marvelous girl."

Joe fixed his gaze on his plate. "I think what Manny means is that Dane's time with Heather will be brief. When the wave of magic comes back, she and I will be returned to our own time. And if we're successful in preventing the downfall of Ormaria, none of us shall meet again."

"I had not thought of that," Shimmer said, taken aback. "What a horrible dilemma—to choose between love and kingdom. I don't envy the two of them."

Joe visualized Wren's pretty face. "Nor do I."

JUST BEFORE MIDNIGHT, Queen Mara, Lady Parker, and Wren gathered at the gazebo. The queen tucked iron-rich spinach leaves into their pockets and waistbands.

"What is the spinach for?" Wren asked, bewildered. "I hope I don't have to eat it."

"It's to ward off malevolent fairy magic," the queen replied. "I want answers, and I'm willing to be ruthless about it. The fairies may retaliate."

"How ruthless, Mara?" asked Lady Parker.

"Utterly."

Lady Parker and Queen Mara lit their crystals to illuminate the path through the forest. Without the power of her dragon crystal, Wren stayed close behind. The rainbow trees marked the entrance to the fairy village known as Fae Glen. Although the true colors of the arches were at their most spectacular during the day, swathes of glittering pigment remained at night. Wren stuck a finger in the band of yellow and came away with a marigold fingertip as a result. She wiped the color onto her skirt. "I used to play in Fae Glen as a child. I thought the fairies were charming at the time."

In a clearing dead ahead, a huge circle of mushrooms marked the perimeter of the fairy village. Clustered next the edge of the circle were a myriad of miniature stone cottages and thatched-roof houses. Fairies were dancing around a Hawthorne tree in the center. Luminescent dust rose from their fairy slippers as they gamboled in their usual midnight ritual. Some of the male fairies perched on a fallen tree trunk nearby, celebrating the witching hour in their own way by hoisting bottomless tankards of ale. The fairies gaped when the queen, Lady Parker, and Wren appeared. In the blink of an eye, the wee folk disappeared.

"I say, that's rude," Wren said. "Not so much as a greeting or anything."

Queen Mara and Lady Parker's dragon crystals flared. On the Hawthorne tree, gleaming ornaments reflected the light. Wren rushed forward to remove one of the sparkling objects.

"So *that's* where my brooch went! I thought I'd misplaced it."

Other familiar ornaments caught Lady Parker's eye. "Oh,

my! The housekeeper warned me that we had a thief in the castle. Now I know who the thieves were."

"Thieves and miscreants, I'm afraid," Mara said.

Wren and Lady Parker hastened to retrieve the purloined items dangling from the tree.

"Who speaks for the fairies?" Mara called out.

"Hush, you'll wake the children," came a disembodied whisper.

"I mean to wake the dead unless I receive satisfaction!" Mara bellowed.

No reply was forthcoming.

"An illness of fairy origin has fallen upon the king, and none of your kind will answer for it?"

Crickets and cicadas filled the silence.

"Your blatant mischief leaves me no choice," the queen said.

Mara beckoned to Lady Parker and Wren. As soon as the three women had stepped out of the circle of mushrooms, the queen murmured a spell. A rumbling noise emanated from deep within the earth, and the wind began to move faster and faster. The ground around the fairy circle rose up like a wave in the ocean—and then suddenly a fairy hill completely covered Fae Glen. The rumbling ceased, and the wind grew still.

Wren gaped. "Are the fairies dead?"

"No, of course not," Mara replied. "Just driven underground where they belong."

"Perhaps when they emerge a thousand years from now they'll think twice about their malicious behavior," Lady Parker said.

"That takes care of our fairy problem, but unfortunately does nothing to help Ansgar," Mara sighed.

The three Ormvalder women returned to the castle. That night, all efforts to sleep came to naught.

RED'S BRIGHT IDEA

*H*eather stood at the prow of the *Dragonslayer*, her eyes trained on the lightning emanating from thunderclouds dead ahead. Although the storm appeared to be some distance away, the ship would eventually have to pass through it to remain on course. Even now, choppy waves were roiling the vessel. More than one crewmember was below deck, fighting seasickness. A harassed Icarus had been obliged to attend his crew, and Heather was relieved of his company.

She'd managed to snag two long pieces of twine that morning, from a bag of bacon Piers had cooked for breakfast. The pungent smell of fried meat permeated the air, doubtless a contributing factor in much of the nausea. After weaving the new strands into her narrow rope, she'd secreted it in her boot. The pitching of the ship began shortly thereafter. The constant retching had driven Heather topside, despite the winds that loosened her hair from its braid. Dark red strands whipped around her face like slender flames.

Towcheez swung from the ropes hanging from the rigging, despite Bast's attempts to dissuade him. Ariel mopped the deck nearby, seemingly unaffected by the waves at all. In fact, the way

SUZANNE G. ROGERS

he'd wolfed down his breakfast would have rivaled Joe for speed, quantity, and enthusiasm.

"You don't get seasick?" she asked him.

He leaned on his mop. "Been a cabin boy on merchant ships since I was six. I've seen worse."

"Where are your parents?"

Ariel shrugged. "I do all right on me own."

"Did anyone tell you where this ship is going?"

"Troll country, I reckon. They told me you're taking us to some kind of treasure. Something that'll make me magical."

"You do know I've been kidnapped, don't you, Ariel? And that these people are conspiring against the king?"

He shrugged again, his thin shoulders pressing against the coarse weave of his oversized shirt. "I'm sorry for you, but I don't much care about who's in charge of the country. King Ansgar never put a crumb of food in my belly."

Heather peered at Ariel. Despite his tough façade, the boy radiated loneliness and deprivation. "If you make it back to Ormaria, call on Lady Parker at the castle. Tell her Heather sent you. She'll help."

Ariel gave Heather a mistrustful glance. "Why should she help me? I'm nothing to her."

"She's very kind," Heather said. "And you're not nothing; you're a person."

Bast's uninjured hand descended on Ariel's shoulder and knocked him to the deck. "You've been told not to talk to Heather. I'll whip you for this."

"You will *not*," Heather exclaimed.

Ariel scrambled backward as she stepped between him and Bast.

"Get out of my way, girl," Bast roared.

"No."

Bast shoved Heather aside and advanced on Ariel, who cowered in a quivering lump of fear. Heather plucked the

218

nearest belaying pin from the pin rail alongside the bulwark and brought it squarely down onto Bast's injured hand. He screamed in pain.

"Run, Ariel!" she yelled. "Hide in the cargo hold."

Bast turned his murderous temper on Heather. The crystal around his neck flared, and she found herself tumbling through the air with the belaying pin still clutched in her hand. When she landed at the base of one of the four cannons, everything went black.

HEATHER CROUCHED flat against Dane's neck as he raced through the forest at Boravagg. Boratures nipped and clawed at his dragon's wings. When he performed a barrel roll, she lost her grip. She crashed through the trees, scrabbling desperately to seize hold of something that would slow her descent. One of her ribs cracked as she fell on a vine stretched between two trees. The vine gave way. Heather grabbed at open air as she rushed toward the ground...

Her arms flailed at nothing as she awoke, screaming. Her pulse was racing, and her head ached. She lay in her hammock, safe, but the sensation of falling had been real. The ship was bucking and rolling like an unbroken stallion. Icarus appeared in the doorway.

"You've been unconscious for some time. You must remain still."

That brought a ghost of a smile to Heather's lips. "Tell that to the ship."

"We've sailed into the storm, and we're taking on water, I'm afraid. If you have any helpful ideas, now would be the time to share them."

Panicked shouts and running footsteps peppered the deck overhead.

"Direct Towcheez to lift the ship clear of the waves. He's

powerful enough to manage, and it's the only way this ship will survive the storm."

Icarus nodded. "It's worth a try."

He left the cargo hold, and a few minutes later, a pressing sensation told her that the ship was rising. Thunder continued to assail her eardrums, and the rainfall fell relentlessly, but the rolling and pitching motion of the ocean had ceased. Heather closed her eyes and fell asleep again. This time she dreamed she was flying alongside Dane, two dragons dancing together in an aerial waltz.

～

BLACK, roiling clouds blotted out the sunlight as the *Bonny Heather II* entered the storm. Shimmer sent the ship even higher in the sky to avoid the worst of the rain. Each time he tried to shield the ship with a spell of protection, a nearby strike of lightning would eradicate it. Because of the lightning storm, the wizards had to take turns making certain the ship was properly enchanted.

After the storm had raged for hours, the atmosphere below deck grew tense. As relentless raindrops drummed against the ship, Joe and Manny played a half-hearted game of cards. To relieve his boredom, Shimmer carved unicorns out of potatoes. Dane, on the other hand, had spent most of the voyage pacing like a caged animal. At the moment, however, he was leaning against a pillar staring out into space.

A loud crack of thunder startled them all.

"I don't envy any poor souls trying to sail in this weather. They'll like as not find themselves on the bottom of the ocean," Manny said.

Joe gave him a kick under the table.

"Ow. What was that for?" Manny exclaimed.

"Your remark wasn't very sensitive," Joe muttered.

Manny shot his cousin a guilty glance. "Oh...sorry. I wasn't thinking." He vacated his chair and headed for the stairs. "Why don't you play my hand for me, Dane? I'll go topside and make sure that last bit of lightning didn't undo the protection spell."

"I think the storm must be letting up," Shimmer said. "I haven't heard any thunder for five or six seconds."

Joe laughed, but Dane's expression remained grim. Shimmer sent another potato unicorn off to gallop freely around the cabin.

"Nice one, Shimmer," Joe said, impressed. "Can you carve a phoenix next? After it bursts into flames and cools down, I'll eat it."

Suddenly Manny stuck his head through the hatch. "You're going to want to see this. Come up here."

The prince joined his cousin on deck, followed by Shimmer and Joe. Manny pointed to a ship far below. The distance made it difficult to see, but Shimmer conjured a spyglass and took a long look. "That's Icky's ship." He handed off the spyglass to Dane.

"How can you be sure?" Joe asked.

"The ship is flying, the same as we are," Shimmer said.

"That would have to be Heather's idea," Dane said, watching the ship through the glass. "I'll transform into a pigeon and fly down. When no one is looking, I'll find Heather."

"Don't be foolish," Shimmer said. "There are no birds this far from land. Bast will surely know you're a wizard in disguise."

"You'd probably get whacked with the nearest mop and wind up in a pigeon stew," Manny said.

Dane's fists tightened in frustration, but Shimmer put a quelling hand on his shoulder.

"Manfred's right. And if we launch an all-out assault, there's nothing to say they won't hurt Heather before we can get to her. It's best to wait until she's out in the open to stage a rescue."

"We'll tail them, out of sight, until they arrive at Boravagg," Manny said.

"When they disembark, we'll rescue Heather," Joe said.

"And then I'll throttle Icky," Dane said.

EVEN AFTER HEATHER'S headache eased, she was reluctant to take meals with the rest of the crew. Only when she learned that Bast had been confined to quarters for the duration of the voyage did she emerge from the cargo hold. The archery master was heartily disliked, so his involuntary isolation came as a welcome development to more than one crewmember. Heather was also relieved to discover Icarus was keeping his distance from her. While he was engrossed in studying a crude map of the island, she crept above deck. Invigorated by the fresh air and sunshine, she climbed the rigging to join Ariel in the crow's nest.

"Hello," she said. "Do you mind if I join you?"

"Suit yourself." Ariel stared at his boots for a moment. "Um...I never thanked you for trying to protect me. Nobody's ever done that before."

"They should have."

Towcheez alit nearby. He practically thumped his chest in pride. "Fancy bit o' magic, keeping this ship in the air, innit? I'm nothing if not resourceful, eh?"

"You're very talented, Towcheez," Heather said. "You deserve more than a royal title for your efforts, don't you think?"

"Icky will make sure I get me reward."

"Really? How can you be sure? After he becomes magical, he won't need you anymore," Heather said. "He might just leave you on Boravagg."

"Icky and me are the best o' friends, and friends stick together."

"Hmmm. Sir Bast thought the same thing and look where that's got him."

Towcheez's wild eyebrows knit together. "Shut up."

The fairy did a swan dive off the crow's nest and began to berate a hapless crewmember.

Ariel squinted at Heather. "You don't really think Sir Icarus would abandon anyone in troll country, do you?"

"I think him capable of anything."

"Er...does anyone know where you are?" Ariel asked.

"No."

Heather bit back a sudden surge of emotion. She missed Joe horribly and hoped he was all right. And then there was Dane. Her expression softened as she pictured his face.

"So nobody would be following you?"

Heather peered at Ariel, taken aback. "Why do you ask?"

"'Cause there's a ship in the sky behind us, a lot higher up."

"Are you sure?" she gasped.

As she craned her neck trying to spot the ship, Ariel yanked on her sleeve. "Don't stare! Someone will notice."

Heather crouched down inside the crow's nest to hide herself from prying eyes. "Where is it?"

Ariel knelt beside her. "Right next to the cloud that looks like a horse."

He pointed toward a dot in the sky. *That must be the Ormvalders!* She couldn't imagine how they could have known how to find her—unless Joe had managed to tell them. The joy inside Heather bubbled out into a broad smile. Ariel gave her a shy, sidelong glance.

"Um...if you're planning to escape, could you take me with you? I don't feel safe with Sir Bast around."

"Don't worry, I won't go anywhere without you."

They stood, and Heather began to climb down the rigging. Ariel's quick intake of breath made her pause. He pulled a whistle out of his pocket and blew it as hard as he could.

"Land, ho!" he cried. "It's Boravagg."

In the distance the volcanic peak was barely visible. Heather hastened down the rigging. While Icarus and his crew clustered at the ship's prow to see the island for the first time, she slipped down the stairs. At the dining table, she paused to pocket a wooden saltshaker. The small round object would serve as ammunition if she couldn't find a rock. In the cargo hold, she worked quickly to finish her rock sling. The *Dragonslayer* would likely reach the island before nightfall, and she had to be ready for anything.

Just as Heather pulled the last loop into place, Towcheez flew into the cargo hold and hovered over her shoulder. "Ye hot-footed it down here fast enough when we was all staring at Boravagg. What's that ye got?" the fairy asked, biting into an apple.

Heather gulped. "It's…it's for my hair. We'll be hiking on Boravagg, and I need to keep my hair under control."

Towcheez peered at her windblown mane and curled his rubbery lip. "Yer hair looks like a nest o' red snakes."

She leveled a reproachful glance at him. "Yes, well, I can always comb my hair, but there's nothing you can do about your face."

He threw his head back and howled with laughter. "Good one, Red. By the by, Icky wants to see ye."

The fairy zipped out of the cargo hold, and Heather breathed a sigh of relief. She hid the sling in her boot and followed. Icarus was in the main cabin, with a map of Boravagg spread out on the table. The physician glanced up as she approached. "You disappeared straight off when we spotted land. What are you planning?"

"Planning?" Heather echoed, to give herself time to think. "No, I just…wanted to be alone for a while. Seeing Boravagg again triggered a few memories."

Icarus peered at her for a few moments before he turned

back to the map. "Perhaps you can tell us where to weigh anchor?"

"In the crater of the volcano."

"Is that a joke? Jovander said something about hot lava."

"That happened six hundred years ago. He and I were brought forward in time since then. The volcano is dormant now, and anyway you don't have much choice. The entire eastern coast is edged by a cliff."

"Then we'll have to circle north until we find a beach," Icarus said.

Towcheez swam the backstroke mid-air while balancing his apple core on his nose. "I can do it, Icky. I can lift the *Dragonslayer* into the crater."

Icarus shook his head. "The consequences of failure would be catastrophic, Towcheez. If you drop the ship, we'll be dashed to our deaths on the rocks."

When Towcheez frowned, Heather took another opportunity to drive a wedge between him and Icarus. "You doubt his abilities, Sir Icarus? Towcheez got us through the storm. The cavern containing the liquid magic is within hiking distance of the volcano, but if we have to travel over land for any length of time our casualties will mount."

"Red's got the idea," Towcheez said. "Lemme show ye."

Heather's knees buckled as the *Dragonslayer* soared skyward. She grabbed onto the table to remain upright, as did Icarus. In the galley kitchen nearby, Piers was caught off-guard. He cursed as he toppled to the floor. Similar shouts of protest came from on deck.

"Stop it, Towcheez," Icarus exclaimed. "This is reckless and unnecessary."

Bast burst out of his quarters, nearly staggering into a pillar. "What in blazes is going on?"

"Hullo, ye lazy wizard," Towcheez exclaimed. "I'm just proving that us fairies are more powerful than wizards."

Piers raised himself onto his hands and knees. "Point taken! Now leave off."

Heather was beginning to regret goading Towcheez into his impromptu display of power. The higher the *Dragonslayer* flew increased the chances that the Ormvalder ship would be detected.

"Towcheez, why don't you save your demonstration for when we get closer to Boravagg?"

Her words came too late. The master gunner came pounding down the stairs to sound the alert. "Sir Icarus, there's another vessel up here. We're being followed."

Icarus tilted his head as he appraised Heather. "The Ormvalders to the rescue, although I can't imagine why. You're more my type than Dane's, you know. He enjoys upper class women—and ones with more feminine figures."

"I don't flatter myself he's come for me," Heather shot back. "I imagine he's here to kill you."

Icarus merely laughed. "Towcheez, bring the *Dragonslayer* level with the Ormvalder ship."

The fairy zoomed up the stairs, cackling with glee.

"Sam, ready the cannons," Icarus said.

"Gladly," the master gunner replied. He joined Towcheez on deck.

"In cases such as these, a preemptive strike is under good regulation," Icarus said with a smirk.

Even with a broken hand, Bast managed to throw Heather into the cargo hold. Try as she might, she could not force the door open. After kicking a crate of oranges in frustration, she sat on her hammock and fumed. When the report of the *Dragonslayer*'s cannons firing reached her ears, however, she wanted to faint.

EVERY OPPORTUNITY

*B*y the time the actual report of cannon fire reached
the *Bonny Heather II*, the first of several cannonballs
had already ripped through the ship. No one was killed, miraculously, but the first of the missiles landed in the galley kitchen
and exploded. The next opened up a long, wide gap in the hull,
and the third exploded just before it hit the prow. While
Shimmer and Joe put out the galley fire, Dane scrambled above
deck to find Manny sprawled on his back—stunned from the
force of the last explosion. After he'd lifted the ship up into the
cover of a fat white cloud, Dane went to help his cousin.

Manny was conscious, but dazed. Shrapnel from the
exploding cannonball had pierced his skin in several places and
cut a gash near his jaw. Dane determined none of the injuries
were life threatening, although he spent a few moments
repeating incantations over each wound to extract the metal
fragments.

"You're going to be all right, but I need my medical kit,
Manny," Dane said.

Dense mist from the cloud swirled around him as the prince
made his way over to the hatch. Eerie fog had crept in below

deck as well, from breaches in the hull. Although Shimmer and Joe had extinguished the fire, black soot coated their face, hair and clothes.

"Manny is hurt," Dane said, coughing from the smoke.

Shimmer hastened up the stairs. Joe followed Dane as he located his medical kit. "So what just happened, Dane? It was like some kind of crazy meteor shower."

"Icky spotted us and opened fire. Since we're facing into the sun, we couldn't see the danger until it exploded right under our noses."

"But the ship is supposed to have a spell of protection on it!" Joe exclaimed.

"That last lightning strike must have undone the spell. Unfortunately, none of us noticed."

"Shimmer thinks we should abandon ship," Joe said.

The creaks, groans, and moaning noises all around them bore out Shimmer's assessment.

"Perhaps sooner rather than later," Dane said, gritting his teeth. "Let's grab what we can, Joe—and hurry."

In the space of less than a minute they'd filled a couple of knapsacks and joined Shimmer and Manny on deck. Dane used an anti-sepsis spell on Manny's wounds, but only a mixture of dried hemlock and pine bark stopped the bleeding. Shimmer helped his son sit up. True to form, Manny made a feeble attempt at a joke. "That was a little too exciting for my taste."

Their relief at Manny's nascent recovery was short-lived when a hideous cracking noise heralded the disintegration of the *Bonny Heather II*. Neither Joe nor Manny were in any condition to fly, so Dane and Shimmer morphed into their dragon forms to ferry them to shore. The two dragons leaped into the fog and circled upward until they'd cleared the cloud. Then, they skimmed the cloud cover all the way to Boravagg.

THE PIT of fear in Heather's stomach tightened at the cheering and whistling from the crew. The door of her cargo hold prison popped open at last, and Bast stuck his pink-tufted head inside. "Your friends are done for. The Ormvalders finally got what was coming to them."

Heather brushed past the man, stifling the impulse to strike him. On deck, most of the crew was clustered at the stern, laughing. Unable to see around them, she climbed the rigging. A bizarre sight awaited her. A puffy cloud some distance behind them was raining bits and pieces of a ship. Several planks fell, and then a large section of hull. With the loss of each piece, a shout of approval went up from the observers. For Heather, however, the disintegration of the Ormvalder ship was like a physical blow. Her face grew pale, and her fingers tightened convulsively on the rope webbing. She scanned the skies, hoping to see dragons, but the clouds made it impossible.

Towcheez hovered nearby. "Pretty fancy shooting, wouldn't ye say?"

Unwilling to let the fairy see her pain, Heather bit back her rising tears. "Did Sir Icarus happen to tell you your future?"

"Er...what future is that?"

"Two hundred thirty-six years from now there's nobody left to work magic. There are no fairies. I grew up believing the wee folk were a myth. What you've done is going to lead to the complete destruction of your kind."

The fairy's wings paused momentarily, and Towcheez bobbled. "That's a lie."

"Is it? Do you remember when we first met?"

"Yeah, yer rude self was oogling me."

"Because I'd never seen fairies before. Don't you understand? Sir Icarus is using you."

"Ye got a big mouth, did ye know that?" Towcheez muttered. He accidentally flew into the mast and bounced off. Rubbing his bumped nose, he gave Heather a dark glance. "Bet ye think that's funny."

As he flew away, hot scalding tears coursed from the corners of her eyes. "None of this is funny."

WITH A BASIN of cool water and a compress in hand, Queen Mara entered King Ansgar's bedchamber. Distressed to discover him missing, she scoured the castle until one of the servants said the king was in the library. The queen found her husband pouring over books on trolls.

"Ansgar, what are you doing out of bed?"

The king shook his head, his eyes glazed, red-rimmed and hollow. "Our whole kingdom has been built on a lie, Mara."

"What?"

"Just last week, Sir Icarus and I were talking about the natural friction between persons who can work magic and those who cannot. If not for happenstance, the Dragonstone would not have come to our shores. There is an element of monumental unfairness to it all."

"Ansgar, you are ill, and Sir Icarus is a traitor."

"Nevertheless, I cannot help but think Icky has a valid point. Where is my brother? I must speak with him."

Lines of worry creased the queen's forehead. "Shimmer has gone with Manny and Dane to Boravagg, don't you remember?"

"Ah, yes, that's right. I wanted to go, too." The king frowned. "Did he take the Dragonstone with him? I cannot find it anywhere."

Mara bit her lip as mulled over her answer. Shimmer was supposed to have hidden the Dragonstone, but she did not know where. If Ansgar believed the Dragonstone to be with Shimmer, however, perhaps it would set his mind at ease. She put a reassuring hand on her husband's arm. "Ansgar, it will do no good to keep looking. Shimmer took the Dragonstone with him to keep it safe. Now come back to bed, my love. You've a monstrous fever."

The king allowed himself to be coaxed away from his books. As she led him back to his bedchamber, Queen Mara kept a serene smile on her face—but she was powerfully worried. King Ansgar's decline was so rapid and marked, it would not be long before rumors began to spread. If the army to the north got wind of the king's weakness, they might be tempted to invade now.

Mara administered a potion to help with Ansgar's fever. His suffering eased, the king was finally able to sleep. She wrestled with herself for several minutes before removing Ansgar's dragon crystal. Ordinarily, her action would have constituted the highest form of treason, but these were not ordinary times. Mara left the bedchamber and summoned Sir Grindol, Dane's second in command. A steely gleam shone from her eyes as she awaited the guardsman. If the northern mongrels attacked, Ormaria must be ready for them. As the fairies had discovered, her brand of justice could be swift—and unmerciful.

NIGHT WAS FALLING when Joe and the Ormvalders finally reached Boravagg. Manny had rallied for a while but now could barely manage to keep his seat on Shimmer's back.

"I'm beginning to suspect that shrapnel that hit Manfred was infected with a toxic enchantment," Dane murmured to Joe.

Joe glanced down at the blood seeping through his bandages and tried not to faint. "I'm not doing that much better, I'm afraid."

"Hang on, Jovander. We'll get you both some liquid magic soon."

Joe guided the Ormvalders to the turtle rock lookout. As the last glimmer of twilight faded to black, the four men ducked into the largest tunnel and began to move toward the cavern. Because of Manny and Joe, progress was deliberate. About halfway there, Manny curled to the ground, unable to continue. Dane shed his knapsack and checked Manny's pulse. His cousin's heartbeat was weak and irregular.

"Shimmer, wait here with Manny," he said. "I'll take my waterskin to the cavern and bring back some liquid magic."

"I'll be right behind you," Joe said.

Dane barreled down the passageway, heartened to see the glow up ahead. He burst from the tunnel, gasping for breath, and then sprinted toward the pool. In his haste he skidded on some loose crystals, nearly losing his footing. Moments later, however, he was kneeling at the water's edge. After he'd emptied his waterskin on some nearby rocks, Dane refilled it with liquid magic. As the prince sprinted back toward the tunnel, Joe had to quickly step aside to avoid a collision.

When Dane rejoined Shimmer and Manny, his uncle's face was etched with anxiety.

"He's barely conscious, and I cannot seem to rouse him."

Dane slapped Manny's face, none too gently. "Open your mouth. You must drink."

Shimmer propped Manny into a sitting position, and together he and Dane got some of the liquid magic down his throat. After a few tense moments, Shimmer grabbed the waterskin and forced his son to swallow more—a lot more.

"Manfred, do you know what your mother will do to me if anything happens to you?" Shimmer shouted. "Come on, son. Save me."

The younger man pushed the waterskin away and belched. "What are you trying to do, drown me? Leave off, old boy."

Shimmer and Dane burst out laughing.

"Can you stand, Cousin?" Dane asked finally.

"Of course I can," Manny replied. "You two act as if I was at death's door."

Dane and Shimmer exchanged a brief glance.

"Sorry about that, Manfred," Shimmer said. "I'm just a little overanxious."

When the Ormvalders emerged from the tunnel a few minutes later, they found Joe pacing near the pool. His face and hair were wet, as if he'd splashed himself with water. As he caught sight of Manny, his shoulders relaxed. "Oh good, Manny, you're better. You had us worried."

"I'm great, thank you," Manny replied. "You seem fit."

Joe grinned as he worked his shoulder and arm. "I could turn handsprings."

"Excellent," Manny said. "Where are we?"

Shimmer stared at the cavern spread out before him, his expression almost one of reverence. "This must be the birthplace of the Ormarian Dragonstone. When Heather told us about this place, I simply could not imagine it."

"Heather!" Dane exclaimed. "We've lost track of her."

He strode toward the tunnel, but Joe grabbed his arm as he passed by. "Where are you going, Dane? It's dark, and there are more predators outside than in here."

"I agree with Jovander," Shimmer said. "Icky's ship won't have arrived until after sunset, and Icky certainly won't be traversing Boravagg at night."

"Relax, Cousin. Now that Joe and I are at full strength, Icky doesn't stand a chance," Manny said. "We'll go search for them at first light."

"Ah...perhaps now would be a good time to mention something else. Along with Heather's rescue, we must also capture Icky's ship," Shimmer said.

"Why bother? The five of us could destroy the ship and then fly to Ormaria in dragon form," Joe said.

Shimmer cleared his throat, a sheepish expression on his face. "I'm afraid there's a little wrinkle."

"What is it, old boy? What aren't you telling us?" Manny asked.

"The fact of the matter is…the Ormarian Dragonstone is gone," Shimmer said. Three pairs of shocked eyes swiveled in his direction. "Ansgar asked me to hide it, you understand, and I thought…what better place than the *Bonny Heather II*?"

"Oh, no," Manny moaned.

"The Dragonstone was hidden under a flour sack in the galley," Shimmer said. "When the first cannonball ripped a hole in the ship, the stone shattered. It was unbelievably bad luck. Nevertheless, we can't leave Boravagg without another Dragonstone."

A leaden silence followed.

"So…we rescue Heather, commandeer Icky's ship, transport a huge Dragonstone on board, and sail home with a quantity of liquid magic," Dane said, ticking off the list on his fingers.

"All without being torn apart by trolls or eaten by wild animals," Joe added.

After a short pause, Dane, Joe, and Manny shrugged and nodded, as if in agreement.

"We can do that," Dane said.

Shimmer breathed a sigh of relief. "Excellent. I thought perhaps you might be annoyed with me."

"Don't push it, old boy," Manny said. "We are."

THE *DRAGONSLAYER* REACHED Boravagg at twilight. After the Ormvalder vessel was destroyed, Icarus was in such a good mood he'd allowed Towcheez to sail the ship into the volcanic crater. To avoid predators, the vessel hovered about twenty feet above ground. The crew dropped the anchor to ensure the ship wouldn't drift with the wind.

At dinner, the crew was loud and boisterous. Although Heather stayed in the cargo hold, she could hear them celebrate as they savored their victory over the Ormvalders. *Celebrate yourselves into a stupor. It will make my escape all the easier.*

Several hours after the last tankard had been drained, she crept from the cargo hold. Many of the crewmembers had retired to their berths, but several had passed out in the main cabin. As Heather tiptoed past in the darkened cabin, the snoring was deafening. Even Towcheez was asleep, curled up inside an empty wooden bowl.

She suddenly realized Piers was staring at her from the galley kitchen. He had been sitting on a stool, reading a book by lamplight. Frozen in fear, she was certain he would sound the alarm. To her surprise, he merely lifted a waterskin from a nail in the wall and emptied a pan of biscuits into a drawstring sack. When he handed the waterskin and biscuits to Heather, she thought he gave her a wink. Since the chef had only the one eye, she honestly couldn't tell.

"Thanks," she whispered. "Please tell Ariel I will come back for him when it's safe."

On her way toward the stairs, Heather was forced to step over Sam, whose prone body lay in her path. The master gunner turned in his sleep, rolling onto her boot. When she worked her foot free, she earned a somnambulant smack.

"Bloody rat," he muttered.

With bated breath, Heather mounted the stairs. A quick glance around the upper deck confirmed that the free-flowing ale and wine had done its work; most of the crew had passed out. Fortunately, the one man on guard duty had his back turned. She loaded the saltshaker into her sling and knocked him out with a well-placed blow to the head. Heather was poised to flee, but even the resulting thud as the man toppled over failed to rouse his shipmates.

After she tied off one end of a coiled rope, Heather leaped over the side of the ship. When her boots met solid ground, she ran for cover in the vegetation, wincing at the crack of every twig under her boots. Eventually the crater sloped upward, and she began to climb. Heather wouldn't truly be able to get her bearings until dawn, but she wanted to put as much distance between her and the *Dragonslayer* as possible.

Toward the top of the crater, Heather paused to glance back. The moonlight gleaming off the surface of the lake told her she wasn't that far from the lava tunnel. She gritted her teeth in frustration. Using the tunnel would help her evade her captors, but with no source of light she would have to feel her way underground in the dark. It would be better to wait for dawn and hike to the turtle rock lookout. She'd still have to traverse an unlit tunnel, but at least the distance would be far shorter.

Heather froze at the sound of someone trampling through the trees nearby. She had her sling, but no rock for ammunition. Never before had she so keenly wanted her knife or bow. As she hid behind a tree, her pulse began to race. *Please let it be a deer.* Moments later, a small moonlit figure came into view.

"Ariel?" she whispered.

The boy let out a sigh of relief. "I thought I'd lost you."

She grabbed him by the shoulders. "What are you doing out here?"

"You said you'd take me with you."

"I would have returned for you. Boravagg is too dangerous for a child."

Something glinted in the moonlight. "I stole this," he said, holding out her hunting knife. "I thought you might need it."

Heather slid the knife into her boot. "You're a very clever boy. Now return to the ship and wait for me."

"I can't climb up the rope. I burned my hands on the way

down. And if Sir Bast finds me off the ship, he'll wring my neck."

"You've put me in a tough spot."

"I'm sorry, but I'd rather brave your displeasure than Sir Bast's."

She made a frustrated noise. "All right, let's go. Just try not to stomp."

"It would be easier to see where we're going with this," Ariel said. Fumbling in a pouch at his waist, he produced a candle.

"That's wonderful, but unfortunately I have no way to light it."

"I do." He dropped a flint and steel fire starting kit into her hand. "And my bag is full of candles. I stole 'em from the galley when no one was watching."

Heather gaped. "Ariel, you're absolutely brilliant."

The lad shrugged. "It was my father's idea."

"What?"

"Er...to be prepared, I mean. He always told me to be ready for anything and to take advantage of every opportunity."

"My father says much the same thing," Heather said. "I'd like to meet your father one day."

As they headed for the tunnel opening, Ariel's upturned face beamed in the moonlight.

LYING EYES

The sky was noticeably lighter by the time Heather and Ariel reached the tunnel. The caved-in opening had widened over the centuries, and ivy creepers were growing downward like a green waterfall. The glimmering dawn allowed Heather to see while she lit a candle with the flint and steel.

"Um...do you have anything to eat?" Ariel asked. "I'm starving."

Heather's stomach had begun to growl too. "Hold my candle a moment."

After she brought two biscuits out from the bag Piers had given her, she suddenly noticed some of the ivy creepers behind Ariel had begun to smolder from contact with the lit candle in his hands. Pulling the boy away from danger, she used her hunting knife to cut the singed vines down. Although she managed to stamp the embers out with her boots, little could be done about the distinctive plume of smoke drifting skyward.

"Oh, no, Heather, I'm sorry," he exclaimed. "I guess I wasn't paying attention. Will the smoke give us away?"

The anguish in Ariel's eyes quelled Heather's irritation.

"Never mind. It can't be helped. Perhaps after last night's revelry, nobody is awake yet to see it."

"I hope not."

"Let's eat while we walk. We've quite a distance to cover, and I don't know how long these candles will last."

Nibbling at a biscuit, Heather strode down the sloping tunnel. Ariel followed, trotting along at her side. Although they moved quickly at first, the boy needed to rest after fifteen minutes. Since her candle was half burned by then, Heather chafed at the delay. When they resumed their journey, Heather lengthened her strides. Unfortunately, Ariel lagged behind, and she was forced to pause more than once to allow him to catch up.

"If you didn't have the candle, would you get lost down here?" he asked.

"This tunnel leads straight to the chamber. I would just keep my hand on one of the walls and keep walking on a downward slope. Nevertheless, I wouldn't want to attempt it without a light."

Ariel shuddered. "Me neither."

After another mile, Heather's candle was nearly spent. "Could you hand me a fresh candle, Ariel?"

But she received no answer.

"Ariel?"

She turned around, but the boy was nowhere to be seen. "Ariel, are you hiding?"

All she could hear was silence. With increasing apprehension, Heather ran back up the tunnel to see if perhaps he'd fallen.

"Ariel, where are you?"

Her voice echoed off the walls of the tunnel.

"Don't do this, lad," she whispered, to no avail. The boy was either unable or unwilling to answer her. Bewildered and confused, Heather had no choice but to keep heading toward the cavern. The last bit of candle stub finally became a mere ember, and she was left in the dark. Gulping back fear, she held her left hand out in front of her and the right one steady against the tunnel wall as she continued her journey downward through yawning blackness.

WHEN DANE, Shimmer, Manny, and Joe emerged into the turtle rock clearing at dawn, they found themselves in the midst of a camp. A dozen large trolls lay snoring next to the remnants of a campfire. With no room to transform, the four men tiptoed past. Their scent woke one of the trolls from his slumber. He sat up, rubbing his eyes, and then howled at the sight of humans. The noise set the other trolls off and soon there was complete panic.

Dane used magic to keep the trolls at bay while Shimmer and Manny sprinted up the trail and jumped off a cliff to transform. Joe, far less confident in his transformative skills, stood teetering at the edge with his arms outstretched. Sweat trickled down Dane's forehead as the rampaging, confused trolls battered against his invisible magical wall.

"Come on, Jovander, I can't hold them much longer," he said through gritted teeth.

"I don't work well under pressure!" Joe yelled back.

Dane turned and tore up the trail. He grabbed Joe around the waist and dove with him over the side of the cliff. As Joe screamed, Dane transformed in the air and flew skyward with the lad gripped firmly in his talons. They barely eluded the trolls, who roared in frustration at the narrow escape.

"Sorry I couldn't give you any warning," Dane said.

"That's all right," Joe managed. "Er...just don't let go."

They joined Shimmer and Manny circling overhead and gained altitude to survey the island. When Dane spotted the *Dragonslayer* inside the volcanic crater, he sped toward it.

"How strange. The ship looks deserted," Joe said.

Puzzled, Dane glided in for a landing. After he transformed, he conjured a sword for Joe and himself. As the prince crept toward the open hatch, Joe glanced skyward.

"Aren't we going to wait for Shimmer and Manny?"

"You can wait. I'm going in."

With a sound of frustration, Joe followed Dane down the stairs. They discovered Piers sitting at a table below deck, rolling out bread dough. The chef stood when Dane and Joe appeared and pointed his rolling pin at them.

"W-who are you?"

"We'll ask the questions," Dane said, his sword at the ready. "Where is Heather?"

Just then, Manny and Shimmer tumbled downstairs. Piers had a sudden flash of recognition. He dropped his rolling pin and bowed.

"Your Royal Highnesses. Chef Piers Wellink at your service. I'm afraid I'm all alone here."

Dane continued to hold the man at the point of his blade while Manny, Shimmer, and Joe verified that the ship was indeed empty. "I ask you again, where's Heather?"

"The poor brave girl escaped early this morning, but Icky and the crew are tracking her. They believe she'll lead them to the liquid magic."

"She's probably heading for the cavern through the crater tunnel," Joe said. "If Sir Icarus manages to follow her, Heather will be trapped between him and that camp of trolls."

"Heather wouldn't try to take that tunnel without a source of light," Dane said. "I have her dragon crystal, remember?"

"She may be with the young lad, Ariel. He followed her with a bag of candles," Piers said.

"Manny, can you hide this ship while Shimmer, Joe, and I go after Heather?" Dane handed his waterskin to his cousin, flicking a significant glance at Piers as he did so. "Piers might find this water especially refreshing," he said, referring to the liquid magic inside.

"Ah, yes, it might be quite restorative." Manny nodded his head.

"I'll leave it with you, then."

While Shimmer and Dane pulled up the ship's anchor, Joe told Manny how to find the crescent cove. As Manny guided the *Dragonslayer* up and out of the volcanic crater, Joe and the other Ormvalders morphed into their dragon forms and went to Heather's aid.

UNNERVED BY THE loss of Ariel's company, each minute in the dark dragged on like an hour. The blackness seemed to have a texture, making it difficult for her to breathe. Even her eyes played cruel tricks by seeing phantom spots of light. Yet despite everything, she continued to move, humming nursery rhymes to calm her nerves.

Heather mistook a faint, distant glow for another hallucination. Unlike before, however, the light grew steadily brighter as she drew closer. At long last, Heather entered the Dragonstone cavern tearstained and trembling. With a feeling of sheer gratitude, she knelt next to the liquid magic and bathed her face. She filled her waterskin, and after drinking from it, she was energized.

Suddenly, a faint noise reached her ears—the echo of shuffling footsteps. Heather reached for her knife, but it was too late. Icarus appeared, flanked by the entire crew of the *Dragonslayer*. Each man was armed with crossbows or swords, and two of the crewmembers carried the case of geyser cake between them. Poised to flee, she stopped when Icarus dragged Ariel into view, pinning him with an iron grip.

"If you try anything, Heather, you'll be responsible for the boy's demise."

One glance at Ariel's pleading face compelled her to lower her knife. "Are you all right, lad?"

The boy managed to nod. Towcheez flew over and plucked the knife from her hand. "Ye won't be needing this," he cackled.

The fairy brought the knife over to Bast, who stuck it in his waistband with a triumphant leer. Icarus released Ariel and let him go free. The boy gave a bewildered Heather a slightly guilty glance. "You said you wanted to meet my father." He cocked a thumb behind him. "Here he is."

Seeing Ariel and Icarus side by side, the resemblance was obvious. With the realization she'd been used and betrayed, something inside Heather twisted into a cold, hard knot. As she bowed her head, Icarus tsk-tsked. "Poor Heather. Didn't I warn you not to trust anyone?"

Feigning dizziness, Heather slumped to her knees next to a pile of loose dragon crystals. Bast hastened to the pool and plunged his injured hand deep beneath the surface. Icarus and his crew pressed closer.

"Well, Bast?" Icarus asked.

Bast chortled with laughter. "Ahh…this feels marvelous. Absolutely fantastic stuff." His glee waned when the surface of the pool froze instantaneously, trapping his hand in the ice. "Stop it, Towcheez. I'm not amused."

All eyes swiveled toward the fairy.

"It ain't me," he protested.

"It *has* to be you," Icarus said.

The fairy's lower lip jutted out. "I done told you I didn't do it."

"Somebody help me. My hand is freezing," Bast complained.

Icarus's brow creased in confusion. "But the only other wizard here is—"

A thick vertical sheet of ice suddenly appeared in the cavern, walling off most of the *Dragonslayer* crew. With a roar of protest, the trapped men began to assail the ice with their hands, feet and the butts of their swords and crossbows. Only Heather, Bast, and three men were left in the clear. Bast could only gape as Heather stood, a dragon crystal blazing in one hand and her sling in the other. With a mighty cry, she launched a rock-shaped ball of ice at the man closest to her. As he went down, the remaining two raised their weapons. A crossbow-launched arrow flew across the cavern, striking Heather in her abdomen. Even as she curled to her knees, Heather caused a stalactite to come crashing down on the archer. The last man, the master gunner, drew his sword and ran toward her across the frozen pool. Heather concentrated on the icy surface, and as Sam approached, the section of ice underneath his feet gave way. After he fell under the surface, Heather froze it again so he couldn't get out. Then she collapsed onto the floor of the cavern, writhing in pain.

"Looks like you're done for, girly," Bast sneered. "I'll make sure to throw your rotting corpse somewhere trolls can feast upon it."

Heather dragged her waterskin toward her with blood-stained fingertips. Praying she wouldn't lose consciousness before the deed was done, she tried to remove the arrow from her body. After three attempts, her throat was raw from screaming—but she'd managed to wrench the arrow free. As she poured liquid magic into the wound, she could hear the ice prison she'd built beginning to crack.

Leaving bloody footprints on the frozen pool, Heather staggered across the ice toward Bast. In his desperation to free himself, the master archer was using Heather's knife to chip away at the ice around his hand. As she approached, he held the blade toward her. "Stay away from me, witch."

"I'll have my knife back now, you pathetic excuse for a wizard."

A crossbow lay next to the man crushed by the falling stalactite. With unblinking deliberation, she loaded the crossbow with another arrow and shot Bast in his other hand. He dropped her knife, cursing and screaming with pain. After sheathing her knife in her boot, she wrenched Joe's dragon crystal from Bast's neck.

"You're friendless and alone," he snarled. "There's no escape on an island such as Boravagg."

"I've no plans to escape." She slipped Joe's crystal around her own neck. "And you're about to find out what hell is really like."

With the ice wall crumbling in earnest, Heather hastened toward the lava tunnels. She nearly stumbled across Towcheez, who'd crawled through a small opening in the ice wall. His pork pie hat gone, the fairy had been abused so badly one of his wings was torn.

"What happened to you?" she gasped.

"Icky thinks I betrayed him," he mumbled.

She knelt to give Towcheez a sip of the liquid magic in her waterskin. When he began to rally, the half-dead creature stared at her in confusion.

"Why would ye help me, Red?"

"I need you to protect Ariel. Get him far away from here," she said. "He's too young to realize what he's done."

With that, the ice wall came tumbling down. Through a volley of arrows, Heather sprinted toward the lava tunnels. Miraculously unscathed, she suspected Towcheez's magic was responsible for keeping her safe. Icarus's voice followed her as she disappeared into one of the tunnels. "Let her go. We don't need her anymore."

Trolls were gathered around a campfire when she burst into

the turtle rock clearing. Heather squeaked with shock and skidded to a stop. After the trolls recovered from their surprise, they stampeded in her direction. In that instant, she transformed into her dragon shape and shot straight upward. A troll managed to grab the tip of her tail, but he got crisped for his efforts.

As Heather soared into the sky, the trolls' rage boiled to a peak down below. She nodded with grim satisfaction. While the trolls remained camped in the clearing, Icarus and his men would be unable to pass. They would linger inside the cavern and wait to harvest the liquid magic after it thawed. When she returned, she would not be alone.

Heading south over Boravagg, Heather scanned the treetops for borature nests. During their time at the dragon rebel stronghold, Shimmer had said dragon crystals allowed wizards to transform into animals—most often dragons. Right now, she needed to transform into something that would fly faster than a dragon, would be small enough to fit into a lava tunnel, and could maneuver quickly enough to save her life. Midair, she transformed into a Peregrine falcon. Although her father had never hunted with falcons, her Uncle Latimar had. Heather had learned to respect the birds for their sheer flying ability. For what she was about to do, she needed the speed, eyesight, and reflexes of a falcon—and nerves of steel.

Finally, she found what she was searching for—the nesting grounds of a large borature colony. Built into the side of a west-facing cliff, the nests were circular depressions dug out of sandstone. Her previous experience with the flying reptiles had taught her they would mercilessly chase an intruder a long way to protect their nests. To lure them back to the cavern, however, she'd have to make them angry.

Plummeting toward her quarry at over two hundred miles per hour, there was no turning back. When the boratures spotted her, they massed to repel the intruder. Heather snatched one of their eggs in her claws and sped upward. Dane had erred before, when he tried to lose them in the trees. Shimmer and Manny had escaped by climbing high into the sky. She did the same. As soon as the boratures began to fall back, she leveled out and headed for the Dragonstone cavern. With scarcely a dragon's length of distance between her and the borature flock leader, she dared not lose focus.

I am the arrow, and I will find my mark.

HARM'S WAY

*M*ara paced in the throne room, her beautiful face etched with anxiety. Suddenly Sir Grindol burst into the chamber. "The invasion has begun, Your Majesty," he said, his chest heaving with exertion. "Our border to the north has been breached. Soldiers are marching in formation alongside cavalry."

The queen grasped her dragon crystal and moments later it glowed with a continuous red light. "I have sent the call-to-arms, Sir Grindol. Within the hour, every able-bodied wizard in Ormaria will assemble in this room. Thereafter we shall fly north to deal with the threat. You will assemble your army to defend the castle, if need be, but I hope it shall not come to that."

"And what of King Ansgar?"

"He is…indisposed," the queen replied.

"Forgive me, my queen, but protocol demands I take orders only from the king."

Mara forced her countenance to appear serene.

"Quite right, Sir Grindol. Before he leads Ormaria in this endeavor, you shall hear it from King Ansgar himself."

Satisfied, the guardsman left the throne room, and Mara had

little choice but to seek help from an unlikely source. With no time to spare, she hastened to the kitchen. After grabbing a handful of spinach from the cooler, she fled the castle and headed for Fae Glen.

~

WITH RELUCTANCE BORN OF DISTASTE, Mara caused a portal to open in the fairy hill. "Who speaks for the fairies?"

A swirling wind swept the queen's flaxen hair back from her face. Moments later a pretty young fairy shot through the porthole. Since the wee folk could appear in many guises, Mara remained vigilant.

"I am Sylvia," the fairy said. "End our torment or leave us in peace."

"If the fairies agree to render me a service, I will free them."

Sylvia peered at Mara. "How do we know you'll keep your word?"

An exquisite bracelet floated from the queen's palm toward the fairy, tantalizing her with its gleaming jewels. Sylvia licked her lips, her fingers twitching.

"King Ansgar gave this to me on the occasion of our son's birth," Mara said. "I never take it off. The fairies may keep it as payment."

The fairy snapped her fingers, and the bracelet disappeared. "We are agreed. Name the service."

"You must transform me into Ansgar for several days, in appearance, clothing, and voice."

"Is that all?"

"No. Soldiers from the north are invading Ormaria as we speak. I give the wee folk free rein to perpetrate whatever mischief they please to repel this invasion—provided it affects our enemies only."

A couple of Towcheez's friends popped out of the fairy hill alongside Sylvia.

"Now yer talkin' sense. I loves me some mischief."

"We'd do it fer free."

Sylvia gave the spinach in Mara's hand a sly glance. "I cannot work magic on you as long as you hold iron. You must rid yourself of those leaves."

The queen laughed. "Iron protects me only from your malevolent magic, not the good. I'm no fool, Sylvia. The iron stays."

The fairy pouted, but in the blink of an eye, Mara was transformed into an exact copy of her husband. In the next moment, the queen undid the magic forces holding the fairy hill in place. The sod eased back from the mushroom circle, and Fae Glen was restored. Fairies burst forth in an excess of exuberance. As King Ansgar, Mara nodded.

"Now that we understand one another, let's go to work."

SHIMMER NUDGED the cut and singed vines on the lava tunnel floor with the toe of his boot. "Somebody's been here recently."

"Sir Icarus's men. Look at all the footprints," Joe said.

Dane peered into the darkness yawning in front of him, alleviated only by the glow from his dragon crystal. "They've had a good head start."

Shimmer and Joe added the light from their dragon crystals to Dane's, and then the three men began to run. After fifteen minutes, the older man's pace started to flag. He bent over, gasping for breath. "At this rate, we'll never catch them. It's time to try something else."

Suddenly Shimmer morphed into a cheetah.

"What an inspired notion, uncle," Dane said.

He morphed into a cheetah as well, but Joe could only

manage a small, spotted kitten. Dane shook his head in dismay. "Remind me to work with you on shape shifting."

Picking Joe up by the scruff of his neck, Dane darted down the tunnel, with Shimmer on his flank. As a cheetah, Shimmer kept up with Dane so well he almost ran into him when Dane came to an abrupt halt.

"What's wrong?" Shimmer asked.

Dane had to let Joe down before he could reply. "I see a fairy light heading this way," he whispered. "It must be Towcheez."

Morphing back into human form, Shimmer and Dane took refuge in one of the small pockets off the main tunnel. At the last moment, the prince remembered to retrieve the kitten.

"Pull yourself together, Joe," Dane said.

Just as Towcheez hovered past with a fairy light in his hand, Joe returned to human form with a loud meow. Startled, the fairy zoomed upward and hit his head on the roof of the tunnel. The fairy light was extinguished, and the tunnel fell into dark once more. When Dane lit his dragon crystal, he was shocked to see a young boy standing there, rubbing his eyes. Towcheez sat on the floor of the tunnel, massaging the new lump on his head.

Dane picked Towcheez up by the collar.

"Ye ain't dead!" the fairy exclaimed.

"No, but you'll be a fairy stain unless you tell me where Heather is," Dane said.

"Where's my father?" the boy demanded. "How did I get here?"

"Yer father's right here, Ariel," Towcheez said, reigniting the fairy light. "See?"

When Ariel stared at the light, he became somnambulant again. Dane gave the fairy a hard shake. "Start talking, Towcheez."

"Calm yerself, Prince. Red done asked me ter get the lad out of harm's way, and that's what I done."

"Heather's alive!" Joe exclaimed.

Dane's shoulders relaxed a little.

"Aye, she's alive. She's quite a girl, Red is," Towcheez said. "She done escaped as far as I know."

"Escaped?" Dane echoed. "Heather didn't come this way?"

"Nah, she went out some littler tunnel, and Icky's boys went after her."

"I hope she didn't run into the trolls," Joe exclaimed.

Dane released the fairy, who made a big show of straightening his clothes.

"Towcheez, the ship has been moved," Shimmer said. "You and the boy should wait here for our return."

"Ye Ormvalders are trickier than fairies. And that's a compliment."

Joe, Dane, and Shimmer resumed their journey on foot. Silence reigned for a few moments.

"I'm guessing Heather is planning something," Dane said finally.

"What?" Joe asked.

"Retribution."

A LARGE PIT remained in the ice from where Bast had been chopped free. One of his hands was bloody and swollen and the other was still wrapped in a bloodstained bit of cloth. Most of the crewmembers knelt on the frozen pond, chipping at the ice with whatever tools they had. The master archer sat on a boulder and glowered at Icarus. "I blame you for this, Icky. If the fairy were here, maybe he could melt this ice."

"I didn't ask him to flit off, did I?" Icarus retorted. "Nor my son."

One of the crewmembers returned from searching the cavern. "I can't find Ariel anywhere, although he might be hiding in the big tunnel."

"Take a few candles and search for him, Kellan," Icarus said. "If you don't find the boy, I'll hold you personally responsible."

Kellan flinched, but he turned on his heel and disappeared behind a stalagmite. Icarus peered at Bast. "I know the girl took your dragon crystal, but there are crystals everywhere. Can't you use another one to melt the ice?"

"It's difficult for one wizard to undo the magic of another, but that isn't the biggest problem. Since I don't have the use of either hand, I can't pick one up, can I?"

"Perhaps we could break the ice with a small portion of the geyser cake," Icarus said.

"Would you have us buried alive? Any explosion could cause the whole place to collapse!"

Both Bast and Icarus jumped when the screaming began. The other crewmembers stopped chipping away at the ice as Kellan darted past at a dead run—a lit candle clutched in one hand. He paused only long enough to shriek, "Snakes!"

His fellow crewmembers laughed as the man skidded and slid across the pond in a panic. After he reached the far side, Kellan careened toward the smaller tunnels that led to the turtle rock clearing. Icarus made a big show of shaking his head, even as his shoulders tensed.

"Go kill the little nest of snakes that has bothered our brave hero," he told the remaining crewmembers in a scathing tone. "The next time anyone sees Kellan, kill him for his cowardice."

No sooner had the crew picked up their swords or crossbows than the leading edge of snakes became visible. The reptiles writhed across the cavern, hissing and undulating like a black carpet of death. The men gasped and backed away. Grabbing a crossbow from one of the deckhands, Icarus gestured toward the snakes. "Deal with that! I'll get Kellan."

Icarus sprinted for the tunnels, with Bast trailing him only by yards. The men who were left behind spent their arrows at the roiling oncoming mass, but their ammunition had no effect.

One by one the men abandoned the effort and made a break for the tunnels. As the snakes continued to slither closer, the atmosphere inside the cavern became one of hysteria. The men fought to reach the tunnels, and several were trampled in the melee.

When the last of Icarus's crew had crawled into the tunnels, Dane, Shimmer, and Joe emerged from the shelter of three fat stalagmites. Most of the snakes magically vanished, but Shimmer sent a few of the bigger specimens through the tunnels to discourage any stragglers from returning.

Dane gaped at the ice, his breath making misty clouds in the chilled air. "I suppose that's one way to prevent Icarus from getting any liquid magic."

"Were those snakes real?" Joe asked.

"Illusions only," Dane replied. "I know how much Icky dislikes snakes."

"I'm surprised Bast was fooled," Shimmer said.

"He didn't expect we'd be around to work magic," Dane said.

"Bast and Icarus believe us to be dead," Joe said.

Dane frowned. "If Heather also thinks we're dead, there's no telling what she'll do."

He started toward the tunnels, but Joe caught him by the arm. "Where are you going?"

"To find her."

"Boravagg's a big place. It took days to find her last time."

"But I have her crystal now," Dane replied. "Its light can lead me to her."

The prince ducked into the largest tunnel, with Joe and Shimmer falling in behind.

ICARUS FOCUSED on the bobbing light in the tunnel several lengths ahead of him. "Kellan? Wait for me."

The man paused to allow Icarus to catch up.

"Do you know where this tunnel leads?" Icarus asked.

Kellan shook his head. "No, but if the girl went this way, it must go outside."

"That's logical."

As they moved forward, Bast huffed and puffed somewhere behind them in the dark. "Icky, hold fast. I'm right behind you."

Kellan hesitated, but Icarus pushed him forward. "Go on. Bast will be fine, and I need air."

They hastened along, but the candle burned steadily lower.

"Move faster, or I'll shoot you myself," Icarus muttered.

Needing no further invitation, Kellan began to sprint. His candle burned out, but the glow of daylight was now visible in the distance.

"We made it," he chortled.

Icarus watched Kellan burst from the tunnel and disappear. Baffled, Icarus hastened the last few yards. When he emerged, the physician squinted his eyes against the afternoon sun. He sighed and took a deep breath.

"I never realized how oppressive it is being underground," he said. "Kellan?"

Something warm and moist dripped on his brow and rolled down his face. His hand automatically went to his cheek and came away bloody. "What in blazes!"

He glanced up.

A headless Kellan hung upside down from a tree root protruding from the cliff face behind him, and the troll who'd put him there wasn't nearly through yet. With shaking hands, Icarus raised his crossbow and shot the troll in the throat. The ugly creature fell with a gurgling yelp, but dozens of other trolls took his place. Suddenly the trolls turned and ran—every bit as panicked as the men inside the cavern had been.

Giddy with relief, Icarus laughed. His one arrow spent, he

tossed the useless crossbow aside. "Ha! That will teach you to threaten *me*, you wretched freaks of nature," he shouted.

Bast staggered from the tunnel, shying away from the steady trickle of blood dripping from above. "What happened to Kellan?" he exclaimed, aghast.

"Trolls," Icarus said. "But I frightened them off."

Just then a huge, twisting shadow appeared on the ground. Although the sun's rays made it difficult to see exactly what was spiraling toward them, Icarus didn't want to take any chances. He edged toward the tunnels but was pushed into the open by the men streaming out.

"Move, damn you!" he exclaimed, to no avail.

"Is that a flock of birds?" Bast asked, peering upward.

Suddenly men began to run in every direction. As the flock drew closer, Icarus whimpered. The incoming mass wasn't comprised of birds, but of large, flying creatures in pursuit of a falcon. Moments later the falcon deposited an egg at his feet and sped away. Icarus cowered as the angry boratures descended.

HEATHER HURTLED SKYWARD, her heart in her throat. Her plan had been to escape the boratures by losing them in the catacombs, but the inopportune appearance of Icarus's crew had blocked her access. After dropping the egg, she had no choice but to flee for her life. As she sped toward a low-hanging raincloud, she hoped the boratures would lose interest in her and attack the men on the ground instead. A quick banking turn, however, confirmed three of the largest boratures were still literally on her tail. Straining with fatigue, Heather ducked into the raincloud and immediately angled left.

A moment of respite followed, but when the boratures discovered they'd lost their quarry they began to emit a high-pitched whine. A reptile scored a glancing hit to her wing with its claws. *The boratures are using sound to locate me.* To stay inside the cloud meant she'd be the only one flying blind—and to remain in falcon form would make her even more vulnerable. Transforming into a dragon, she soared higher until the cloud was underneath her.

Sensing the boratures had followed, Heather turned and spewed a vicious gust of dragonfire. The leading borature was caught in the blast and plummeted toward the ground. Unfortunately, the other two reptiles had circled around to either side. One clamped onto her back and pierced her neck with needle sharp claws while the other attacked her softer underside. She managed to kill the borature within reach, but not before he'd gouged her hide. Although she flipped frantically through the air in an effort to dislodge the borature on her back, she continued to hurtle toward the island—and certain death.

TRIAL BY TROLL

*D*ane, Shimmer, and Joe flinched as screams began to echo through the tunnel. Dane swallowed hard. "Trolls must be tearing Icky's men apart."

When bird-like cries reached his ears, Joe gasped. "It's not trolls; it's boratures!"

"I *knew* it. Heather must have led them here," Dane said. "She needs my help."

The prince darted away, with Joe hard on his heels. When Dane reached the end of the tunnel, he paused. The boratures had scattered overhead, but bloody men and body parts were flung everywhere. Joe gagged and promptly clapped a hand over his mouth to stave off nausea.

Dane murmured a spell, and a beam of light shone from Heather's dragon crystal. The beam drew his attention skyward, to a flailing red dragon barely visible beyond the swarm of boratures. Joe emerged from the tunnel and followed his glance.

"Go!" he yelled. "I'm right behind you."

His transformation instantaneous, Dane shot through the boratures before the reptiles had the chance to react. The creatures coalesced into a mass and pursued the prince. To his frustration, Joe remained on the ground. "Don't *think* about it, Jovander, just *do* it."

When he suddenly managed to morph into a dragon, Joe flew faster than he ever had before. He gained on the boratures, belching long tongues of dragonfire at the trailing edge of the flock. After he'd picked off several reptiles, a large part of the flock abandoned their pursuit of Dane and turned on Joe instead. As he hovered in the air, he flamed boratures until he became lightheaded with the effort. Finally Joe admitted he would soon be overcome, until Shimmer came to his aid at last.

The black dragon tore through the flock like an avenging angel. Recognizing the greater threat, the boratures descended on the older dragon. As they attacked, a white-hot fury possessed Joe. Thereafter, he battled the reptiles with renewed purpose—burning, biting, and clawing valiantly as he fought to protect the only real father he'd ever known.

～

I CANNOT FAIL HER AGAIN.

Dane hurtled toward the falling red dragon, straining against the drag of the wind. As he drew near, he could see the reason for Heather's distress. A borature had attached himself to her back, his muscular claws clamped down on her spine. Her wings were still moving, so the creature had not yet severed her spinal cord, but the reptile was making it impossible for her to keep aloft.

With his outstretched talons, Dane took hold of the borature and tried to wrench it off. The creature screamed but did not loosen its deadly grip. The ground was rapidly approaching, and Dane was out of options. After biting the borature in half, he flung the pieces to either side. Unfortunately, Heather was barely conscious. With her bloodied body gripped in his claws, he beat his wings in a desperate attempt to slow their descent. The red dragon, half-conscious, squirmed with fright.

"I've got you, Heather," Dane said, through gritted teeth.

His muscles tore with the strain, but mere yards away from the treetops, the two dragons leveled out. As soon as he found a small clearing, he landed. After releasing Heather from his grip, Dane morphed into his human form and knelt by her side.

"Heather, you must transform so I can tend your injuries."

Although she made no outward sign she'd heard him, moments later Heather morphed into human form. When he saw her condition, Dane could not suppress a gasp of dismay. Soaked with blood, Heather's clothes were torn to shreds and hideous gouges marred her skin. The severity of her condition precluded the efficacy of a simple healing spell, but that didn't stop the prince from trying. At the same time, he cursed himself for leaving the liquid magic with his cousin. When Heather's lips moved, he bent close to listen.

"Drink," she murmured.

"Of course."

He freed her waterskin from its strap and turned her gently, until she was propped up against him. After he dribbled some of the water into her mouth, she managed to swallow it. Then Dane cradled Heather's dying, broken body in his arms.

How am I ever going to live without her?

In the guise of her husband, Mara returned to the castle. Ormarian wizards were waiting in the throne room. The queen strode through the crowd, feigning her husband's usual good-humored air of command. Sir Grindol stood next to the throne, an expression of relief on his face at the king's appearance.

"Your Majesty, it is good to see you well again."

Mara nodded. "Not to worry, Dolly," she said, using the

king's favorite nickname for the guardsman. "I wouldn't have wanted to miss the fun."

She turned to address the Ormvalders. "My friends, Ormaria is under attack by Great Faturia—"

Suddenly a wan and weak King Ansgar appeared in the doorway, clad in his nightshirt.

"I missed the call-to-arms because somebody stole my crystal," he cried. "Let us all fly to Boravagg together."

When the assembled wizards recognized the king, there were gasps of astonishment. Confusion ran rampant throughout the throne room.

"What is this, Your Majesty?" someone called to Mara.

"Damnable fairy mischief," she replied with feigned annoyance. "Although the fairies have agreed to join our fight, they continue to create havoc here at the castle. Sir Grindol, detain that man—but treat him well. The poor soul is bewitched and likely does not know who he is. I'll sort him out upon my return."

King Ansgar was escorted from the throne room, and Mara continued her address to the wizards of Ormaria. Her husband would want her to protect the kingdom at all costs, even if that included his arrest. Nevertheless, it pained her to see Ansgar treated like a trespasser in his own home. After the invasion was repelled, and Dane returned with liquid magic to heal his father, she and Ansgar would have a good laugh about the whole affair.

PIERS LOOKED through a spyglass as Manny navigated the *Dragonslayer* down the coast of Boravagg. "I believe the rocky cove is dead ahead, but it's awfully difficult for me to tell with only the one eye." He handed the spyglass to Manny, who confirmed the sighting.

The wizard settled the ship in the center of the cove and weighed anchor.

"Although my father and cousin are powerful wizards, Icky has a great many men with him—not to mention a wayward fairy," Manny said. "I'm going to fly back to the island as a dragon."

"I'd like to tag along. I'll scrounge a crossbow from below deck. I used to be a fair shot before I lost my eye."

"I warn you, Boravagg is right dangerous—or so I've been told. There are trolls and nasty boratures to contend with."

Piers squinted at Manny. "I don't care. Heather's bravery puts me to shame."

The chef located a battered crossbow and a quiver of darts in the back of the weapons locker. Before they left, Manny offered Piers the waterskin Dane had given him.

"Thanks," Piers said, quaffing a mouthful. "Fresh spring water is always welcome." He shivered as the liquid magic slid down his throat, and then he stifled a burp. "Oh, pardon me. I've been among rough company far too long."

"Have some more. I've seen for myself its beneficial effects."

A peculiar expression crossed Piers's face after he lowered the waterskin the second time. The scar running underneath the man's eyepatch was knitting itself together. Confused, Piers tore off the patch and stared at his own fingers with both eyes.

"Is this a cruel trick?" he gasped.

"No trick. Liquid magic," Manny said with a chuckle. "Without it, I would have died from Icky's poison. I didn't want to get your hopes up, but it's amazing stuff."

A muscle in Piers's jaw worked as he struggled to contain his emotions. "I've been cursing the Ormvalder name since Lord Gaston Ormvalder took his revenge two years ago. It seems I have misjudged you."

"What happened between you and Gaston?"

"Hanna Ormvalder and I became fond of one another. Her father thought the match beneath her and so maimed me."

"Why didn't you seek redress with King Ansgar?"

Piers shook his head. "I thought you royals would stick together. I suppose I was blinded by more than Gaston's sword."

"There is a great deal of prejudice to go around," Manny said, extending his hand in friendship. "Let us begin anew."

"Agreed." Piers gave Manny's hand a strong shake, and then took up his crossbow. "With two good eyes I'll be far more useful now."

MANNY AND PIERS flew away from *The Dragonslayer* and headed toward the volcano. Unused to flying on a dragon, Piers had Manny's neck in a tight grip. As the chef gained confidence, he gradually pushed himself up into a sitting position. He even managed to admire the island as they flew over the mountain range. About halfway to the crater, Piers suddenly noticed a strange phenomenon in the sky.

"How odd," he said. "That's unlike any lightning I've ever seen before."

Although the chef was not dragon apt, Manny could understand *him* full well and shot forward. Piers dropped down to grab the dragon's neck as they sped toward the firefight. When they arrived, Shimmer and Jovander were in the middle of a swirling mass of boratures. Although the two dragons were crisping dozens of reptiles with each gust of dragonfire, the sheer number of boratures threatened to overwhelm them. With a fierce dragon cry, Manny swept into the fray. He forgot for a few moments that Piers was on his back—until the darts from the man's crossbow began to fly. True to his word, the chef was a good shot. But Shimmer's stamina had begun to ebb. As they sensed the older dragon's growing weakness, the boratures descended on him and slashed his tough hide with their claws and beaks. After Manny and Joe turned their efforts to protecting Shimmer, the boratures attacked their blind sides.

"Where the devil is Dane?" Manny shouted. "We're getting our tails handed to us!"

"He went to help Heather," Joe yelled.

"We should retreat," Manny said.

"No! The boratures will follow," Shimmer said. "We must stand and fight."

A reptile swooped past Manny and scored Piers on the shoulder. To his credit, the man managed to wound the creature with a dart. With no spell of replenishment on his quiver, however, Piers would soon be out of ammunition.

HEATHER CAME to full consciousness with a gasp. Dane stared in amazement. "You're all right! That must have been liquid magic in your waterskin."

As Heather rolled to her feet, she drew her hunting knife and leveled it at Dane. "I should carve you up and feed you to the boratures. How *dare* you play tricks on me again!"

Dane held his hands up. "No tricks, Heather."

"*Never trust anyone*, isn't that what you told me, Sir Icarus?"

"I'm Dane."

Unmoved, she flipped the knife until she was holding it by the blade. Although Dane was seconds away from feeling its cruel caress, he lowered his hands.

"You healed my soul, Heather. I remember."

The knife dropped slightly. "What?"

"I love you. If you don't believe that, kill me. Without you, I'm already dead."

Her eyes locked onto his, Heather crept closer. Dane held his arms wide in invitation.

"You were right. The universe has a way of arranging things," he said.

The knife dropped from her fingers and fell to the earth. With a strangled cry, Heather rushed into Dane's arms. No words were exchanged, but he held her close until she stopped trembling. Several long, tender kisses later, he pulled back.

"This belongs to you." He slipped her dragon crystal around her neck. "It was our crystals that brought us together again."

"I knew it. The magic really is alive," she whispered.

He gave her another kiss. "Wait for me, Heather. Joe and Shimmer need my help with the boratures."

She retrieved her blade from the grass and tucked it safely away. "If you're going to fight, so am I."

His lips curved in a smile. "Won't you ever let me protect you?"

She returned the smile with one of her own. "As long as I can protect you right back."

The two lovers transformed into dragons and streaked toward the swarming clot of boratures. The periodic eruptions of dragonfire in the center of the reptilian tornado resembled a lightning storm. Heather and Dane joined the battle, burning a wide path through the boratures. Several boratures peeled away from the flock and fled right away. As the reptiles sustained more and more casualties, many of the creatures retreated. After a few more minutes of fighting, the demoralized flock finally broke off their attack completely and retreated.

"Just in time, Cousin," Manny said, casting a worried glance at his father.

"I'll be all right, Manfred, although I could use a cup of tea," Shimmer admitted.

"For the moment, liquid magic will have to suffice. I suggest we continue our conversation on the ground," Dane said.

The dragons circled toward the turtle rock clearing and took human shapes. Heather winced at the damage the boratures had inflicted on Joe.

"You've looked better, Jovander, but I'm awfully glad to see you."

The two embraced.

"And I'm relieved you're safe," Joe said.

"As am I," Shimmer said.

"We're all happy to find you sound, Heather," Manny said.

"I'll echo the sentiment," Piers said.

The chef was still clutching a crossbow. His clothes were bloody and torn, but he stood straight. With a slight scar visible from above his eyebrow to just below his eye, Piers's countenance had taken on a rakish character.

"Piers, is that you?" Heather exclaimed.

"The very same. Thanks to the Ormvalders, I've got two good eyes again. I just wish the scenery was more pleasant."

The carnage spread out before them was horrendous. Between the trolls and the boratures, the crew of the *Dragonslayer* had been literally torn apart. Although they checked for survivors, there were none to be found—the flying reptiles had devoured much of the remains. Heather shuddered and averted her eyes from what was left of Sir Icarus, but could not muster much regret.

"Sir Icarus planned to blow up the Dragonstone cavern after he plundered what he could. I had to find a way to stop him."

"Don't apologize, Heather," Manny said. "I think your plan was very effective."

"You made a weapon out of the island itself," Dane said. "That was amazingly clever, but it nearly cost you your life."

"And the rest of you as well, unfortunately," she said. "And if it weren't for you, Dane, I wouldn't have survived. I feel sorry for Ariel, however. Because of me, he doesn't have a father anymore."

"You did a good deed in saving the boy, Heather," Shimmer said.

"Although I'm not convinced Towcheez was worth the effort," Joe said.

"Icky never mentioned any children to me," Dane said.

"Ariel told me he'd met his father for the first time only a few days ago," Piers said. "Apparently the child was unacknowledged until Icarus needed him."

A ripple of anger crossed Joe's face. "I know how that feels— except my father never needed me."

The wizards used magic to pile human remains into the fire pit and then set them ablaze. That done, Shimmer passed a weary, bloodstained hand over his eyes. Heather gave him the last of the liquid magic in her waterskin.

"Let's return to the Dragonstone cave. I'll thaw the liquid magic, and then you can go for a nice swim."

CURLED up in a quivering mass a few yards inside the lava tunnel, Bast scrambled to his feet when he heard footsteps. His smile more closely resembled a grimace.

"Your Highnesses! Praise the heavens you're all right. And what a smart girl we have here. I knew you would find a way to prevail, Heather."

"Excuse me, Sir Bast, but as I recall you'd planned to throw my rotting corpse somewhere trolls could feast upon it. Weren't those your exact words?"

Forced laughter bubbled up from the man's lips. "Ah, well, I was angry you'd injured my hand. Let's put that quarrel behind us."

"I ought to kill you myself," Dane said, the knuckles on his fists showing white.

Bast blanched, but Heather put a quelling hand on the prince's arm. "No, Dane. Sir Bast has learned a valuable lesson. I think we ought to set him free."

Everyone, including Sir Bast, was taken aback.

"Um...what was that again?" Manny asked.

"Why, I *knew* you were a good girl," Bast said, beaming. "Just and merciful as well as beautiful."

"Go," she said, jerking her head toward the turtle rock clearing.

Jovander laughed, but horror dripped from Bast's reply. "What? You can't mean to send me out there! You'd be committing murder!"

"It's as much mercy as you're going to receive," Dane said.

"And more than you deserve," Manny added.

"Go on, Bast, before I turn you into a pink rabbit," Shimmer said.

As Heather, Joe, Piers, and the Ormvalders continued their trek into the mountain, Bast stumbled out of the tunnel. He whimpered when he saw the bloodstains on the ground, and the flaming funeral pyre for his former crewmates. Bast slipped in a pool of gore and fell, cursing—until he spied an unexpected treasure within arm's reach. Crying with relief, the master archer used the heels of his hands to pick up an amethyst dragon crystal dropped by one of Icky's crewmen.

"Ha! Now I can take the ship and get away from this God-forsaken place," he muttered. "Alone."

Bast used magic to bring debris down from the mountainside, blocking each of the lava tunnels entrances.

"May the cave become your crypt, Your Highnesses."

With the dragon crystal clamped between his teeth, Bast hiked up the trail toward the crater. A grunting noise stopped his progress, mid-step. Trolls were filing down the trail in his direction. Although he turned and ran, more trolls were closing in on the other side. He backed into the turtle rock clearing and transformed into a crippled dragon. As he leaped into the air, one of the trolls grabbed his tail and slammed him into the side of the rock wall. Bast fell to the ground, stunned, until the troll raised his enormous foot over Bast's head and brought it down with all his strength.

PRECIPICE

*T*he crystal cavern resembled a half-frozen battlefield. Heather thawed the liquid magic and melted the remnants of the ice wall. Afterward, the men went about the grisly business of sealing up the dead bodies and leftover weapons inside a lava tunnel pocket. Shimmer magically rendered the crate of geyser cakes inert and buried it several yards underground. Thereafter, Shimmer, Manny, Joe, and Piers took off their boots and shirts and dove into the now-warm pool. Dane and Heather relaxed together on a nearby boulder, their shoulders touching.

"There was enough geyser cake to destroy this whole cavern," Dane said. "I wonder what Icky was thinking?"

"He believed, wrongly, that the liquid magic would give him magical powers. I'm guessing he was planning to blow up his crew along with the cave so there would be no one left to tell tales."

"I never suspected Icky's true nature," Dane said, shaking his head with regret. "I considered him a friend, but he cared for no one but himself."

"We should decide what to say to Ariel," Heather said. "He won't take the news of Sir Icarus's death very well."

"No!" Ariel's voice echoed throughout the cavern.

Towcheez fluttered nearby with a sheepish expression. "Ooh, sorry, Red. I heard yer voices, and I thought it was safe to bring the lad back."

Ariel's face was twisted in pain, and Heather's eyes filled with tears of pity.

"I'm so sorry, Ariel. I didn't mean for you to find out about your father this way."

"Liar! You don't care about me at all!"

Stricken, the boy snatched up a handful of stones and began to hurl them at Dane and Heather. The prince used magic to sweep the incoming missiles safely aside. Towcheez bobbed nervously in the background.

"Now, Ariel, ye want to be settling down. Oof!" The fairy took a pebble in the head for his troubles.

Shimmer, Manny, Joe, and Piers climbed out of the pool to intervene. Albeit dripping wet, the chef tried to calm the boy. "Come on, lad, stop that. You'll be putting my eye out again."

But because Ariel was filled with rage, the admonition fell on deaf ears. When he'd thrown all the stones within easy reach, Ariel lunged for a fistful of loose crystals instead. Before he could hurl them, the crystals in his hand began to glow. The boy's eyes grew wide as he stared at them. Heather and Dane exchanged a startled glance, while Towcheez gurgled in glee.

"Looks like yer a wizard, lad. Wouldn't Icky be surprised?"

"But that's impossible!" Ariel sputtered. "My mother isn't magical, nor my...my father."

The crystals slid from his limp fingers onto the ground. As he dissolved into tears, Heather hastened to wrap the child in a comforting hug. Shimmer shook his head and sighed.

"It truly never occurred to me before Heather and Joe came along that commoners might have magical abilities."

"Nor I. The Ormvalders have an obligation to serve the people of Ormaria. Going forward, that will include identifying wizards regardless of class," Dane said.

Towcheez's rubbery lips formed an O. "What, are ye daft? That's all Ormaria needs—more pesky wizards."

The fairy skulked over to the pool so he could skip dragon crystals on the surface of the water.

"Perhaps we should take a load of crystals with us," Joe suggested.

Manny cleared his throat. "Yes, that's a good idea, seeing as how the original Dragonstone has been destroyed."

"What?" Heather gasped.

Shimmer winced. "How was I to know a cannonball would split our ship in two?"

"I suppose you couldn't, but why didn't you simply stash the Dragonstone under your bed?" Manny groused. "That's what I would have done."

"Because that's the first place Ansgar would have looked," Shimmer huffed. "When we were children, he always won at hide-and-seek."

"With the original Dragonstone blown to bits, will that diminish the power of your dragon crystals at all?" Heather asked.

"No, fortunately, since each crystal carries its own individual power," Shimmer replied.

"But how did the king draw back the magical energy in Ormaria—the way it happened before?" Joe asked.

"Ansgar would have used some sort of gathering spell to withdraw the energy from the crystals and store it in the Dragonstone," Shimmer said.

"Nah, a calling spell would've done the trick. That's fairy mischief, that is," Towcheez said. As all eyes turned in his direction, he clapped his hand over his mouth.

"That explains quite a lot," Manny said.

"I suppose the loss of the original Dragonstone doesn't matter so much now. We have more Dragonstones than we'll ever need," Dane said.

"Transporting said Dragonstones to the ship will be a challenge," Shimmer said.

Joe grimaced. "I hadn't thought of that."

"What we need are a couple of elephants," Heather said.

"We're a bit short on elephants," Shimmer said, "but we do have wizards."

WHILE DANE CONJURED a cask and filled it with liquid magic to take back to Ormaria, Heather returned Joe's dragon crystal to him. The corners of her mouth tugged upward when she glanced at Wren's crystal around his neck.

"You wear the dragon crystal of another, Joe? I wager I know whose crystal it is," she teased.

Joe flushed pink. "I wouldn't take that wager."

Heather giggled at Joe's discomfiture. Then, as her attention focused on Dane working nearby, her eyes took on a dreamy glow. Joe's brows knit together.

"Manny warned me to stay away from Wren because he understands what will happen when the wave of magic returns. Do you?"

A flicker of pain crossed Heather's beautiful features.

"I've forgotten nothing. But I *will* savor the few sweet days I have left with Dane. He's the only man I will ever love."

Joe caught her arm. "And what of Dane's feelings?"

The lump in her throat made it difficult for Heather to form the words.

"When I am gone, another woman will ease his loneliness," she said, swallowing hard. "Please, Joe. Let's not speak of this again."

Suddenly Dane was at her side. "Don't worry about Ariel, Heather," he said, misunderstanding her expression. "Piers has taken him under his wing."

Indeed, Shimmer had enchanted a wide flat amethyst Dragonstone for Ariel to ride. To the child's delight, Piers was pushing him along as if he were perched upon an airborne sled. With the sound of Ariel's laughter echoing about the chamber, Heather closed her eyes and rested her cheek against Dane's broad chest. She breathed in the scent of his tunic to memorize its fragrance. He kissed the top of her head and then nuzzled her neck.

"I almost wish we could stay a while, just like this," he murmured.

"Why can't we?"

"My father is in dire need of liquid magic."

Heather stepped back, stunned. "But when I left the king, he was well!"

Towcheez pirouetted on top of a stalagmite formation nearby. Dane cast a dark look in his direction. "The king's illness is the result of fairy magic as it turns out. The wee folk were working with Icky to overthrow the monarchy."

Joe overheard. "Gah! I knew there was a good reason I didn't like Towcheez, but I didn't realize the other fairies were just as wicked."

"Are Wren, Lady Parker, and the queen safe?" Heather asked, aghast.

"My mother was on her way to deal with the fairies as we left Ormaria. She is a formidable wizard. The wee folk will feel her wrath."

Heather took Dane's hand, interlacing her fingers with his. "By all means, let us make haste. We've several days journey as it is."

The wizards enchanted several additional boulder sized Dragonstones and the cask of liquid magic to fly. Piers rode the cask through the lava tunnel. Astride the amethyst Dragonstone, Ariel made a race out of it. Heather surveyed the beauty of the Dragonstone cave one last time before she mounted a huge ruby red Dragonstone alongside Dane. Together they brought up the tail end of a very strange, floating caravan.

As the walls of the lava tunnel sped past, Heather asked Dane about his childhood and growing up in the castle. She leaned into him and listened to his answers—laughing at the occasional tale of mischief and smiling at his many triumphs.

I want to know everything about this man.

At length, he paused.

"I've talked far too long. Tell me your earliest memory, Heather of the Jagged Peaks. Talk to me of your dreams and nightmares. I want to know your favorite color, and who gave you your first kiss."

Heather giggled. "Surely my first kiss is not as important as my most recent," she replied, her gaze lingering on Dane's lips.

"I'm going to consider that a very welcome invitation," he said, leaning in to accept.

Although Heather and Dane freely shared details about their past, neither spoke about anything beyond the next few days. Albeit an unvoiced reality, they both knew they had no future.

When they reached the *Dragonslayer*, Piers took Ariel below deck and gave him something to eat. Although the cask of liquid magic managed to fit in the cargo hold, none of the newly harvested Dragonstones could be brought below deck. The huge, glowing stones were covered with a tarp at the stern of the ship. Heather laughed when she remembered Gumm sleeping under a tarp in that exact spot for his voyage across the ocean. Joe caught her eye and grinned.

"We're bringing a troll-sized lot of Dragonstones back to Ormaria, aren't we?"

"And more where that came from—although I'm not sure I'd want to return to Boravagg too soon."

Heather and Joe stepped back as Shimmer, Manny, and Dane carefully de-masted the ship. The sun shone in a cloudless sky while the Ormvalders worked, raising a fine sheen of sweat on Dane's brow. When he stripped off his shirt and hung it from a belaying pin, Manny followed suit. Both Ormarian princes had impressively well-muscled torsos, but Heather only had eyes for Dane. She smiled to herself when he kept glancing over his shoulder to make sure she was watching. Joe was too preoccupied to even make a joke about preening, blue-eyed peacocks.

"Heather, do you think we've done enough to change the future?" he asked finally. "Do you suppose everything will be different when we return to our own time?"

"I truly hope so, Joe. Otherwise, all of our sacrifices will have been for naught."

The Ormvalders succeeded in separating the mast from the deck. They sent it overboard and onto the rocks before weighing anchor. Towcheez fluttered here and there during the proceedings—offering unwanted and unheeded advice. At last Manny instructed everyone to make ready for departure.

"I renamed the ship the *Bonny Heather III*, if you please." He gave Heather a little bow.

"Maybe we should call it something else. The *Bonny Heathers* don't seem to meet a good end," Heather quipped.

"Nonsense," Dane said. "The name is perfect, as is the lady herself."

"That is something we can agree upon," Joe said.

Shimmer lifted the *Bonny Heather III* from the cove. "I confess I am glad to be leaving this brutal island."

"Really? I'm going to miss the wildlife," Manny quipped.

As the ship rose into the air, Towcheez flitted past. "Er... whatever happened to the others, Yer Highnesses? Is Icky's crew staying here without him?"

"Haven't you been paying attention? There *are* no others, unless Bast manages to survive," Manny said. "The island took all of them."

Towcheez's eyes grew wide. "The crew was nearly a score strong!"

"Be under no illusion, Towcheez, I am mindful of your part in this mayhem," Shimmer said, glowering at the fairy. "When we return to Ormaria, you and the rest of your kind will be dealt with harshly."

"If you want my advice, you'll stay on Boravagg," Manny added.

"I say we chuck him overboard halfway to Ormaria," Joe said.

"Capital idea, Jovander," Dane said. "I like it."

Towcheez blanched. "Let's not be hasty, Yer Highnesses. I have a wife and family, see? And Red here'll vouch for me, won't you lass? I saved the boy, I did."

"You protected Ariel, Towcheez, that's true," Heather said. "But I will not stand in between you and whatever justice King Ansgar sees fit to mete out."

"Aye, I'll take what's coming, fair and square," Towcheez said, nodding his potato head so vigorously he resembled a hummingbird. "In the meantime, I'll make meself useful in the galley." He zoomed through the hatch, out of sight.

As *The Bonny Heather III* picked up speed, Joe ducked through the hatch to alert Piers and Ariel that the ship was getting underway. Dane and Heather stood at the prow of the ship, looking toward the eastern horizon. Her hand rested on the railing, and the prince covered her hand with his.

"*The Bonny Heather III* carries the most valuable cargo ever seen," he said.

"Yes, these Dragonstones will furnish enough dragon crystals to last Ormaria for centuries."

"I wasn't referring to the Dragonstones." Dane put his arms around Heather and kissed her.

IN DRAGON FORM, Queen Mara and a phalanx of Ormarian wizards flew north to repel the Great Faturian invasion. Many Ormarian dragons also sped alongside the wizards, doubling their numbers. Like warriors charging forth on steeds, a few wizards remained in human form to ride on dragonback. Although most of the fairies had gone ahead, eager to work the mischief Mara had promised them, sharp-eyed Sylvia rode on Mara.

"Look there, below," the fairy said.

The leading edge of invaders was not difficult to spot. Clad in red and gold uniforms, the soldiers stood out against the lush green of the grassy northern hillsides like drops of blood. Some were mounted on tall horses and others were on foot, but the forces were slowly moving south. Curls of black smoke in the distance meant the hordes had already burned through several border towns. Flames of anger shot from Mara's nostrils as she led the charge.

The wizards on dragonback masked their approach with an illusion of roiling clouds. When they attacked, however, the guise became impossible to maintain. As dragons and wizards became visible, enemy soldiers scrambled into a defensive position. Archers began to send arrows skyward, but the wizards' magic caused the flying darts to explode into goose feathers. The wee folk darted fearlessly among the enemy combatants, intent on wreaking their own havoc. Suddenly men morphed into red and gold mushrooms the size of sheep. Slower fairies were swatted for their efforts, and Sylvia dove toward the ground to help her kinsmen.

Dragons and wizards fanned out, spurting long fingers of flames. Mara circled south and landed on a hillside. She morphed into human form, still in Ansgar's guise.

"Ormaria herself will repel its attackers."

A fiery intensity built in Mara's dragon crystal as she wove her spell. When her arms flung wide, the ground before her seemingly turned liquid, like an ocean of grass. A swell built at her feet and picked up strength, flowing toward the invaders with an ominous rumble. The tsunami of soil grew higher and higher, until the crest was taller than the towering giraffe topiary bush in the castle garden.

The advancing cavalry fared the best in the oncoming onslaught of earth since they were able to turn tail and gallop in the opposite direction. The foot soldiers and archers attempted to run, but the huge curl of dirt buried them before they could get far. The earthen wave crashed in a crescendo of dust, but the Great Faturian cavalry streaked north without stopping. Dragons and wizards picked screaming riders off their horses and flung them like fish. One by one, wizards turned the horses into pigs, and the remaining cavalry soldiers were left to the mercy of the wee folk.

When the upheaval in the Earth's crust subsided, the light in Mara's crystal ebbed. Ormaria's enemies were routed, but the queen failed to notice the scouting party creeping up from behind. As their arrows pierced her body, she gasped slightly and crumpled to the ground.

A STRANGE STORM

*A*ided by fortuitous weather and accommodating air currents, the *Bonny Heather III* sailed toward Ormaria at top speed. An ebullient mood danced in the wind. Piers, buoyed by his newly restored vision, hummed in the galley kitchen when he prepared their meals. Dane, Manny, and Joe took turns above deck, practicing swordplay. The sound of clashing metal lured Ariel away from Piers's side, where he'd lingered since returning to the ship. Although the lad crept on deck to watch Joe and Manny face off, he carefully avoided Heather's gaze. Undeterred, she came over to stand beside him.

"How are you feeling?" she asked.

He flicked her a sharp glance and hunched his shoulders. "Why are you being nice? I threw rocks and tricked you. You probably hate me."

"The way I see it, Ariel, you were used—same as I was. We have something in common."

A sword clattered to the deck just then, followed by Joe jumping up and down in glee. Manny pursed his lips. "Now that's what I call unsportsmanlike conduct, Jovander."

SUZANNE G. ROGERS

Dane laughed and clapped his cousin on the back. "The loser always says that."

Manny lifted his chin in a mock display of swagger and gave Dane a salute with his sword. "Then let's make a loser out of you," he challenged.

"Give it your best effort," Dane replied, taking a stance.

The two princes went at it with good-humored zeal. Shimmer climbed through the hatch, narrowly avoiding the tip of Manny's swooshing blade.

"Have a care, Manfred!"

"Oh, sorry, old boy."

An air of concentration quickly replaced Manny's sheepish demeanor as Dane pressed him into a defensive posture. Shimmer hastened out of danger and toward Joe, Heather, and Ariel. The sunlight gleamed off the first strands of silver just beginning to form in his hair and beard. He laughed at Ariel's rapt expression.

"What say you, lad? Do you yearn to practice the noble art of swordplay?"

Ariel gaped at him, his expression a mixture of longing and suspicion. "Not much use for that in the ghetto, but thanks anyway."

"Nonsense. We can't have Ormaria's newest wizard skulking about in undesirable company," Shimmer said. "You must come to live at the castle."

Ariel's thin face twisted in a sudden display of emotion. "You're having me on."

"Lady Parker will adore taking you under her wing. You'll be washed, fed, fussed over, go to school, and taught how to be a gentleman," Shimmer said.

"Wren will treat you like a little puppy," Manny called out, never taking his focus off Dane's advancing blade.

Shimmer nodded his agreement. "No doubt it will become quite tiresome."

"I...I can't imagine it would," Ariel said. "But I'd like to find out."

The boy's tremulous smile brought tears to Heather's eyes. *A little kindness makes all the difference.* A clatter of a sword dropping onto the deck was followed by Dane's triumphant cry.

"That was luck," Manny groused, massaging his wrist.

Dane winked in Heather's direction. "You're so right, Cousin."

∿

ORMARIA CAME into view a little over two days' voyage across the sea. Lit by the rising sun, the castle shone clean and bright. Shimmer lowered the ship in front of the castle. Although the occupants of the *Bonny Heather III* were bursting with hopeful optimism, a muted hush greeted their arrival. Several sober-faced servants came at a run to slide the gangplank in place. When the steward appeared, his eyes red-rimmed with sorrow, Dane seized the older man by the arms.

"What's wrong, Bybee?"

"It's the king, Your Highness. He routed the Great Faturian invaders yesterday in a mighty battle but was felled by several arrows. The surgeon does not expect him to live."

Shimmer grew ghastly pale, and Manny stared at the steward, stunned.

"Where is my father?" Dane asked, a muscle in his jaw working.

"He lies in his bedchamber."

Dane called out a command to the ship. "My waterskin!"

Ariel, who had been watching at the railing, scrambled through the open hatch. Moments later, he emerged with the waterskin, scrambled down the gangplank, and pressed the bag of liquid magic into Dane's hands. The prince set off for the castle at a dead run.

A stab of fear ricocheted inside Heather as she watched him go.

"How in the world was Ansgar able to ride into battle, Bybee? When Dane saw him last he could barely stand," Shimmer said.

"He must have recovered from his illness," Manny murmured.

The steward shook his head. "I cannot say. One moment King Ansgar was in a decline, and in the next he had raised the call to arms and was leading the wizards north. From all reports, his sorcery was a sight to behold."

"Queen Mara must be out of her mind with worry," Manny said.

A rattle of distress escaped Bybee's throat. "The queen has been missing these few days. No one knows where she is."

Manny and Shimmer exchanged a horrified glance. They hastened toward the castle, flanked by the steward and servants. Heather, Joe, Piers, and Ariel were left in the courtyard. Towcheez buzzed past, wearing a hat he'd fashioned from discarded cornhusks. The thatched head covering lent him the appearance of a scarecrow. He swept the hat from his head and bowed mid-air.

"Not quite the hero's welcome you'd anticipated, eh? Can't say it's been a pleasure," he said with a cackle.

The fairy zoomed off just as Wren burst from the castle.

"Jovander!" she cried, tears flowing down her pretty cheeks.

Joe met her halfway. Heather averted her eyes from their tender reunion, glad that Wren's older brother wasn't there to spoil the moment.

Ariel plopped down onto the gangplank, forlorn. "What's going to happen now?"

Although Heather forced herself to smile, she rather wondered the same thing. "If we go to the kitchen, maybe the cook will give us breakfast."

"Capital idea," Piers said.

But Ariel hung back. "What if they won't let me inside the castle?"

"That won't happen," Heather said. Casting a glance down at herself, however, she grimaced. *Perhaps I should ask Shimmer about his cleansing spell when the opportunity next presents itself.*

Lady Parker emerged from the castle. "Heather! Joe!" Her long skirts swished as she hastened toward the ship. Purple shadows were visible under the woman's eyes. Her greeting, although genuinely warm, was strained.

"I'm glad you've returned."

"I'm sorry to hear of King Ansgar's injuries, Lady Parker," Heather said.

"Yes, it's a very bad time for Ormaria I'm afraid. And with Mara gone missing too, we are all in uproar." A ripple of anxiety crossed the woman's face, but she gave herself a little shake. "Who are your friends?"

After Heather introduced Piers and Ariel, Wren dropped Joe's hand and put her arm around the child's thin shoulders instead.

"Aren't you just the cutest thing!" she cooed. "Let's take you inside and get you something to eat." The princess led Ariel toward the castle. "I always wanted a little brother, you know."

"I guess Manny was right," Heather said to Joe.

"It's the first time I wished I were a puppy."

A SURGEON from the hospital was pacing in the king's bedchamber when Dane arrived. When the prince burst into the room, the surgeon blocked his path.

"Brace yourself, Your Highness."

"Step aside, Sir Quincy."

Dane brushed past the surgeon and pulled back the coverlet

so he could examine his father. The king was barely breathing, and his pallor matched the milky white pillowcase underneath his head.

"He was attacked from behind. One arrow pierced his kidney, and the other lodged near his heart. I managed to remove the arrows, but it's a miracle the king is still alive," Sir Quincy said. "Your father has an incredible constitution."

Dane paid the surgeon no heed as he uncorked the waterskin.

"Father, I need you to drink."

Although he tried to lift Ansgar's head, Sir Quincy stayed his hand. "The king has been unconscious since he was brought home."

"Help me turn him on his side."

Dane winced at the wounds on his father's back, but as he doused the incisions with the liquid from the waterskin, the torn flesh knitted itself together.

Sir Quincy gasped. "What strange medicine is this?"

"Liquid magic from Boravagg. We may yet be able to save the king if he wakes enough to swallow some of it."

Ansgar stirred just then, responding to his son's voice. "Dane..."

"Yes, I'm here. You must drink, Father."

The king shook his head slightly, but he allowed Dane to pour a bit of the liquid down his throat. When Ansgar's features began to blur and transform, Dane blinked in confusion.

"The wee folk kept their bargain to help repel our enemies. Do not punish, but send them to Boravagg," the king whispered.

"Yes, Father."

"Find Ansgar. Dolly will know..."

As the breath left the king's body, the liquid magic lifted the fairy enchantment at last. The anguished cry that escaped Dane's lips when he recognized his mother echoed throughout the castle.

Lady Parker had just ushered the group into the dining room when the castle suddenly erupted into shouts and chaos. Manny thundered down the stairs and darted toward the double doors that led to the guardhouse.

"Manfred, what is happening?" Lady Parker called out.

Her son skidded to a stop on the marble tiles, his normally jovial expression clouded by grief. "It's Aunt Mara. She is dead, and it is the king who is missing."

"What?" Lady Parker sagged against the doorjamb, her hand pressed to her mouth. "No. Not Mara!"

"Dane is calling for Sir Grindol. I'm on my way to fetch him."

Manny darted off once more. Heather followed Lady Parker as she mounted the wide floating stairs up to the second level. When they reached the king's bedchamber Lady Parker disappeared inside, but the guardsman held Heather back.

"*You're* not allowed."

At once she felt like she was eight years old, confronted by King Chance's porter. To Heather's relief, this time Dane's commanding voice rang out to break the impasse.

"Let her through."

Inside the bedchamber, Shimmer and Lady Parker were locked in a grief-stricken embrace. The surgeon had collapsed onto a settee, and Queen Mara lay in repose on the king's four-poster bed. Dane held out his hand to Heather and pulled her to his side. He cleared his throat several times before he could speak.

"Heather, meet my mother—one of the finest women ever born. She would have loved you, like I do."

Queen Mara's stunning beauty took Heather by surprise. She glanced at Dane, whose expression was a study in granite. Only the slightest quiver in his jaw muscle revealed his turbulent emotions. As she studied his profile, her heart bled for him.

"You...you have her looks, Dane," she said, blinking back tears. "She's very handsome."

Dane noticed two dragon crystals tangled in his mother's flaxen locks. With a furrowed brow, he gently lifted the larger onyx crystal from around his mother's neck.

"This is my father's crystal. I wonder—"

Sir Grindol hastened into the bedchamber just then, his footsteps faltering when he saw Queen Mara. He exhaled from shock but stood at attention in the face of Dane's decisive demeanor.

"You called for me, Your Highness?"

"The king is missing, Sir Grindol. Before she died, my mother said you would know his whereabouts."

The guardsman peered at Dane. "I don't understand."

Dane held up his father's crystal. "My mother took my father's place on the battlefield, Dolly."

"But how could—" Grindol broke off, confused. "There's a man in detention who resembles the king, but your father assured me he was a hapless stranger enchanted by fairies."

Almost before the man finished speaking, Dane snatched up the waterskin and took Heather by the hand. "I need you with me. Please."

"Always."

"Sir Grindol, lead us to this man."

WHEN GRINDOL USHERED Dane and Heather into his cell, King Ansgar was conducting a lively conversation with several unseen and imaginary companions. Although the king's hair and clothes were unkempt and in disarray, a broad smile lit his face at the sight of his newest visitors.

"Dane! Is it time to leave for Boravagg? Can my friends come too?"

"Give us privacy," Dane told Grindol, who shuffled away from the door.

The king smiled at Heather. "You'd make a very pretty red dragon, dear. Has anyone ever told you that?"

Despite her best efforts, hot scalding tears threatened to spill from Heather's eyes.

"Yes, once, Your Majesty."

The prince helped his father to drink from the waterskin. When the older man regained his senses, Dane very quietly told him about Queen Mara. Heather stood at the window staring out at a far-off lightning storm as a maelstrom of gut-wrenching grief was loosed behind her.

QUEEN MARA LAY in state in the castle rotunda over the next three days. Enclosed in a glass sarcophagus, her glorious beauty was on full display. Commoners and wizards alike came to pay their respects in a never-ending line. Ansgar was so distraught, Dane took over his father's duties. Except for a few stolen moments, Heather rarely managed to see him alone. She watched from afar as the prince received dignitaries and dispatched guardsmen north to patrol the border. Although Ormarian wizards reported that the Great Faturian army had been decimated, Dane left no detail unattended. For her part, Heather made no effort to hide her pride.

"The man was born to lead," she said to Joe.

They'd taken a walk in the garden to escape the activity in the castle. Joe paused next to a topiary elephant as it shifted its balance from one foot to the other.

"I haven't always felt warmly toward Prince Dane, I admit. But you're right, he's done extraordinarily well in the face of his loss. I remember being unable to eat for a week after my mother died."

SUZANNE G. ROGERS

Heather frowned. "I feel horrible about Queen Mara. I was so determined to help the king, I didn't realize she would be in danger."

"Don't feel guilty, Heather. The queen died to save her country."

"I pray she did not die in vain."

"We have done all we could. It will have to be enough. And think of Piers and Ariel. Their lives would have been far different had we not intervened."

A whisper of mirth lit Heather's face. "Yes, Piers has completely transformed the kitchen, and Ariel is going to school for the first time in his life."

Joe chuckled. "We'll see how long it takes for the lad to complain about his schoolwork."

Wren appeared. "There you are!" She grabbed Joe's hand. "I must say, Heather, you look like a queen in that dress. Even if it's a mourning gown, the black is stunning with your hair."

Heather managed a smile, even as she tried unsuccessfully to pull the high, tight collar away from her neck.

"Thank you, Wren. It took Bette nearly twenty minutes with a button hook to fasten all the buttons up the back."

Wren's gaze fell to the stunning bracelet on Heather's wrist. "I'm glad Sylvia saw fit to return Aunt Mara's bracelet—the wretched fairy. It looks well on you."

"Yes, Dane told me about the bargain his mother made with the wee folk," Heather said.

"I'm shocked they returned the bracelet. Fairies have certainly proven themselves very untrustworthy up until now," Joe said.

"I'm very happy Dane gave Aunt Mara's bracelet to you, Heather," Wren said. "She would have wanted you to have it."

"It really should belong to you, Wren. Something this valuable ought to stay in the family."

Heather started to remove the jewelry, but Wren wouldn't let her.

"You *are* family, Heather. Which is why I'm here, actually. Dane has sent for you. Aunt Mara is to be entombed tomorrow, and he wants you to lay the wreath."

Taken aback, Heather was momentarily speechless.

"I would be honored," she said finally.

Wren glanced over her shoulder. "We should get indoors quickly. A strange storm approaches."

Heather wheeled around, gasping at the black wall rolling in from the west. "No! It's too soon!"

His eyes riveted on Wren, Joe took the crystal from around his neck and pressed it into Heather's hand. "I'm staying here."

Heather's throat closed up. "Joe?"

"There's nothing for me back home, Heather. And if we've succeeded in saving Ormaria, I might not even exist. My place is here." He grasped Wren's hand and brought it toward his heart.

Heather staggered backward, as if she were being torn asunder. The pitiless, inexorable wave was seconds away.

"Stay with us, Heather," Wren pleaded. "Take off your crystal."

"Yes...yes, I want to stay. I must."

In a panic, she tried to reach the cord underneath her collar but the fabric would not yield. Wren scrambled to help, but as the wave descended, Joe yanked the princess clear.

"Dane!" Heather screamed.

And then it was too late.

IN REMEMBRANCE

"*A*re you hurt, Lady Heather?"

"Oh, look, she's waking up."

"Somebody get Sir Saltimar. Tell him we found her."

Heather opened her eyes. A crowd of children was clustered around her as she lay in the garden. Confused, she sat up. "Hello. What are you little wizards doing out of school? And how in the world did I get here?"

For some reason her throat was raw, and there were tears on her face.

"Everyone went looking for you when you went missing, Lady Heather," Christian said. At fifteen, he was the eldest of the group. "Wizard Lippy let us out of runes to help search."

"*I* saw you first," bragged little Odette. "Your sparkly bracelet caught my eye."

"My *what?*" Heather stared at the bejeweled silvery bangle around her wrist, startled.

"Heather!" Sir Saltimar's voice carried throughout the garden and the children parted to let him through. He practically lifted Heather to her feet.

Regent Hennings was right behind him.

"Thank heavens you're all right," the regent said. "Can you tell us what happened to you?"

"I don't really know, Regent," she said. "One moment I'm finishing lessons with my archery students in the practice field, and then I woke up here...dressed like this."

Heather spread her arms wide to show her old-fashioned, high collared dress.

The regent blanched when he saw the bracelet on her wrist. He peered at her a moment, and then averted his eyes. "If you'll excuse me, there is an urgent matter I must attend to. I'm glad you are safe, Heather."

"Thank you, Regent."

The regent hastened toward the castle. Saltimar's gaze fell to the green crystal clutched in Heather's hand. "Whose dragon crystal have you got there?"

A frown creased Heather's brow as she examined the crystal hanging from a cord intertwined in her fingers. "I've no idea, but it looks familiar somehow."

"Even in a kingdom full of wizards this strikes me as strange business," Saltimar said.

"Maybe it's fairy mischief?" Odette suggested with a delicious shudder.

A ripple of fear crossed the faces of the school children. Heather smiled.

"No. Perhaps some wizard is playing tricks on me, but it's not fairy magic. The wee folk were banished from Ormaria centuries ago."

"Well, now, children, thank you for finding Lady Heather," Saltimar said. "Shouldn't you go back to school?"

"No lessons for the rest of the day," Christian said.

The children cheered.

"I'm going for a swim. Last wizard to the beach is a rotten troll!" Christian cried.

"Christian, I'll expect you first thing tomorrow morning in

archery," Heather called out.

But Christian had darted away, followed by all but one. Odette tugged on Heather's skirt and pointed to the marble statue in the center of the garden. "Dressed like that, you look like *her* now—Heather of the Jagged Peaks."

"That you do, lass," Saltimar said. "And you being named after her."

Heather giggled. "Too bad it's not All Troll's Day. I'd win a prize for the best costume."

"Do you think the legends about her and the Ormarian prince are true?" Odette asked.

Heather tweaked Odette's chestnut braids. "Just pretty fairy-tales, lass. Now take yourself to the beach for a swim. If you hurry, you can catch up with your friends."

Odette scampered off, and Saltimar gave a relieved sigh.

"I'm glad you're safe and sound, Heather. When I heard you'd disappeared, it gave me quite a turn. I went straight to the regent, and he put out an alert."

"It wouldn't do for the castle gamekeeper to lose his only daughter, now would it?" Heather laughed.

Sir Saltimar wrapped his daughter in his arms and kissed the top of her head. "I'll tell my men to call off the search."

As her father strode away, Heather tilted her head to examine her namesake statue. Although she'd passed the monument hundreds of times before, she had never fully appreciated how much she really *did* resemble Heather of the Jagged Peaks. Protected from the elements by magic, the marble was as pristine as the day it was carved.

Every schoolchild knew the story of Heather and Prince Dane. Two hundred thirty-six years ago, or so the legend went, the prince lost his true love to some evil magic. This was during the Great Faturian Rout, which claimed the life of Queen Mara. Since King Ansgar never recovered from the loss of his wife, the prince ruled Ormaria for five years as its first regent. After the king died, Prince Dane left to search for Heather, vowing never to return until she reappeared. The royal family faded from view, and Ormaria was ruled by regency ever since. Many a forlorn ballad was sung in remembrance of the two lovers, and an annual pageant at the castle always featured a play that recreated the tragedy. Heather had always done her best to avoid it.

"Romantic nonsense for tourists," she scoffed. "The Hennings family has done a fine job as regents. What would Ormaria do with a king?"

Without a backward glance, she hastened toward the castle and her rooms. Her duties as Archery Master were done for the day, but her strange ordeal had left her a little shaken.

A peacock feather lay in her path, and Heather paused to pick it up. As she traced the beautiful pattern that formed the eye at the top of the plume, a moment of disorientation swept over her.

"I'm forgetting something, I just *know* it," she exclaimed in exasperation.

The jewels in her bracelet caught the sunlight, dancing like butterflies. Heather wondered again how the beautiful piece of jewelry had come to be on her wrist. She giggled.

"The jokester who put it there will come forward to reclaim it eventually. By then, however, I will be reluctant to part with it."

REMOVING the fancy black dress did not prove a simple task. The tiny buttons in the back would not yield to Heather's fingers, nor those of the maid. After an exhaustive search, one of the maids finally located an antique buttonhook, and used it to free Heather from the gown.

"Thank you, Sally. I was about to cut the dress off with my knife if I could not remove it any other way."

The maid giggled. "'Twas a wicked trick, I grant you, to wrap you in this shroud. Seems like there are easier ways to catch your eye."

"You think this was done by an admirer?"

"None but an admirer would go to the trouble to recreate Queen Mara's bracelet so faithfully."

"Queen Mara?"

"Aye. She's wearing this exact bracelet in the big portrait over the drawing room fireplace. Since I dust the painting once a week, I knew it right away."

"No wonder the regent seemed startled to see it." Heather showed the green dragon crystal to Sally. "You wouldn't happen to recognize this, would you? It was in my hand when I awoke."

Sally shook her head. "Why don't you ask the Head Wizard when he arrives? I've been told to expect him for dinner."

"The Head Wizard of Ormaria? Is he still alive?" Heather gaped.

"I hear he spends most of his time as a dragon to extend his life. It doesn't seem like much fun to me."

"I've never actually met the man. Dinner should be interesting."

The maid left, and Heather changed into a pretty blue gown with the new shorter hemline that brushed her boots just above the ankles. The trousers she preferred were awfully tempting, but since the dinner hour was near, she reluctantly left them in the wardrobe. She stuffed the green dragon crystal into a pocket, and with the bracelet sparkling on her wrist, Heather hastened downstairs and into the unoccupied drawing room.

The castle had been her playground growing up, so she was quite familiar with the oil paintings hung on the walls. This time, she tried to see the artwork with fresh eyes. Queen Mara's portrait was perhaps the most impressive painting in the castle, and the bracelet on her wrist was depicted in detail.

"You were a beauty, Queen Mara," Heather mused. "And if I didn't know better, I'd say this really *was* your bracelet."

Her gaze focused on a smaller portrait of Prince Dane, off to one side. A smile tugged at her lips, and a slight blush stained her cheeks as she gazed at him. His clean-shaven face was certainly unusual for the era, but the look suited him well.

"I daresay you were far too handsome for your own good, Prince Dane."

Suddenly the sensation of having forgotten something came over Heather, even more strongly than before.

She shook her head, as if trying to clear it. "Why can't I remember?"

"Remember what, dear?"

Heather jumped and glanced around to identify the voice. An extremely elderly man had ambled into the drawing room, nursing a small glass of sherry in his withered hand. As he stared at her, his glass slid from his fingers and crashed to the tile.

"It's Heather of the Jagged Peaks, returned at last."

"No, of course not. I'm Lady Heather, the Archery Master here at the castle. Let me help you clean that up."

But before she could move, a quick gesture of the man's fingers had reassembled the glass and made the spilled sherry disappear. The impressive bit of magic took Heather aback.

"You must be the Head Wizard of Ormaria, then. I've been looking forward to meeting you," she said.

"Don't you know me, Heather? It's Ariel."

"I don't believe I've had the pleasure, sir."

"So you remember nothing? Dreadfully inconvenient, but it gives me the opportunity to test a theory of mine."

Regent Hennings appeared just then. "Oh, good, you're both here. Heather, I sent for Wizard Ariel to sort out what has happened today. I believe it to be an important sign."

"Not merely a sign, dear Regent, a sledgehammer," Ariel said.

"This is Heather of the Jagged Peaks, without a doubt. The magic returned her to her own time today, but she has no recollection of what has gone before."

"Come, now, gentlemen, this jest has gone too far. I know who I am," Heather said.

"You returned with Jovander Chance's dragon crystal, did you not?" Ariel asked.

Bewildered, Heather produced the green crystal and gave it to the older man. Regent Hennings's eyes grew wide. "*The* Jovander Chance Hennings, the second Regent?"

"The very same," Ariel replied.

Heather shifted her weight as she tried to conceal her impatience. "I've read your books and treatises on time travel, Head Wizard. The concept is fascinating, but there is no way to prove your theory."

"*You* are the proof, Heather. Magic is the living force that binds all living creatures together. A wizard's essence intermingles with his or her crystal. Where there is a very deep connection between wizards, their memories can be shared—across time and space."

"Forgive me for being blunt, Sir, but this is ridiculous."

Regent Hennings stepped in. "Heather, every Regent swears a sacred oath to Ormaria. Our duty is clear—when the bracelet of Queen Mara reappears, it will herald the restoration of the monarchy."

"Long ago, you showed me kindness and mercy when I deserved none, Heather of the Jagged Peaks," Ariel said. "I have lived long enough to return the favor. Trust me when I tell you that your memories are the key."

"But I'm no one special!" Heather blurted out. "I've some small talent with a bow, that's all. How can you expect *me* restore the monarchy?"

The Head Wizard chuckled. "Jovander told me once you were the spark that ignited a revolution."

"Gah! If I'd ever met Joe, I'd know it," she said, without thinking.

The regent and Ariel exchanged a glance.

"Heather, how did you know his nickname was Joe?" Ariel asked.

No ready answer came to her lips. Over the regent's shoulder, Prince Dane gazed at her—his handsome face at once arrogant and kind. Regent Hennings and Wizard Ariel's notions were absurd. And yet ever since waking up in the garden, she'd felt the need to remember...something. Queen Mara's blue eyes held a look of encouragement. Heather slowly reached for the green crystal resting in the old wizard's palm.

"What do you want me to do?"

"Hold the two crystals together," Ariel said. "I warn you, Dane said the experience is disorienting."

Heather slipped the green pendant around her neck until the green crystal hung next to hers. With a deep, shuddering breath, she reached up and gripped them with a trembling fist. She smiled when nothing happened. "You see? I—"

The world tilted on its axis and spun Heather around. Memories of another lifetime flooded her mind, *her* life—memories of what could have been, and once was. Friendships forged and now lost...and a love ripped away by a tidal wave of magic and the passage of time. Heather sank to her knees and sobbed.

"I'VE DONE what I can, but she's inconsolable," Sir Wize whispered. "The only thing that will help now is time."

No, time is the problem. Everyone I grew to love died centuries ago.

Although the physician had used a sedative spell on Heather, her grief was stronger than his magic. She lay on her bed with tears sliding out from under closed lids, pretending to sleep.

"I had no idea she would react to the return of her memories this way," Regent Hennings murmured. "This is inhumane."

"We have to understand that Heather has just experienced a great loss," Ariel replied.

Great loss? Her head was fuzzy from the sedative, but those words held importance somehow. *If only everyone would leave me alone to think.* Sir Saltimar's booming voice echoed outside in the hallway. A commotion ensued when the gamekeeper tried to force his way through the door. Sir Wize held him at bay, however, and moments later the physician insisted that Regent Hennings and the Wizard Ariel leave the room as well. Sir Wize filed out last and closed the door behind him.

Heather turned on her side and stared at a spot on the opposite wall. The return of her memories was supposed to lead to the restoration of the monarchy? What a horrible joke. No kind of magic, liquid or otherwise, would bring back people who'd long since turned to dust. If only she'd managed to remove her dragon crystal, she could have stayed with Dane. They would have married and had beautiful children together. Her memories of what should have been would torture her for the rest of her life.

"I used to believe magic had a plan and a purpose. Now I know it's pitiless and cruel."

Heather sat up. A sudden, overwhelming need to visit the Ormvalder mausoleum had taken hold. Touching Liam Ormvalder's tomb had made his life meaningful to her once upon a time. The regents and royals were buried in the mausoleum, too. Perhaps she could derive some small comfort from being there now.

Night had fallen, and the castle residents were at dinner when Heather left her room and crept down the stairs. Somewhat unsteady from the sedative spell, she was forced to keep one hand on the wall the whole way. Her destination was neither secret nor forbidden, but Heather wished to avoid questions or company. After her emotional meltdown this afternoon, Sir Wize would probably feel compelled to cast another sedative spell if he saw her out of bed.

The path through the garden was well lit by copious number of moonflowers glowing softly. Heather still wore Joe's dragon crystal in addition to her own, and both crystals emitted a bright white light. The eyes of the topiary animals, gleaming in the reflected illumination, followed her as she hastened toward the mausoleum. The lion-shaped bush yawned and shook its fern mane as Heather passed.

Several minutes later, the columns of the large white mausoleum came into view. Her hand reached out to grip the iron gate, but Heather paused. Would seeing the tombs add to her pain or help alleviate it? With a sigh, she pulled the gate open.

"Perhaps a second sedative spell would have proved beneficial after all."

Heather began at the back of the mausoleum, where she knew Liam Ormvalder was entombed, and searched until she found the tomb of Regent Jovander Chance Hennings. A whimper escaped her lips as she rested her forehead against the cool marble.

"Joe," she whispered. "You've been here my whole life, and I never knew it." Fresh tears traced a path down her face, unchecked. "I miss you, Joe, so much."

Dragging a sleeve across her eyes to stanch the flow, Heather stepped back to read the entire inscription. Wren Ormvalder Hennings was entombed alongside Joe, and the names of their ten children were inscribed as well. A laugh escaped Heather's lips when she discovered their eldest daughter had been named

Heather. Joe must have obtained another dragon crystal because it was set in a marble sconce along with Wren's.

Thereafter, Heather found the tombs of Shimmer and Lady Parker, and that of Manny—who'd never married. In the center of the mausoleum, in a place of honor, were King Ansgar and Queen Mara. The very next sarcophagus had been reserved for Dane. When Heather saw his name, she grew faint. His crystal was set in a sconce, along with an inscription.

"In Memoriam of Dane Ansgar Ormvalder, the last Crown Prince of Ormaria. He will wait until the end of time to be reunited with his one true love."

With her back resting against Dane's sarcophagus, Heather slid to the ground and stared off into space. Numbness permeated her soul, and she wept without ceasing. Minutes passed... or perhaps hours, she was unsure. Time had no meaning for her anymore. *Great loss*, Ariel had said. The words resonated in Heather's mind, but again she could not remember why. Had it been this lifetime or the other one that had come before? Why couldn't she just die, right now, and be reunited with Dane that way?

A passing movement caused her to blink. An incredibly beautiful woman in a shimmery gown knelt before her and took Heather's hand.

"Remember, Heather. There is treachery, deceit, and great loss ahead of you, but wherever you go, your heart will follow."

"Queen Mara?"

The woman smiled. "Dry your tears, little one. The path has been difficult, but your journey is at an end. Trust the magic, always. You know what to do."

Queen Mara bent forward to kiss Heather's brow, and then she was gone. Heather scrambled to her feet. "Don't leave me! I *don't* know what to do!" she shouted, her voice echoing off the cold marble walls. "How can you say that and just—"

She froze as a bit of conversation between her and Shimmer came into her mind.

"Do the Ormvalders in crystal stasis wake automatically?"

"No. I must touch my crystal to theirs and speak their name to break the spell."

Heather jerked her dragon crystal from her neck, breaking the cord. Wheeling around, she touched the crystal to the one on Dane's empty sarcophagus.

"Dane! Dane Ansgar Ormvalder," she cried, sobbing so hard she could barely get the words out. She gulped and tried to calm down. "Dane Ansgar Ormvalder, it's time to wake."

The ebony crystal began to glow with a blue light, and Heather stumbled back. Suddenly Dane was standing there, more mature than before, but handsomer than ever. Tears filled his eyes as he gazed at Heather. Then he opened his arms wide and pulled her close.

"Don't leave me again," he murmured.

"I won't. Not ever."

"I love you, Heather of the Jagged Peaks."

"And for some strange and marvelous reason I love you, too, Dane Ormvalder," she teased.

He gave her a long slow and unhurried kiss, full of promises and tenderness and future happiness. Then he scooped her up and spun her around.

"It seems like we've done this before," he said, his blue eyes crinkling at the corners.

"You're older this time around!"

"And you're exactly the same...the most beautiful girl I've ever seen." Dane frowned at the tearstains on her face. "You've been crying? Not over me, I hope."

Heather laughed. "It's a long story, but we have all the time in the world now."

"I may have something to cheer you up," he said, setting her down. "Some old friends have been waiting to talk to you."

He touched his crystal to Joe's. "Jovander Chance Hennings, awaken."

When a silver-haired Joe materialized, Heather shrieked with happiness and threw herself into his arms. Dane proceeded to wake a now-matronly Wren, a still-youthful Manny, and an elderly Shimmer and Lady Parker. Everyone was talking at the same time, and no one was listening, but the smiles said all that needed to be said.

The cacophony was interrupted by a booming voice.

"There's so much magic in here I could feel it all the way up in the castle!" Ariel said. "It's making my hair stand on end."

"Mine, too, and I'm not all that magical," Regent Hennings said. "I nearly spilled my after-dinner coffee due to the vibrations."

Another round of introductions and reunions took place, which ended with Joe and the regent peering at one another.

"You must be my great-great-great grandson or something," Joe said.

"I believe I'm a tenth-generation Hennings," the regent replied.

"Really? Nevertheless, you have my good looks," Joe said.

Raucous laughter ensued.

"Is there a vicar in the castle, Regent?" asked Dane.

"Vicar Foster resides in the village. I'll send for him first thing tomorrow to arrange your coronation," the regent replied.

"You'll send for him tonight! The coronation can wait, but my wedding cannot," Dane said.

He gave Heather a long and lusty kiss, interrupted only by the arrival of Sir Saltimar. The gamekeeper strode into the mausoleum holding a lantern in one hand and a crossbow in the other.

"Oi! Who's that kissing my daughter?" he shouted.

Heather gazed into Dane's blue eyes and beamed. "It's all right, Papa. Dane is to be my husband...and the king."

I finally found my mark.

ABOUT THE AUTHOR

Suzanne G. Rogers is a California native, but she changed coastlines and now lives in romantic Savannah, Georgia, on an island populated by deer, exotic birds, turtles, otters, and gators.

ALSO BY SUZANNE G. ROGERS

HISTORICAL ROMANCE

Graceling Hall Series

Larken (Book One)*

Lord Apollo & the Colleen (Book Two)

The Vanishing Beauty (Book Three)

The Beaucroft Girls Series

Ruse & Romance (Book One)*

Rake & Romance (Book Two)*

The Mannequin Series

The Mannequin (Book One)*

Grace Unmasked (Book Two)

The Star-Crossed Seamstress (Book Three)

A Chance of Rayne (Book Four)

The Substitute (Book Five)

The Gilded Age Series

Duke of a Gilded Age (Book One)

Lady of a Gilded Age (Book Two)

Standalone Titles

*Spinster**

Lady Fallows' Secrets

A Gift for Fiona

*My Fair Guardian**

*Jessamine's Folly**

*The Ice Captain's Daughter**

An American in Paris of the West

Rumer Has It

Courtship on Eaton Square

One Little Kiss

The Prettier Sister

The Glass Heart

*Available in Audiobook Format

www.ingramcontent.com/pod-product-compliance
Lightning Source LLC
Chambersburg PA
CBHW051517260626
47170CB00003B/657